NASRULLAH

Kalila and Dimna

NASRULLAH MUNSHI

Kalila and Dimna

Translated from the Persian by

WHEELER THACKSTON

Hackett Publishing Company, Inc.
Indianapolis/Cambridge

For further information, please address
Hackett Publishing Company, Inc.
P.O. Box 44937
Indianapolis, Indiana 46244-0937

www.hackettpublishing.com

Cover design by Rick Todhunter and E. L. Wilson
Interior design by E. L. Wilson
Composition by Aptara, Inc.

Library of Congress Cataloging-in-Publication Data
Names: Naòsr Allåah Munshåi, active 12th century, author. | Thackston, W. M.
    (Wheeler McIntosh), 1944– translator. | Ibn al-Muqaffaʿ, –approximately 760,
    compiler.
Title: Kalila and Dimna / Nasrullah Munshi ; translated from the Persian by
    Wheeler Thackston.
Other titles: Tarjumah-i Kalåilah va Dimnah. English | Fables of Bidpai. Persian.
Description: Indianapolis : Hackett Publishing Company, Inc., 2019. | English
    translation of the Persian version of the Arabic text of Kalåilah wa-Dimnah.
Identifiers: LCCN 2019010478| ISBN 9781624668081 (pbk.) | ISBN
    9781624668098 (cloth)
Classification: LCC PK6495.N33 T3713 2019 | DDC 891/.5531—dc23
LC record available at https://lccn.loc.gov/2019010478

Contents

Kalila and Dimna

Contents

Contents

Introduction

The history of the fables known variously as *Kalila and Dimna* and the *Bidpai Fables* is long and involved. It began in India with a collection of animal fables that became known as the *Pañćatantra* 'Five Sections' set in a frame story, some version of which is thought to have been composed around the third century before our era.[1] Over time the Sanskrit *Pañćatantra* has inspired at least twenty-five recensions and many translations into regional languages in India, but this preface is concerned instead with the westward migration of the tales.

According to the oft-repeated legend, a version of the tales was brought to Iran from India and translated into Middle Persian by a physician named Burzoë at the behest of Chosroës I Anoshirvan, who ruled Persia from AD 531 to 579. The Middle Persian translation and the Sanskrit text from which it was purportedly made have both disappeared without a trace.

Not long after the Middle Persian version was produced it was translated into Syriac. This version is known as the Old Syriac to distinguish it from a later one, and so far as is known, it gave rise to no other versions.[2]

In the middle of the eighth century, an Arabic-writing Persian scholar named Ibn al-Muqaffaʿ translated the Middle Persian into Arabic.[3] One of the earliest examples of literary narrative prose in Arabic, the translation

---

1. The version of the *Pañćatantra* that exists today almost certainly contains many accretions and has been massively reworked over time. The *Pañćatantra*, the *Mahābhārata*, and the *Hitopadeśa* all contain elaborated parts of an original collection or stock of stories and fables. What was translated into Middle Persian and thence into Syriac and later into Arabic represents an earlier version of—or selection from—what became the *Pañćatantra* and not the *Pañćatantra* as it is now known.
2. The Old Syriac was edited and translated into German by Gustav Bickell with a long introduction by Theodor Benfey in 1876: *Kalilag und Damnag: Alte syrische Übersetzung des indischen Fürstenspiegels* (repr., Amsterdam: APA-Philo Press, 1981). A later edition of the Syriac was made by Friedrich Schulthess, *Kalila und Dimna* (Berlin: G. Reimer, 1911).
3. Among the numerous editions of Ibn al-Muqaffaʿ's text are *Calila et Dimna, ou Fables de Bidpai*, ed. Silvestre de Sacy (Paris: Imprimerie Royale, 1816), and Louis Cheikho's Beirut edition of 1905, *La version arabe de Kalīlah et Dimnah, ou, Les fables de Bidpai* (repr., Amsterdam: APA-Philo Press, 1981). An English translation

became a model of elegant writing and achieved such lasting popularity that it is still read in schools all over the Arab world. Translations of it were made into (1) Syriac, (2) Greek, (3) Persian, (4) Hebrew, and (5) Spanish.

(1) A Syriac translation of Ibn al-Muqaffaʿs Arabic was made by an unidentified Christian priest in the tenth or eleventh century (the New Syriac version).[4]

(2) A Greek translation was made around 1050 by Simeon, son of Seth, and that was rendered at some point, perhaps as early as the twelfth century, into Old Slavonic and later into Italian.[5]

(3) The first rendering of *Kalila and Dimna* into Persian was made by the poet Rudaki in the mid-tenth century, but only a few scattered lines of his work remain. Around 1120 Abuʾl-Maʿali Nasrullah, a writer employed in the court chancery of the rulers of the Ghaznavid Empire, freely translated Ibn al-Muqaffaʿs Arabic into New Persian and dedicated his work to the ruler Bahramshah (r. 1117–1157).[6] It is apparent that Nasrullah found the economy of expression that characterizes Ibn al-Muqaffaʿs Arabic—not to mention the elegance of diction—difficult to capture in Persian. His version is significantly expanded, and what was expressed in one pithy phrase in Arabic may run to a page of Persian, not counting the lines of epigrammatic poetry, often Arabic, that were inserted in conformity with the approved style of the time. Nasrullah's version is also replete with quotations from the Koran and hadith, "all of which [sound] rather quaint in the mouths of animals in the jungles of India."[7]

---

of the Arabic was made in 1819 by Wyndham Knatchbull, *Kalila and Dimna, or The Fables of Bidpai* (Oxford: W. Baxter, 1819).

4. The Syriac *Book of Kalilah and Dimnah* was edited by William Wright in 1884 (repr., Amsterdam: APA-Philo Press, 1981). An English translation was made by Ion G. N. Keith-Falconer, *Kalilah and Dimnah, or the Fables of Bidpai: Being an Account of Their Literary History* (Cambridge: At the University Press, 1885).

5. The Greek text was edited by Sebastian Gottfried Starke, *Specimen sapientiae Indorum veterum: Id est, liber ethico-politicus pervetustus, dictus arabice كليلة ودمنة, graece Στεφανιτης και Ιχνηλατης* (Berlin: Johann Michael Rüdiger, 1697). The Italian translation, *Del governo de' regni, sotto morali esempi di animali ragionanti tra loro*, was edited by Dominico Mammarelli and published in Ferrara in 1583.

6. Nasrullah's translation, known as *Kalila u Dimna-i Bahrāmshāhī*, was edited by Mujtabā Mīnuvī-Ṭihrānī, *Tarjuma-i Kalīla u Dimna* (Tehran: Dānishgāh, [1343] 1964). It has often been reprinted with various titles.

7. François de Blois, *Burzōy's Voyage to India and the Origin of the Book of Kalīlah wa Dimnah* (London: Royal Asiatic Society, 1990), p. 5.

At the end of the fifteenth century, Nasrullah's Persian having become hopelessly old-fashioned, Husayn Va'iz Kashifi, a Timurid polymath, composed a new version in the fashionably elegant prose of the period and called it *Anvār-i Suhaylī* 'The Lights of Canopus.'[8] After lavishing praise on Nasrullah's prose style, Kashifi adds:

> However, because he introduces strange words, embellishes his prose with Arabic features, overdoes the use of various metaphors and similes, and is too wordy in obscure locutions and expressions, the mind of the listener fails to enjoy the purpose of the book and to comprehend the contents, and the reader is also unable to connect the beginning of a story to the end. All this inevitably leads to weariness on the part of the reader and listener, especially in this elegant time, when people have reached such a level of subtlety that they can comprehend meanings without their being decked out in verbiage, not to mention the fact that for some words one has to thumb through dictionaries and search to discover the meaning. For all these reasons, such a valuable book was almost abandoned and nearly became obsolete, and the people of the world were on the verge of being deprived of its benefits.[9]

In addition to being completely reworded in a much more fluid Persian, Kashifi's version is considerably expanded from Nasrullah's. While he retains the basic framework and stories of the earlier version, Kashifi added a number of stories, making his version considerably longer than Nasrullah's. A hundred years after Kashifi, it was once again felt that it was time for a stylistic revision. This time the Mughal emperor Akbar's friend and biographer Abu'l-Fazl composed a new version entitled *'Iyār-i dānish* 'The Assay of Knowledge' in the Persian style prevalent in India at that time.

---

8. Suhayl is Canopus, a star (α Carinae) of great auspiciousness and the second brightest in the sky, but it is never visible north of the latitude of Athens. Suhaylī was the poetic pen name of a Timurid dignitary, Amir Shaykh-Ahmad, to whom Kashifi's version was dedicated. *Anvār-i Suhaylī* was translated into English by Edward B. Eastwick, *The Lights of Canopus* (Hertford: S. Austin, 1854), and later by Arthur N. Wollaston (London: Wm. H. Allen, 1877). For a recent study of *Anvār-i Suhaylī*, see Christine von Ruymbeke, *Kashefi's Anvar-e Sohayli: Rewriting Kalila wa-Dimna in Timurid Herat* (Leiden: Brill, 2016).

9. Kamāluddīn Ḥusayn Vā'iẓ Kāshifī, *Anvār-i Suhaylī* (Tehran: Amīr Kabīr, [1362] 1983), p. 7.

(4) A Hebrew translation of the Arabic was made in the twelfth or thirteenth century by a Rabbi Joel.[10] Toward the end of the thirteenth century, Giovanni da Capua made a Latin translation of the Hebrew.[11] A German translation was made from the Latin, and the earliest printed edition is from around 1480.[12] From the German were produced translations in Danish in 1618 and in Dutch in 1623.[13] A Spanish translation of the Latin appeared in 1493.[14] On it is based Agnolo Firenzuola's *Discorsi degli animali ragionanti tra loro,* first published in Venice in 1548, and that was translated into French in 1556.[15] An Italian translation of the Latin was made in 1552 by Anton Francesco Doni, and part of that was translated into English by Sir Thomas North in 1570.[16]

(5) In 1251 Ibn al-Muqaffa''s text was translated into Old Spanish by an unknown author.[17] It and Giovanni da Capua's Latin formed the basis of a later Latin version in 1313.[18]

As a testimony to the enormous worldwide popularity of *Kalila and Dimna,* there are today versions to be found in Arabic, Armenian, Azerbaijani, Chinese, Croatian, Danish, English, French, Georgian,

---

10. Joseph Derenbourg, ed., *Deux versions hébraïques du livre Kalîlâh et Dimnâh* (Paris: F. Vieweg, 1881).

11. Giovanni da Capua, *Directorium vitae humanae: Parabola antiquorum sapientum.* The earliest known printed copy, in the library of Trinity College, Cambridge, dates from before 1483. The standard edition is by Joseph Derenbourg (Paris: F. Vieweg, 1887–1889).

12. Antonius von Pforr, *Das Buch der Beispiele der alten Weisen,* ed. Wilhelm Ludwig Holland (Stuttgart: Litterarischer Verein, 1860).

13. Christen Nielssen, *De gamle vijses exempler oc hoffsprock* (1618; repr., Copenhagen: J. H. Schultz, 1951–1953); *Voorbeelsels der oude wyse* (Amsterdam: Broer Jansz, 1623).

14. *Exemplario contra los engaños y peligros del mundo* (Zaragoza: Pablo Hurus, 1493).

15. Agnolo Firenzuola, *La prima veste de' discorsi degli animali di messer Agnolo Firenzuola,* ed. Pier Carlo Tagliaferri (Imola, Italy: Angelini, 2009); Gabriel Cottier, *Le plaisant et facétieux discours des animaux, nouvellement traduict de tuscan en françois* (Lyon, 1556).

16. Anton Francesco Doni, *La moral' filosophia del Doni* (Venice: Francesco Marcolini, 1552); Thomas North, *The Morall Philosophie of Doni Drawne out of the Auncient Writers* (London: Henry Denham, 1570).

17. *Calila e Dimna,* ed. Juan Manuel Cacho Blecua and María Jesús Lacarra (Madrid: Castalia, 1984).

18. Raymond de Béziers (Raimundus de Biterris), Liber de Kalila et Dimna, MS, Latin 8504, Bibliothèque Nationale, Paris.

German, Greek, Hungarian, Indonesian, Italian, Karakalpak, Kashmiri, Kurdish, Laotian, Lebanese, Malay, Marathi, Nyanja, Old Church Slavic, Portuguese, Punjabi, Russian, Spanish, Tatar, Thai, Tongan, Turkish (both Ottoman and modern), Uighur, Urdu, and Uzbek.

The collection is often known in the West as the *Bidpai Fables* after the philosopher Bīd(a)bā, who serves King Dabshalīm, as Ibn al-Muqaffaʿ calls them.[19] In Nasrullah's version, those names are dispensed with. The philosopher becomes the Brahman, and Dabshalīm is simply the "Raja of India." Kashifi transposes the setting to "olden days in the farthest reaches of the realm of Chīn," which is the equivalent of "long ago and far away," but he retains the emperor Dabshalīm and calls his vizier Bīdpāy, or Bidpai, an adaptation of the name given by Ibn al-Muqaffaʿ.

The *Pañcatantra* belongs to an Indian genre called *nītiśāstra*, a treatise on *nīti*, or right, wise, and moral behavior that leads to security, prosperity,

---

19. The frame story of the king and the philosopher is not found in the *Pañcatantra* as it exists today. In the Old Syriac, the king is called דבשרם *DBŠRM*, which looks like it could reflect a Middle Persian form that might well have been interpreted as Ibn al-Muqaffaʿ's Dabshalīm since *l* and *r* are written with the same letter in Middle Persian. What it could have come from in Sanskrit is not known, since modern versions of the Sanskrit have no such character. The Old Spanish Dicelen is a transcription of the Hebrew דיסלם *DYSLM*, which must have resulted from a miscopying or misreading of دبشليم *DBŠLYM* (Dabshalīm) as ديسلم *DYSLM*. In Giovanni da Capua's Latin, the Hebrew is misread as דיסלס *DYSLS* and becomes Disles. Ibn al-Muqaffaʿ's بيدبا Bīd(a)bā has a variety of names. In the Old Syriac, he is ܒܝܕܘܓ *BYDWG*, which is probably to be read as Bēdawāg and could represent an assumed Middle Persian form like Wēda-wāga, Wēda-nāka, or Wēda-nāga (*n* and *w* are represented by the same sign in Middle Persian, as are *k* and *g*). The final *-ka* or *-ga* of Middle Persian would have been dropped in New Persian, so it could have been read as Wēdawā and written in Arabic as Bīd(a)bā. In the Hebrew version, the translator gave up on the Arabic altogether and called the philosopher סנדבאר (Sandabār), a mistake for סנדבאד (Sindbād), a name with which the translator would have been familiar from the well-known book *Sindbad the Sage and the Seven Wise Masters* (a different character altogether from Sinbad the Sailor of the *Arabian Nights*). Sandabar became Sendebar in Giovanni da Capua's Latin translation. The variants in Old Spanish—Bundobet, Barduben, Burduben, and Bendubec—are all garbled versions of Bīd(a)bā. See Keith-Falconer, *Kalilah and Dimnah*, p. 271. In the fifth chapter of the Old Syriac version (Bickell, *Kalilag*, p. 57 of the Syriac text = Nasrullah chapter 7), the two characters are called ܙܕܫܬܪ (Zedashtar) and ܒܫܡ (Bisham), names that betray the original Indic names Yudhiṣṭhira and Bhīṣma from the *Mahābhārata*, and it is likely that the Middle Persian version had names much like those. Bidpai is what was turned into Pilpay, the name of the Indian sage to whom Jean de La Fontaine attributed his second collection of fables in 1671.

resolute action, friendship, and learning to produce joy. The five sections of the *Pañcatantra*, into each of which are embedded numerous stories, are as follows:

(1) *mitrabheda* 'breach of friendship': The lion king Pingalaka (unnamed in Arabic and Persian) and the bull Sanjīvaka (Shanzaba) become friends, but the king's scheming jackal retainer Damanaka (Dimna) breaks up the friendship.

(2) *mitralābha* 'acquisition of friendship': A crow sees a mouse free a pigeon from a snare and befriends the mouse against the mouse's initial objections. A turtle and a gazelle join them. When the gazelle is trapped, they set him free, and then they work together to save the turtle when he is caught.

(3) *kākolūkīya* 'crows and owls (natural enemies)': A crow gains access to a group of owls and betrays them to the crows, who set the owls' cave ablaze.

(4) *labdhapraṇāśa* 'loss of gain': A crocodile conspires to get a monkey's heart to heal his wife, but the monkey escapes through guile.

(5) *aparīkṣitakāraka* 'ill-considered action': A Brahman's wife leaves her child with a mongoose. Mistakenly believing that the bloodstained mongoose that greets her on her return has killed the child, she kills it, whereas the mongoose actually saved the child from a snake.

Ibn al-Muqaffaʿ's Arabic version also contains these five chapters, but after the first chapter, to accord with Islamic sensibilities, which demanded justice for Dimna's outrageous scheming against the bull, he inserts a chapter on the trial of Dimna. After those six chapters, Ibn al-Muqaffaʿ's version also contains another eight chapters, (7) Īlādh (the minister), Shādram (the king), and Īrākht (the king's wife); (8) the cat and the mouse; (9) the king and the bird Finza; (10) the lion and the fasting jackal; (11) the traveler and the goldsmith, and the monkey, the snake, and the tiger; (12) the king, the nobleman's son, the merchant's son, and the husbandman's son; (13) the archer, the she-wolf, and the jackal; and (14) the ascetic and the guest. The cat and the mouse of chapter eight, the king and the bird of chapter nine, and the lion and the jackal of chapter ten are all found in the *Mahābhārata*. These three stories are found already in the Old Syriac translation, so whatever text the Syriac translator had must have included them.

In Nasrullah's version there are, in addition to Ibn al-Muqaffaʿ's fourteen chapters, four prefaces: (1) Nasrullah's preface outlining the history of the book, (2) a Persian adaptation of Ibn al-Muqaffa''s preface, (2) Buzurjmihr's preface to Burzoë's translation, and (4) the testament of the physician Burzoë.

Major themes that are stressed throughout versions of *Kalila and Dimna* in their Islamic guise are *ḥazm*, a quality that is a combination of resolve, firmness, judiciousness, and prudence, and *muruvvat* 'gallantry.' *Muruvvat* is etymologically connected to the Arabic word for 'man' (*mar'*) and would be the equivalent of 'manliness' were not modern notions of manliness at such odds with the medieval ideal. It would also be the equivalent of 'virtue,' which is derived from the Latin for 'man,' *vir*, if the modern understanding of virtue were not limited to moral excellence. The ideals of chivalry are not far from those of *muruvvat*, but chivalry conjures up images of knights in armor and is inappropriate. The best modern word for *muruvvat* is probably 'gallantry' because it still contains implications of moral excellence, bravery and courage, and good manners, all of which are implied in *muruvvat*. The Persian equivalent of *muruvvat* is *hunar*, and both words are often found on the pages of *Kalila and Dimna*.

Another quality that is often mentioned is 'ignorance' (*jahl, nādānī*). For the Arabic- and Persian-writing authors of *Kalila and Dimna*, 'ignorance' is not so much the lack of knowledge as it is the lack of self-control—that is, impetuosity and incautiousness. Anyone who rushes into action not fully prepared and without judicious reflection on the consequences of his actions is guilty of 'ignorance.'

Much advice is given throughout concerning master-servant relationships. Few people these days have servants, and that relationship is a thing of the past, but if employer-employee relationships are substituted, much will be immediately recognizable.

In the various versions, one animal is sometimes substituted for another. For example, the *Pañćatantra* story that is chapter five in Nasrullah's version is the story of a monkey and a crocodile. In Ibn al-Muqaffa''s version, the crocodile is a tortoise (*ghaylam*) and remains a tortoise or turtle in subsequent versions. While some substitutions may have been made because the animal in question, like the mongoose or the crocodile, was unfamiliar in Arabic- and Persian-speaking environments, usually it makes little or no difference since the animals, while being appropriate to their settings, behave less like animals and more like human beings. In Nasrullah's chapter twelve, the King and the Brahmans, there are no animals at all. The purpose of the chapter was originally to excoriate Brahmans, and it is thought to be thoroughly Buddhist in origin.[20] Ibn al-Muqaffaʿ and, following him, Nasrullah have expanded this chapter into a long and tedious exchange between the king and his minister Bilar before the resolution of the tale. Kashifi, as usual more interested in good storytelling than in faithfully reproducing an old tale, reduced the exchange to the bare minimum.

Changes in other respects, too, have been made in the various translations. In the Old Syriac version, the various holy men of the Sanskrit are called *mguše* 'Magi,' or Zoroastrian priests. In the Islamic versions, they have all become *nāsik* 'ascetics,' since in the Islamic world there was no priestly caste, and there was certainly nothing analogous to the hermits and Brahmans of the Sanskrit.

This translation has been made from Nasrullah's version, but Ibn al-Muqaffaʿ's text has also been taken into account, and Kashifi's interpretations have been relied upon when Nasrullah's text is ambiguous or obscure.

Some liberties have been taken with the translation. Nasrullah uses a heavily Arabicized vocabulary in his Persian, "decked out in verbiage," as Kashifi says. He quite often uses Arabic words in metaphorical senses far removed from the usual meanings of the words—particularly the meanings they normally have in Persian. I have tried to render these in an understandable fashion in modern English. It is impossible, given Nasrullah's style, to fix a specific meaning to a given word and to translate it uniformly throughout the work. Routinely omitted from translation are the quotations of Arabic poetry with which Nasrullah embellished his text. However apropos they may be to the topic at hand, they rarely sound good in translation and wind up sounding either obtuse or silly. Kashifi omitted the Arabic lines altogether, perhaps because few in his milieu would have understood them, and added a lot of Persian poetry of his own. There are also a few places in the text that are insolubly problematic. They were deleted altogether by Kashifi, a fact that may well indicate that these places in the text were already corrupt in his time.

---

20. The premise of the basic frame of this story, the Brahmans' exploitation of the fear of dreams and their intentional misrepresentation of the king's dream to further their own aims, is shared by the *Mahāsupina Jātaka*. See E. B. Cowell, ed., *The Jātaka, or Stories of the Buddha's Former Births* (Cambridge: At the University Press, 1895), 1:187.

Manuscripts of *Kalila and Dimna* were often copiously illustrated. For a catalog, see Ernst Grube, "Prolegomena for a Corpus Publication of Illustrated *Kalīlah wa Dimnah* Manuscripts," *Islamic Art* 4 (1990–1991): 301–481.

Concordance of Versions of the Tales

	Panch.[21]	Syriac[22]	Muq.[23]	Nasr.[24]	Kashifi[25]
Nasrullah's introduction	—	—	—	2–27	—
Ibn al-Muqaffa''s preface	—	—	46–52	28–43	—
Anoshirvan sends Burzoë to India	—		19–29	30–37	—
Buzurjmihr's preface	—	—	—	38–43	—
Testament of the physician Burzoë	—	—	30–44	44–58	—
I. On causing dissension among allies: The lion and the bull, and the jackals Karataka (Kalila) and Damanaka (Dimna)	19–25	Chap. 1 1–50	Chap. 1 53–101	Chap. 1 59–126	12–166
The monkey that pulled the wedge	25–41	3	55	62	75
The jackal that tried to eat a drum	41–48	10	62	70–71	87
The adventures of an ascetic	58–62	12	65–67	74–79	92–97

---

21. *Panch.* = *The Panchatantra*, trans. Arthur W. Ryder (Chicago: University of Chicago Press, 1925). This is the *Pañćatantra* as it exists today.
22. Syriac = *Kalila und Dimna,* ed. Friedrich Schulthess (Berlin: G. Reimer, 1911). The Old Syriac translation is assumed to be the version closest to the lost Middle Persian translation.
23. Muq. = Ibn al-Muqaffa', *Aqdam nuskha makhṭūṭa mu'arrakha li-kitāb Kalīla wa-Dimna,* ed. Louis Cheikho (1905; repr., Amsterdam: APA-Philo Press, 1981).
24. Nasr. = Abū'l-Ma'ālī Naṣrullāh Munshī, *Tarjuma-i Kalīla u Dimna,* ed. Mujtabā Mīnuvī-Ṭihrānī (Tehran: Dānishgāh-i Ṭihrān, [1362] 1983).
25. Kashifi = Kamāluddīn Ḥusayn Vā'iẓ Kāshifī, *Anvār-i Suhaylī* (Tehran: Amīr Kabīr, [1362] 1983). The late fifteenth-century reworking of Nasrullah's translation of Ibn al-Muqaffa''s version.

	Panch.	Syriac	Muq.	Nasr.	Kashifi
Battling rams kill a greedy jackal	61–62	12	65	75	92
A weaver cuts the nose of a bawd	62–71	13–17	66–67	76–78	94–97
The crow that killed a snake	74–76	17–20	69–72	81–85	103–6
The crab cuts off the heron's head	76–81	18–20	69–71	82–85	104–7
The hare that outwitted the lion	81–89	20–23	72–73	86–88	110–12
How the louse got killed trying to be nice to a bug	119–22	25	77–78	—	—
How the lion's servants killed the camel	—	32–36	84–85	106–9	136–40
The sandpiper that defeated the ocean	145–62	36–37	88–91	110–13	141
The turtle and the geese	147–49	37–38	89	110–12	141–44
The fate of three fish	149–53	23–25	75–76	91–92	115–17
The bird that tried to advise a monkey	184	43–44	94	116–17	150–51
The duck that saw the reflection of a star in the water	—	—	—	102	126–27
Two friends and betrayed trust	184–97	44–46	95–98	117–20	152–56
How the mongoose ate the heron's chicks	188–89	46–48	97	118–19	154–55
The iron-eating mice	192–95	48–49	99	122	162–64
The trial of Dimna	—	—	Chap. 2 102–24	Chap. 2 127–56	167–219
The woman who couldn't tell the difference between her lover and his slave	—	—	109–10	137–38	194–95
The quack physician	—	—	—	146–47	205–7
The scheming gamekeeper	—	—	—	153–54	213–16

	Panch.	Syriac	Muq.	Nasr.	Kashifi
II. On securing allies: The crow, rat, tortoise, and deer that became friends	213–72	Chap. 2 51–73	Chap. 3 125–42	Chap. 3 157–89	220–64
The ascetic and the mouse	231	59–66	131	170–80	243
The woman who traded husked sesame for unhusked	234–38	60	132–34	171–73	244
How the greedy jackal died eating a bowstring	235–37	61	133	172	245
How the deer got caught in a trap	279–88	70–73	140	184–89	260
III. On war and peace: The enmity between crows and owls	291–304	Chap. 6 92–122	Chap. 4 143–66	Chap. 4 191–236	265
The ass in leopard's skin	409–12	—	—	—	—
The birds who wanted to make the owl their prince	304–8	97–98	147–48	201–11	280
The hare that fooled an elephant	308–15	98–101	148–49	202–5	281
The partridge and hare take their case to the cat	315–24	101–4	149–51	206–8	287
Three rogues who fooled a Brahman	324–26	104–7	152–53	211	295
The old merchant and his young wife	341–43	107–8	155	214	300
The thief, the ogre, and a Brahman	343–46	108–10	155–56	215	301
How the unfaithful wife tricked her foolish husband	348–53	110–13	156–57	217–21	303
The marriage of a mouse that turned into a girl	353–59	113–18	159–60	224–26	317
The frogs that went for a ride on the back of a snake	368–70	118–22	162–63	230–32	323–25

	Panch.	Syriac	Muq.	Nasr.	Kashifi
IV. On losing what you have gained: The friendship between a crocodile and a monkey	381–422	Chap. 3 74–81	Chap. 5 167–74	Chap. 5 238–59	333–60
The ass without ears or a heart	—	78–81	172–74	253–57	353–59
V. On hasty actions: Killing a mongoose in haste	432–34	Chap. 4 82–85	Chap. 6 175–77	Chap. 6 261–65	362–73
The dreamy beggar	453–54	82–83	176	263	366–67
Escaping calamity by being kind to an enemy: The cat and the mouse[26]	—	Chap. 5 86–91	Chap. 8 205–10	Chap. 7 266–81	375–97
Enemies who are best avoided	—	Chap. 7	Chap. 9	Chap. 8	398–422
The king and the bird Finza[27]	—	123–30	211–16	283–303	—
The old woman and her daughter	—	—	—	288–90	406–7
Kings and their intimates	—	Chap. 8	Chap. 10 217–27	Chap. 9 304–33	426–59
The lion and the jackal[28]	—	131–43	—	308–33	—
One who has to harm others to preserve his own life	—	—	Chap. 13 239–42	Chap. 10 334–39	462–75
The archer and the she-lion	—	—	—	335–39	462–74
One who foolishly abandons his own calling	—	—	Chap. 14 243–44	Chap. 11 340–46	476–92
The ascetic and his guest	—	—	—	340–45	477–85
The washerman and the crane	—	—	—	—	481

26. The story of the cat and the mouse is found in *Mahābhārata* XII, vv. 4930 sqq. (section CXXXVIII).

27. The story of the king and the bird is found in *Mahābhārata* XII, vv. 5133 sqq. (section CXXXIX).

28. The story of the lion and the jackal is found in *Mahābhārata* XII, vv. 4084 sqq. (section CXI), where the lion is a tiger.

	Panch.	Syriac	Muq.	Nasr.	Kashifi
The man who lost his beard	—	—	—	—	482–83
The crow that wanted to walk like a partridge	—	—	244	344–45	490–91
Clemency is the best quality in rulers	—	Chap. 9	Chap. 7	Chap. 12 347–96	493–533
The king and the Brahmans	—	144–79	178–204	351–96	496–533
The pair of doves that stored up grain	—	159	—	377–78	527
Who deserves the king's trust?	—	—	Chap. 11 228–32	Chap. 13 397–407	534–58
The goldsmith and the traveler	—	—	—	402–6	557
The role of destiny	—	—	Chap. 12 233–38	Chap. 14 408–17	559–82
The prince and his friends	—	—	—	409–16	560–80
The man who bought a pair of parrots and set them free	—	—	—	416	577–79

Nasrullah's Preface

Thus says Nasrullah Muhammad, son of Abdul-Hamid Abu'l-Ma'ali[1]

When, thanks to the emperor's good fortune, my master's house became the resort of learned men, and he granted the requests of every one of them more cheerfully than one could imagine (this being far too well known to need any elaboration), consequently all attained contentment with him and entered into friendship with him. A group of well-known persons, each of whom possessed abundant erudition and renown, were habitués of that house. . . . I became accustomed to sitting and conversing with them, and I was so greatly inclined to acquire skills that would be of use in my job that my fondest wish was to meet with them and spend an hour in their company in conversation, which I reckoned as the greatest felicity. These words may be attributed to boasting and swagger, but since fairness necessitates that one remove the veil of envy from one's own beauty, and when one reflects on the miracles of rhetoric that this book contains, it will be recognized that unless one is high-minded in acquisition and the greatest pains are taken in learning, one will not attain that level of speech by which humankind is distinguished from other animals. It being the custom of destiny always to take back what it gives, when it dispersed that group, I saw that I could be guided only by reading books, and it is proverbial that the best narrator is a book. Inasmuch as it has been said that being serious all year long wearies people, occasionally there was levity, and I turned my attention to histories and stories. During that time the jurist Ali Ibrahim Isma'il, one of His Majesty's outstanding jurists who is exceptionally virtuous and wise, brought a copy of *Kalila and Dimna*. Although there were already several other copies among the books, it was taken as a good omen and I thanked him as a good friend. In short, I gained an intimacy with that copy, and as its good features

---

1. Much irrelevant material in Nasrullah's excessively long-winded introduction has been deleted in translation.

became better known with reflection and contemplation, I had an even greater desire to peruse it, for after books of law no more beneficial book has ever been made in the history of the world. Its chapters are based on wisdom and advice, and it is couched in a jocular tone so that the elite might be inclined to recognize experiences and the common folk might also read it because of its light tone and its sage advice might gradually take root in their minds.

Truly it is a mine of wisdom and perspicacity and a storehouse of experience and practical knowledge. By listening to it kings can learn policy for ruling a realm and ordinary people can read it and benefit from it to preserve their possessions. They put the following to one of the Brahmans of India: "They say that next to India are mountains on which grow medicinal plants that can bring the dead back to life. How can one obtain them?" He replied, " 'You learned one thing and missed many' is something the ancients said. By 'the mountains' they meant learned men, and by 'the medicinal plants' they meant their words. By 'the dead' are intended the ignorant, who come to life by hearing those words and gain eternal life through knowledge. There is a collection of those words called *Kalila and Dimna*, and it is in the treasuries of the kings of India. If you can get hold of it you will attain your goal."

The good features of this book are endless, and what greater distinction could it have than that it passed from nation to nation and community to community without being rejected? When the rule came to Chosroës Anoshirvan,[2] whose renown for justice and clemency is inscribed on the pages of time, and whose bravery and wise policy are writ large in histories to such an extent that the rulers of Islam are likened to him in beneficence—and what greater luck could he have had than that the Prophet himself said, "I was born during the time of the Just King"?—he ordered the book brought by subterfuge from India to Persia and translated into the Pahlavi language. He based affairs in his kingdom on it and made its advice and counsel a model for benefits of religion and this world and an exemplar for policy toward the elite and the common folk. He counted it as a precious article in his treasury, and so it remained until the end of the days of Yazdgird Shahryar, the last of the kings of Persia.[3]

---

2. Chosroës I Anoshirvan "the Just" reigned over the Sassanian Empire AD 531–579.
3. Yazdgird III, r. 632–651.

When Iraq and Persia were conquered by the armies of Islam and the dawn of the nation of the truth broke over those territories, mention of this book reached the hearing of the caliphs, and they were much intrigued by it. During the reign of the Commander of the Faithful Abu-Ja'far Mansur son of Muhammad son of Ali son of Abdullah son of Abbas, the second caliph of the house of the uncle of the Prophet,[4] Ibn al-Muqaffa' translated it from the Pahlavi language into Arabic, and it was well received by him and was taken as a guide by the grandees of the nation. . . .

In sum, the gist of this is that such a monarch was desirous of this book, and when the rule of Khurasan came to Abu'l-Hasan Nasr son of Ahmad the Samanid,[5] he ordered the poet Rudaki to versify it because people were more inclined to read poetry. That monarch was very expansionist, and during his reign Kirman, Gurgan, Tabaristan, and as far as Rayy and Isfahan were added to the kingdom of the Samanids, and he enjoyed ruling for thirty years. If even a bit of his history were to be given it would take too long. He venerated this book and read it with care.

Dabshalim was the raja of India at whose order the collection was made, and Bidpai was the Brahman who composed the original.[6] His perfect wisdom can be judged by this book . . . since its excellence will not be hidden from anyone who has an iota of wisdom, while anyone who does not possess intelligence will be excused by people of insight. "How can the blind see the light of Moses? How can the deaf hear Jesus' words?"

If volumes were filled with the good features of this book it would still not be given its due, but surely we have wearied our readers beyond all bounds. From the point at which Anoshirvan was mentioned to here is all extraneous and has nothing to do with the flow of the book, but we wanted it to be known that wisdom has always been precious, especially in the view of kings and grandees, and in truth if any effort is made in that direction or any expense borne, it will not be wasted because knowledge of the code of good policy is a firm basis for ruling the world. Permanence of one's name throughout the ages is a precious commodity and cheap at whatever price it is purchased.

---

4. The second Abbasid caliph, Abdullah son of Muhammad al-Manṣūr, r. 745–775.

5. The Samanid Nasr son of Ahmad ruled from Bukhara 864–892.

6. Dabshalim and Bīd(a)bā, which became Bidpai in Persian, are names introduced by Ibn al-Muqaffa'. In Nasrullah's Persian translation, neither is named, and they are called simply "the Raja of India" and "the Brahman."

After Ibn al-Muqaffa's translation and Rudaki's poetry this book was retranslated, and everyone who stepped onto the field of expression acquitted himself according to his ability, but it appears that their goal was to tell stories, not to make wisdom and advice understandable, for they wrote in quite an abridged manner and limited themselves to the fables.

In short, now that people's desire to read Arabic books has waned and they have become deprived of the wisdom and counsel contained therein—indeed they are in danger of becoming lost altogether—it occurred to me that it should be translated and expanded and have Koranic verses, sayings of the Prophet, lines of poetry, and proverbs added to give new life to this book, which is a condensation of several thousand years of wisdom, so that people would not be deprived of its benefits.

Thus was it begun. The text was embellished by adding proverbs, lines of poetry, explanation of obscurities, and advice, and the translation and introduction were done. The one chapter that is limited to a mention of Burzoë the Physician and attributed to Buzurjmihr was done as succinctly as possible because it is based on a tale. A meaning that is devoid of major sagacity and basic wisdom gains nothing in beauty if somebody dresses it in borrowed clothing, and any time one bypasses wise critics and masterly stylists and pays no attention to them one will of course be exposed to disgrace. The rhetorically expanded version and subtle conversation begin with the story of the lion and the ox, which is the beginning of the book proper, and there the gate to the garden of knowledge and wisdom is opened to readers of this book.

When some of the work had been done, a mention of it reached the hearing of His Majesty, and several quires were honored to be perused by him. Since His Majesty is perfectly conversant with and discriminating of writing styles he approved of it, deigned to praise it, and issued a generous order that it should be continued in that vein and a preface be added in his name. I was thus encouraged and honored, and with great trepidation I plunged into that service since servants have no choice but to obey orders. Otherwise it is certain that the first thoughts in the regal mind of the monarch of the world are exemplars of the prime intellect and a route to the holy spirit, and neither does he need reflection on the experiences recorded in this book nor can perusal of these expressions add anything to the pearls of his regal wisdom. . . .

With this command he honored me and my progeny and assured himself of the reward for his regal times. If the kings of the past . . . had such success and held the words of the wise dear so that remembrance of them would last through the ages, today the world obeys the lord of the world, the just, most magnificent sultan of humankind, the reins of rule have been turned over to his justice, mercy, awesomeness, and regal policy, and the superiority of this king of kings over the kings of the age and monarchs of the past is too obvious to need elaboration. "In a hundred thousand generations the plodding celestial sphere does not bring a cavalier like him onto the field of time." May his name and the renown of his felicitous reign, which is a field day of excellence and superiority, last forever and perpetually across the expanse of time. May God make the ultimate ambition of the kings of the world only the beginning of the fortune and felicity of this monarch, and may he grant him enjoyment of the season of youth and the fruits of kingship.

Ibn al-Muqaffaʿ's Preface

Thus says Abu'l-Hasan Abdullah Ibn al-Muqaffaʿ, after praising the Creator and extolling the Lord of Apostles:

God created the world with his perfect power and wisdom and graciously distinguished humankind from other animals by intelligence and wisdom because intelligence is absolutely the key to goodness and happiness, and to it are tied the interests of this and the next life and success in this world and resurrection in the next. It is of two sorts: innate, which God gives, and acquired, which is obtained through experience. Innate intelligence in humans is like fire in wood: just as its appearance is not possible without tools for lighting fire, its effect does not appear without experience and practice. The wise have said, "Experiences are seeds for the mind." Anyone who has a share of heavenly grace and innate intelligence and is careful to acquire virtue and reflect upon the experiences of the ancients will get his wishes in this world and be fortunate in the next as well. "God leads to what is the clearest way and the best guide."

It should be known that God has a reason for everything, for every reason there is an efficient cause, and for every efficient cause there is a place and a time to which the eventuality is tied and the lifetime of a specific person of fortune to whom it is slated. The reason and cause for translating this book and bringing it from India to Persia are as follows. The Creator gave the just monarch and successful prince of the world, Anoshirvan Chosroës son of Kavadh, a large share of intelligence and justice and granted him penetrating insight and a sharp mind to know things and recognize their proper order, and he adorned his character with heavenly assistance so that he might acquire knowledge and apply its principles and thereby attain a station no monarch after him has ever been able to acquire or been worthy of attaining. In him were combined such regal splendor and ambition for world conquest that he brought under his control most of the realms of the world and rendered the tyrants of the day obedient to his will, and the worldly glory people seek he found.

It reached his hearing that in the treasuries of the kings of India there was a book written in the language of the birds and beasts that was useful to kings for managing their subjects, spreading justice and clemency, exterminating opponents, and conquering enemies. They considered it a major source for every good, the basis of all knowledge, a guide for every benefit, and the key to all wisdom, and just as kings could benefit from it, so too could ordinary people profit from it. They called it the book of Kalila and Dimna.

That just monarch was determined to see it. He ordered that a skilled person should be sought who knew both Persian and Indian and who was known for his quest for knowledge so that he could be sent on that mission. They sought long and hard, and finally they heard of a young man named Burzoë who had all the qualifications and also had gained some renown as a physician. He was summoned and told, "After reflection, augury, planning, and consultation we have chosen you for a mission, for your wisdom and perspicacity are known and your desire to acquire knowledge and skill is certain. They say there is such a book in India, and we desire that it should be brought to these parts along with other books of the Hindus. Make yourself ready to go on this mission and get it. Much money will be sent with you so that you will be able to cover any expenses you may have. If your sojourn is lengthy and you need more, tell us so that more may be sent, for all our treasury is at your disposal."

Then he ordered that an auspicious day and favorable ascendant should be found for his departure, and on that day he left. With him were sent fifty purses, each holding ten thousand dinars. All the army and grandees of the realm escorted him off.

Burzoë set out on his mission in all eagerness, and when he arrived at his destination he frequented kings' courts, assemblies of the learned, and gatherings of citizens and asked about the intimates of rajas, the dignitaries of the city, and philosophers. He frequented every place and conducted himself with kindness toward all, and he represented himself as having left his home on a quest for knowledge and going everywhere as a student. Although he knew something about every branch of learning he delved into his search as though he knew nothing, took advantage of every opportunity, made friends, and put each to various tests. Finally his choice fell upon one of them who was exceptional in his virtue and wisdom, and he developed such intimacy with him that over a period of time he had taken the measure of his friendship and compassion and knew for certain that if he put the key to his secret in his hand and opened its lock to him he would repay him for his friendship nobly and gallantly.

When they had spent enough time together for the bonds of friendship to be as firm as could be and for him to know that his friend could be trusted with his secret, he said one day, "Brother, I have kept my purpose concealed from you until now. 'For the intelligent an indication is sufficient.'"

"So it is," replied the Hindu. "Although you have kept your purpose hidden, I have seen signs of it. Yet my affection for you has not allowed me to reveal it. Now that you have divulged it, there is no reason for me not to tell you. It is as clear as the sun in the sky that you have come to carry off precious stores from our realm and enrich the monarch of your land with treasures of wisdom, and you have been deceitful and cunning. I, however, have been watching you patiently and carefully, and I have been waiting for a word to drop that would reveal your purpose. Of course it never happened, and for that reason my trust in your friendship grew stronger, for no one exercises so much prudence, wisdom, and self-control as when he is in a strange land and among people who do not know him and of whose customs he is unaware.

"Intelligence can be discerned by eight things. First, clemency; second, self-awareness; third, obedience to kings and the desire to please them; fourth, knowing the place of secrets and being aware of the confidentiality of friends; fifth, taking care to keep one's own and others' secrets hidden; sixth, being eloquent and sweet-tongued at kings' courts and winning friends by good speech; seventh, keeping one's tongue under control and speaking only when necessary; and eighth, maintaining silence in gatherings and avoiding revealing what is not asked or what might result in regret. Anyone who has these qualities may obtain what he needs and succeed in that for which he has adopted friends.

"All these qualities coalesce in you, and it is certain that your friendship with me was for this purpose, and no one who has such excellent qualities, if in all cases his pleasure is sought, will fall far from the path of wisdom. However, this request causes me trepidation, for it is very dangerous."

When Burzoë saw that the Hindu was aware of his deception he did not deny it but responded calmly and kindly, saying, "I had thought up many convincing things to say to reveal this secret. As though deploying an army, I had looked at it from every angle. I reinforced the right and left wings with friendship and sincerity, the vanguard with our oaths and compacts, and I strengthened the flanks with respect for each other in separation. With such array I set out for the battlefield to remove the veil of fear from my desire and achieve success with your assistance, but with one indication you became aware of all of my ideas and made it unnecessary for me to go on at length, voicing your willingness to grant my wish. It was worthy of your virtue, and that was what I hoped for in my friendship with you. If a wise man trusts in a stronghold with a firm foundation or if he is secure on a mountain that can be moved by neither wind nor water, he cannot be accused of a fault."

The Hindu said, "The wise say that nothing can be compared to friendship. Even if friendship is adorned with affection, and even if friends support each other with their lives and possessions, it will still fall short of what is required. The key to all purposes is the keeping of secrets, and any secret that is not revealed to a third person is safe from exposure, while any that reaches the ears of a third person will undoubtedly become public knowledge, and then it will be impossible to deny it. It is like a springtime cloud that is dispersed in the sky with patches in every direction. If someone tells about it, necessarily he must be believed since it cannot be imagined that it could be denied. I have derived such pleasure from your friendship that nothing can be compared to it. However, if anyone learns of this, our brotherhood will be so ruptured that nothing, no amount of money or goods, can ever make up for it. Our king is severe and strict. He punishes cruelly for the slightest offense, so you can imagine what would happen for a major infraction."

Burzoë said, "The firmest foundation for friendship is the keeping of secrets. I have no other confidant in this affair and trust only you. I can imagine that the danger is great, but it would be more virtuous for you to grant me my wish. If some pain must be borne you will count it as slight and attribute it to the cost of friendship. It is certain that it is an impossibility for me to divulge this talk, but you are thinking of your family and friends, who, if they knew, would expose you to the king's wrath. Most likely no news of it will ever leak out."

The Hindu agreed and gave him the books. Burzoë worked in constant fear for a long time copying them and spent a lot of money on it. He made copies of this book and others of the Hindus' books and informed Anoshirvan by trusted messenger. Anoshirvan rejoiced, and since he wanted Burzoë to get back to court as fast as possible before untoward events could cloud his happiness, he immediately sent him a letter ordering him to make haste and to be strong of heart and great of expectation. He also worried about the books and told him that he would have to make an intelligent plan to bring them out. The letter was sealed and entrusted to a messenger, who was instructed to avoid the highways lest the letter fall into inimical hands.

As soon as the letter reached Burzoë he returned in haste to the court. The king was informed, and he immediately summoned him. Burzoë bowed, kissed the ground, and received a warm welcome. The sight of the travails that were apparent in Burzoë distressed the king, and he said, "Be strong of heart, good and faithful servant, and know that your service is appreciated and praised. You must withdraw and rest for a week. Then come to court so that we may order what is necessary."

On the seventh day the learned men and nobles were commanded to assemble. Burzoë was summoned and told to read the contents of the book for those present. When he read it all were amazed, and they praised Burzoë and expressed their gratitude to the deity for making it possible. The Chosroës ordered the doors of the treasury opened and commanded Burzoë to go in and take without reservation what coins and jewels he wanted.

Burzoë kissed the ground and said, "The king's good opinion of and favor toward me go beyond wealth. What riches could equal the king's favorability toward me? However, since an oath has been given, I will take from the royal wardrobe one robe of the Khuzistan type that is worn by kings." Then he added, "If I confronted any difficulties in this service or had any fear and dread, it was easy for me to bear when I had hopes of the king's pleasure. All effort and striving on the part of servants are done out of loyalty. Otherwise tasks are carried out only by the felicity of the king's person and the favorability of the king's fortune. What service could be equal to the favors that were granted to my family while I was away? There remains one request, which, in comparison to the king's favors, is insignificant. If it is in conformity with destiny, eminence in this world and glory in the next will be joined together, and reward and praise will adorn the king's felicitous days."

Anoshirvan said, "Even if you had expectation of sharing in our kingdom, it would be granted. You must ask for anything you want."

"If the king please," said Burzoë, "let Buzurjmihr be ordered to write a preface for this book containing an account of my adventures and my profession, lineage, and sect. Then, by order of the king, let it be assigned a position to be a lasting honor for me, your servant, for all time and so that a record of my good service to the king may be eternalized."

The Chosroës and those in attendance were greatly astonished and fully convinced of Burzoë's high-mindedness and intelligence. They agreed that he was worthy of that honor. Buzurjmihr was summoned and was told, "You have realized Burzoë's true counsel and great loyalty, and you have learned of the great task he has carried out at our command. We wanted him to have a large share of worldly reward and of our treasury, but he paid no attention to that and only requested that a preface should be added to this book in his name detailing his history from the day of his birth until this moment, when he has the honor to be addressed by us. When it is finished it should be announced so that an assembly may be held and it can be read out in public, and your efforts and deeds, which go beyond the ability of the people of the age, should also be made known to the learned men and nobles of the realm."

When the king gave this order Burzoë prostrated himself in gratitude and lauded the king. Buzurjmihr wrote a preface as has been described, ornamenting it with various rhetorical devices, and informed the king. That very day open court was held, and in the presence of Burzoë and all the people of the realm Buzurjmihr read out his preface. The king and all those present approved of it highly and were eloquent in their praise of what Buzurjmihr had said, and the king gave him a hefty reward of cash, jewels, and fine garments, but Buzurjmihr accepted only a robe.

Burzoë kissed Anoshirvan's hands and feet and said, "May God always grant the king success and combine his splendor in this world with glory in the next. This your servant has been honored, and there will be benefits for readers of this book that will cause it to be related. They will know that obedience to kings and service to monarchs are the most excellent of deeds, and noble indeed is he whom the rulers of the day ennoble and take into their service."

The book of Kalila and Dimna contains fourteen chapters, ten of which are part of the original book that the Indians made: (1) the lion and the bull, (2) the trial of Dimna, (3) the ringdove, (4) the owls and the crows, (5) the king and the bird Finza, (6) the cat and the mouse, (7) the lion and the jackal, (8) the monkey and the tortoise, (9) the archer and the lioness, and (10) the ascetic and the guest.[1] What the Persians

---

1. These ten constitute Chapters 1–4, 8, 7, 9, 5, 10, and 11 of this translation.

appended to it consists of five chapters: one on Burzoë the Physician, one on the ascetic and the weasel, one on Bilar and the Brahmans, one on the traveler and the goldsmith, and one on the prince and his friends.[2]

When we saw that the people of Persia had translated this book from the Indian language into Pahlavi, we wanted to give the people of Iraq, Baghdad, Syria, and the Hejaz the benefit of it, and so it was translated into the Arabic tongue, which is their language. When our labor was finished, insofar as possible it had been couched in terms that would enable learners to understand and would inculcate benefit in order that readers might profit from it more easily, God willing.

---

2. These five are the testament of Burzoë and chapters six, twelve, thirteen, and fourteen in Nasrullah's version. Chapter six actually belongs to the *Pañcatantra* as it is now, but apparently when this part of the preface was written, it was thought that it had been added by the Persians. It is chapter six in Ibn al-Muqaffaʿ's version.

Buzurjmihr Bokhtagan's Preface[1]

This book, *Kalila and Dimna*, which was collected by the learned and the Brahmans of India, contains various pieces of advice, wise anecdotes, and fables. Wise men of every sort strove to produce a collection containing good advice for the present and future and for this life and the next until they achieved this good result, and they set it down in eloquent language put into the mouths of beasts, birds, and wild animals, and in that they achieved several benefits. First, they took advantage of the opportunity to arrange words so that every topic that was initiated was brought to a satisfactory conclusion. Second, advice, wisdom, sport, and jest were combined so that wise men could profit by reading it while the ignorant could read it as fable. Young learners could look upon it as knowledge and advice, and it would be easy for them to memorize. When they reached maturity they could reflect upon what they had memorized and see that the pages of their minds were filled with benefits and they could avail themselves of a precious storehouse. It is like a man of mature years who stumbles across a treasure his father left for him. He rejoices over it and is freed from the necessity of working for a living for the rest of his life.

The reader of this book should know the original purpose for assembling and composing it, for if he does not he will not reap the benefits. First, it is necessary that it be read correctly, for if that is neglected how can the meaning be understood? Writing is the mold into which meaning is poured, and if mistakes are made in reading, how can the meaning be comprehended? Once one is able to read it, one should reflect upon it and not try to get to the end as quickly as possible. One should rather allow the benefits to become part of one's nature slowly. If not, it would be like a man who found a treasure in the wilderness. "If I transport it by myself," he said to himself, "I will spend my life doing it and only a little will be transported. It would be better to hire laborers and rent many pack animals to take it all to my house." That is what he did, and he sent several loads off ahead of himself. The hirelings thought it would be better to

---

1. Buzurjmihr Bokhtagān was minister to the Persian kings Kavadh I (r. 498–531) and Chosroës I Anoshirvan "the Just" (r. 531–579) and is known to history as an embodiment of wise counsel.

take the treasure to their own houses, and when that man, who thought he was so foresighted and wise, got home he had nothing of the treasure but regret and remorse.

Truly one should realize that the benefit lies in understanding, not in memorizing, and anyone who initiates a labor without understanding is like the man who wanted to speak Arabic. He put a slate in the hands of a learned friend of his and said, "Write something for me in Arabic." When it was done he took it home, looked at it from time to time, and thought he had acquired perfect eloquence. One day in an assembly he made a mistake in Arabic. One of those present smiled. The man laughed and said, "My tongue makes a mistake because the slate is at home."

One should strive to acquire knowledge and know that understanding is key, for searching for knowledge and storing provisions for the afterlife are necessary tasks. A person who is truly alive must have knowledge and good action, and the light of good manners should also illuminate his mind. The medicine of experience saves people from the death of ignorance just as the light of the sun illuminates the face of the earth and the fountain of youth gives eternal life. Knowledge is adorned by good deeds, for beneficence is the fruit of the tree of knowledge.

Anyone who possesses knowledge and does not act upon it is like a man who knows the dangers of a road but takes it anyway and is robbed and plundered, or like a sick person who knows the ill effects of certain foods but eats them anyway and dies. Of course anyone who knows the detriment of a thing and throws himself into it anyway will be a target for blame—like the two men who fell into a pit. One was sighted and the other was blind. Although death was common to both, the blind man's excuse was more acceptable to persons of wisdom and insight.

The benefit in learning is first and foremost for self-respect and self-improvement and only then for teaching others, for if one benefits others and neglects oneself it is like a spring: it benefits everybody, but the spring itself is unaware of it. There are two things with which one should first assist oneself and then give to others: knowledge and money. That is, when all aspects of experiences are known, first one should strive to improve one's own moral character and only then that of others. If an ignorant person thinks this is a joke, he is like a blind man who chides a cross-eyed one.

An intelligent person must keep before his eyes his goals and purposes at the beginning of a labor and determine his destination before setting foot on the road. Otherwise he will suffer confusion and regret.

A wise man would do better always to put the quest for the afterlife ahead of desire for this world, for he who aspires less for this world has less regret when he departs it. He who strives for the afterlife gets both his worldly desires and life eternal, while he who limits his striving to this life has a miserable life here and is deprived of reward in the afterlife. The striving of the people of the world to achieve three things is praiseworthy: to store up provisions for the afterlife, to acquire the wherewithal for living, and to have good relations with others by doing as little harm as possible.

The most pleasing of all qualities are piety and the acquisition of money by licit means. Although one should in no situation despair of the mercy of the Creator and the favorability of fortune, to rely on them and to neglect effort are far from wise. To acquire happiness and felicity one does better to be steadfast in one's labors and earnest in one's endeavors. If, as happens due to the quirkiness of fate, an indolent person achieves something or a heedless person gets somewhere, one should pay no attention to that and not be misled by it, for fortunate is he who follows the fortunate and wise in never being far from trust in God or unmindful of the excellence of striving.

One does better to be guided by the conduct of the ancients and to make the experiences of the moderns one's model for conduct, for if one learns lessons only from one's own experiences one will spend one's life in tribulation. While it is said that "in every loss is a gain," it is better to see others' losses and to benefit from their experiences. If one deviates from this path one will encounter something unpleasant every day, and by the time one has acquired certainty through experiences it will be time to depart.

Anyone who ignores these precepts will be deprived of the integrity of life. Opportunity will be lost, one will be lethargic in time of need, things will be believed that may or may not be true, false assumptions will be made based on irrationality, one will pay attention to the blather of informants, one's family and people will be injured on the say-so of seditious troublemakers, one will not do good to the poor, one will chase after lusts—and for the intelligent there is no error greater than following one's lusts—and one will quit the field of certainty.

When an intelligent person is beset by vicissitudes he should take refuge in correctness and not persist in error, mistakenly calling it steadfastness and sticking to one's word. When you proceed blindly down an unfamiliar road without a guide and stray from the right way, the farther you go the more lost you become. If a splinter falls into your eye and you neglect to take it out and rub your eye, doubtlessly you will become blind. A wise person should believe in heaven-sent destiny and not neglect prudence. He should not approve for others what he does not approve for himself, for every action has a reward, and when one's time comes it cannot be hastened or delayed.

Readers of this book should focus their attention on understanding its underlying meaning and recognize what lies beyond the metaphors so that they may not need other books and experiences and not be like someone who gropes in the dark or tosses a stone over a wall. Once they understand they can base their labors and plan for this life and the next on that understanding so that the benefits can accrue and be perpetual. God grants success in what pleases him through his wide grace.

The Testament of Burzoë, Physician of Persia

My father was a military man, and my mother was from a family of scholars of the Zoroastrian religion. The first blessing God bestowed upon me was my mother and father's love, and their affection for me was such that I was singled out from among my brothers and sisters for greater attention and care. When I was seven years old they encouraged me to study medicine, and once I had gained some knowledge of it and realized how excellent it was I pursued it eagerly until I acquired a certain amount of renown and began to treat patients. Then I was faced with a choice among four things that are sought by people of the world: wealth, comfort, fame, and eternal reward.

Now it should be known that the art of medicine is commended by all wise people and in all religions. In medical books it is said that the most excellent of physicians is he who takes care in his treatment to store up for the afterlife, for by doing that he will attain a significant share of this world and also attain salvation in the next life, just as a farmer's object in sowing seed is the grain that gives him sustenance, but hay, which is fodder for animals, is also obtained as a by-product.

In short, I had great success, and any time I was shown a patient who had any hope of recovery I undertook to treat him. When some time had passed and I saw that some of my peers had surpassed me in wealth and status, I too started yearning for those things, and a wish for this-worldly rewards began to invade my mind. I almost went astray, but I said to myself, You are not making a distinction between the things that benefit you and the things that are detrimental. How can an intelligent person wish for something that involves much pain and retribution and gives little benefit or enjoyment? If you think sufficiently about the end of things and the journey to the grave you will realize that the desire for this ephemeral world comes to an end. The most powerful reason to abandon the world is that you have to share it with this handful of noxious vileness by which you have been deceived. Forget this mistaken thought and concentrate on acquiring eternal reward, for the path is dreadful, companions are disagreeable, and departure is nigh even though its hour is unknown. Do not be remiss in building stores for the next life, for the human body is a weak vessel filled with four incompatible corrupt humors, and life is only a prop. It is like a golden idol, the limbs of which are held together by a peg: when the peg is pulled out the whole thing collapses. Although a temporal body can be animated with life, it quickly disintegrates. Do not pride yourself on friends and brethren either, and do not be eager for their company because good times are never free of grief, and sadness outweighs happiness. Moreover, the pain of separation is only to be expected. For the comfort of one's family and children and for supplying the necessities of life one may need to acquire wealth and sacrifice oneself entirely to that. It is just like incense placed on fire: a breeze carries its aroma to others while its own body is burned up. It would be better to be careful in your treatment and pay no attention to the fact that physicians are under-appreciated. Look instead to the fact that if you succeed in saving one person from suffering you will ensure your salvation. In a world in which many are deprived of the enjoyment of water, bread, and the company of wives and children and are afflicted with chronic diseases and debilitating pain, if effort is made to treat them and health or alleviation is obtained, who knows what rewards there may not be? If a low-minded person forgoes such effort for the sake of the chattel of this world he would be just like the man who had a room full of aloeswood. He thought, "To sell it by weight and to be scrupulous about its worth will take too long," so he sold it by estimate and got only half of what it was worth.

When I persisted in opposing my carnal soul I got back on the right track and treated the ill with true willingness and for a modest fee, and I filled my days with that. Thanks to it I made a living and was rewarded by kings. Before I traveled to India, and after that too, I achieved great success and surpassed my peers in wealth and status. Then I reflected on the results and fruits of the medical profession. No remedy could be imagined that would bring essential health or by which total security from any one malady could be had in a way that would prevent its recurrence. This being so, how could wise people be so confident of it and consider it a means of healing? Good works and storing provisions for the afterlife, however, do bestow healing from the disease of sin such that it cannot possibly recur.

In accordance with the preceding I gave up the art of medicine and focused my attention on seeking religion. I found the way to be truly long and without an end and filled with terror and difficulty, and there was neither helper nor guide. Nothing had been seen in my medical books by which I could come to any conclusion or find release from the bonds of perplexity. The disagreements among the nations were perfectly clear: some clung to a weak branch hereditarily, others placed their feet on a shaky foundation to follow monarchs and in fear for their lives, and still others put their reliance on a rotten support and trusted in decaying bones for the chattel of the world and high status among men. Their disagreements on the definition of the Creator and the beginning and end of things were innumerable, but everyone was convinced that he was right and the others wrong.

With such thoughts I spent some time wandering in the wilderness of confusion. Of course I found no way to my goal and discovered no guidepost to lead me on the right way. I therefore determined to make an inquiry into what the scholars of every sect had to say about their beliefs and doctrines and thereby try to gain a satisfactory foothold. When I persisted in my efforts and research I found that every nation had much to say about the preference for their own religion and the superiority of their own sect and spent a lot of time vilifying opposing creeds and anathematizing their opponents. In no way did I find anything helpful to me, and it was clear that everything they said was full of hot air and had nothing to say that an intelligent person's mind could accept. I thought to myself that if after all this disagreement I were to follow any one group and believe the rantings of some self-seeking foreigner, I would be like the ignorant man who went out one night with his comrades to commit burglary. The owner of the house woke up hearing their movements and realized there were thieves on the roof. He gently shook his wife awake and told her what was happening. Then he said, "I'm going to pretend to be asleep. You start speaking to me in a voice they can hear and be persistent in asking me how I got so much wealth." The wife agreed and began asking him.

"Don't ask," the man said, "because if I told you the truth somebody might hear and people would find out." When the wife persisted in asking he said, "I got all this wealth from burglary, at which I was a master. I knew a spell, and on moonlit nights I would stand by the walls of a rich man's house, say '*shaulam*' seven times, and grab hold of a moonbeam. In an instant I would be on the roof. Then I would stand by a window and say '*shaulam*' another seven times, and I would be transported on a moonbeam into the house. I would say '*shaulam*' another seven times and all the valuables in the house would be revealed to me. I would take as much as I could, say 'shaulam' another seven times, and get back up through the window on a moonbeam. Thanks to that spell no one could see me or ever suspect me. Gradually I got all this wealth you see. But do not reveal that word to anyone because it can be perilous."

The thieves heard all this and rejoiced over learning the spell. They waited a while, and when they thought the household was asleep the ringleader of the thieves said 'shaulam' seven times, and no sooner did he step into the window than he fell into the house. The owner picked up a cudgel and beat him, saying, "Did I work hard all my life and get some money so that you could take it? At least tell me who you are."

"I am that ignoramus who was taken in by you and believed I could spread a carpet on water, but I got burned," he replied.

I got no certainty from my inquiry. I told myself that if I clung to the religion of my ancestors without any certitude I would be like the magi, who persist in nonsense and entertain hopes of salvation by imitating their ancestors. Were I to set out on another search the days of my life would not suffice since my term was running out. If I spent my days in confusion opportunity would be lost and I would have to set forth without provisions. It would be best for me to concentrate on good works, which are the best part of all religions, and do what is praised by reason and agreeable to nature.

I therefore avoided cruelty to animals, killing people, arrogance, wrath, treachery, and theft. I kept my loins from impropriety and turned away entirely from women. I stopped my tongue from telling lies, snitching, and uttering words that could be harmful, like cursing, backbiting, gossip, and false accusation. I saw the necessity of abstaining from annoying people and from loving the world, sorcery, and other evil things, and I banished from my heart any wish to give pain to others. I said nothing slanderous about prophecy, resurrection, or reward and punishment. I cut myself off from evil people and clung to good ones. I made rectitude and chastity my companions, for there is no friend like rectitude. Its acquisition, when one's ambition is in accord with destiny, is easy and quick, and it does not decrease with any amount of expenditure. If it is used it does not grow old but rather gets fresher every day, and there is no fear of monarchs' taking it away. Water, fire, beasts, and other destructive things cannot make any dent in it. Anyone who would turn away from it and cease doing good and storing up for the hereafter in pursuit of immediate enjoyment and thereby squander his wealth and life in worldly delights is like the merchant who had many pearls and hired a man at a hundred dinars a day to pierce them. When the hireling entered the merchant's house he saw a harp and kept staring at it.

"Do you know how to play?" asked the merchant.

"I do," he said, and he was proficient at it. He picked it up and began to play a beautiful melody the merchant enjoyed listening to, meanwhile forgetting about piercing the pearls. When the day came to an end the man asked for his wage.

"The pearls are as they were," the merchant said. "You don't get paid when you haven't done any work."

The man insisted and said, "I was hired by you, and I did what you told me to until the end of the day."

The merchant had to pay him and was left in stupefaction. The day had been wasted, money had gone to naught, the pearls were still unstrung, and expenses had yet to be borne.

When the good features of rectitude were fixed in my mind, I wanted to adorn myself with religious practice so that my words and actions would be in conformity with each other and I would be adorned with knowledge and action both externally and internally. Practice and abstinence are powerful breastplates for warding off evil and long lassos for drawing in good, and if one encounters a stumbling block or a steep hill, one can persevere with them. One of the fruits of piety is that one can live free of any worry over death and the end of this life, and when a pious person reflects on the works and pleasures of this impermanent world he envisions its ugliness, focuses his attention on doing little harm and following the road to the next life, is content with his lot in order to have less grief, divorces himself from the world to escape its consequences, eschews lust in order to acquire purity of body, abandons envy to be beloved in the hearts of others, acquaints himself with generosity to be free of remorse when parted from worldly goods, bases his actions on reason to escape regret, remembers the next world to be content and humble, keeps consequences of action before his eyes in order not to stumble, and gives no one any cause for fear in order to live in safety. The more I reflected on the fruits of abstinence the more I wanted to acquire it, but I feared it would be difficult to rise above lusts and renounce the pleasures of the here and now, and to embark on that path would pose great danger since, if anything impeded my progress, it would not be in the best interests of my life in this world or the next, like the dog that found a bone on the bank of a river. No sooner had it taken the bone in its mouth than it saw a reflection of the bone in the water and thought it was another bone. It opened it mouth greedily to snatch it from the water, and what it already had in its mouth was lost.

In short, these worries almost swamped me and cast me into such waywardness that both worlds would have been lost to me. Once again I reflected on the ends of things in this world and took into account what it had to offer. It was clear that the rewards of this world are as impermanent as the brightness of a flash of lightning. This world is like salt water: the more you drink of it, the thirstier you get. It is like wine laced with poisoned honey: drinking it delights the palate but results in death. It is like a good dream: doubtless during the dream you are happy, but after you wake there is only regret and sorrow. In acquiring the goods of this world one is like a silkworm: the more it spins its cocoon, the tighter it gets and the more escape becomes impossible.

I also told myself that it was not right to flee from this world for the sake of the next or from the next for the sake of this one. My mind was like a crafty judge who gives a verdict in favor of both parties in a single case.

Finally I settled on practice since the difficulty involved was of no importance in comparison with eternal salvation. Of course a little bitterness that yields much sweetness is better than a little sweetness that brings about much bitterness. Anyone who is told that to have eternal salvation he will have to spend a hundred years in constant torment, having his limbs torn from his body and restored ten times a day, would choose that torment because that period, with its hope of eternal pleasure, would pass in an instant, and if a few days have to be spent in rigor and in the strictures of the law, how could an intelligent person refuse or even think it difficult?

It must be known that the world is surrounded by calamities and torments. From the day a person is formed in the womb until the end of his life, not for one moment does he escape tribulation. In medical books it is found that when the liquid that is the origin of the creation of children mixes with the liquid of the woman it becomes dark and thick. It swells and then begins to move until it becomes like whey. Then it becomes like yogurt. Next it develops limbs, and a boy turns toward the mother's back and a girl toward her belly, hands over the eyes and chin on the knees.

The limbs are folded up and contracted as though tied up in a purse. It breathes with difficulty. Above it are the warmth and weight of the mother's belly; beneath it are darkness and tightness that need no description. When the gestation period is up and it is time for the birth of the child the womb swells and movement appears in the child, enabling it to turn its head toward the exit. From the tightness of the aperture it experiences unimaginable pain. When it emerges, even if it falls into soft hands or a pleasant breeze blows over it, the pain is equivalent to having one's skin stripped off. Then it is afflicted with all sorts of torments. When it is hungry and thirsty it cannot ask for food or drink. If it is in pain it cannot express it. There is no end to the amount of being picked up and put down, being rocked in the cradle, and having diapers changed. When the days of infancy are over it then faces the tortures of education, the affliction of medicine and abstinence, and the agony of pain and illness. Upon maturity one has to worry about possessions and children, suffer through greed and cupidity, and fret over making a living. In addition to all this the four conflicting inimical natures are one's constant companions, and accidental afflictions like snakes, scorpions, wild beasts, heat, cold, wind, rain, snow, devastation, murder, poison, flood, and storm lurk in ambush, and the torments of old age and feebleness—if one gets that far—are the worst of all. There are also attacks by foes and the malignity of enemies to contend with. Even if there were none of these things, and if one had been given every assurance that one would live healthy, the thought of the moment when one's time is up and one has to bid farewell to friends, family, and children and quaff the bitter potion of death would embitter one to love of this world, and no reasonable person would waste his life in the quest for it, for it would be great madness to sell an eternal thing for an ephemeral one or to sacrifice one's pure soul for the sake of a vile body.

This is particularly true in these dark days when good is in retrograde and people are not inclined to good works. Despite the fact that King Anoshirvan the Just, son of Kavadh, possesses felicity of person, preponderance of reason, steadfastness of purpose, exaltedness of ambition, perfect power, truthfulness, justice, clemency, generosity, mercy, and love of learning and the learned, is philosophical and employs the wise, defeats his enemies, rewards his servants, eliminates the unjust, and empowers the downtrodden, I see that the world is on the decline. It is as though charity has bid farewell to people and praiseworthy deeds and good character have been effaced. The right way is closed, and the path to error is open. Justice is nowhere to be seen, and cruelty is apparent. Learning has been abandoned, and ignorance is sought. Vileness and baseness are dominant, and nobility and virtue have withdrawn. Friendships are weak, and enmities strong. Good people are belittled and demeaned, and the evil are comfortable and respected. Deceit and cunning are awake, and fidelity and magnanimity are asleep. Lies are influential and fruitful, and truth is rejected and exiled. Right is routed, and wrong is victorious. Following lusts is the beaten path, and ignoring the dictates of reason is the highway taken. Tyrannized persons in the right are debased, and tyrants in the wrong are dignified. Greed overwhelms, and contentment is overwhelmed. The deceitful world rejoices over all these things and smiles at their acquisition.

When my thought had encompassed all these works of the world and I realized that humans are the noblest of all creatures and yet they do not appreciate the days of their lives and do not strive for the salvation of their souls, I was greatly amazed to see this condition. When I looked closely I saw that what prevented this happiness was the small comfort and mean ambition with which people are afflicted, which are the pleasures of the senses, eating, smelling, seeing, touching, and hearing, and their needs and desires can never be satisfied. It is impossible to find safety from death and annihilation in these things, and if it were possible it would mean loss of both this world and the next. Anyone who desires this world and ignores the next is like the man who ran from a mad camel and took refuge in a pit, hanging on to two branches growing over the pit and with his feet suspended over something. When he looked closely he saw that his feet were over four snakes that had put their heads out of a hole. He looked at the bottom of the pit and saw a horrible dragon with its mouth open waiting for him to fall. When he looked above the pit he saw black and white rats gnawing away at the branches. In such a state he should have thought of some way to save himself, but instead he found a beehive with honey, some of which he put to his lips and was so distracted by the sweetness that he forgot about his situation and gave no thought to the fact that his feet were over the heads of four snakes and he could not know when they would strike, that the rats were intent on gnawing away the branches and were not going to stop, and when the branches broke he would fall into the dragon's maw. That momentary pleasure so distracted him and clouded his judgment that when the rats finished gnawing, the poor fellow fell into the dragon's mouth.

I liken the world to that pit filled with horrors and terrors. The black and white rats and their constant gnawing at the branches are night and day, whose relentless sequence wears down living beings and brings their demise ever closer. The four snakes are the natures that are at the essence of human existence, and when one of them moves it is lethal poison and present death. The tasting of the honey and its sweetness are the pleasures of this world, the benefits of which are few and the pain and consequences of which are many. They distract people from working for the next world and block the way to salvation. The dragon is the final end that cannot be avoided, and when the draft of death is quaffed and the angel of death comes knocking, of course one must join him and face terror, danger, fright, and horror. It will be too late then for remorse, and repentance will be to no avail. There will be no way back or any excuse for shortcomings. The Koran records the wail that will go up: "Alas for us! Who hath awakened us from our bed? This is what the Merciful promised us; and his apostles spoke the truth" [Kor. 36:52].

In short, I finally reached a stage at which I gave in to my destiny and did what I could to pave the way to the next life, and I live in the hope that perhaps someday I will find a guide and helper.

When a journey to India was proposed I went there and had many discussions and held as many deliberations as I could, and when I returned I brought with me books, one of which is this book, *Kalila and Dimna.*

Kalila

&

Dimna

Chapter One

The Lion and the Bull

The Raja of India said to the Brahman, "Tell me a story of two individuals who had a friendship that was ruptured by the machinations of a treacherous schemer and turned into enmity and separation."

The Brahman said, "When an evil person comes between two friends, they will of course be parted. An example is the following."

There once was a rich merchant, and he had sons who refused to learn a trade and squandered their father's wealth. The father advised and chided them, saying, "My sons, the people of this world seek three things they cannot attain unless they have four traits. As for the three they seek, they are easy living, high status, and reward in the afterlife. The four things by which those goals can be attained are, one, the acquisition of wealth in an honest way; two, perseverance in keeping it; three, spending it to ensure a good life, the contentment of one's family, and as provision for the afterlife; and four, protecting oneself from the vicissitudes of fate insofar as possible. Anyone who neglects any one of these four things will have a veil of misfortune drawn over his goals by fate. No one who refuses to acquire wealth will be able either to make a living for himself or to provide for others. A person who acquires wealth but neglects to make it productive will soon be poverty-stricken—like collyrium: no matter how sparingly it is used, ultimately it is all used up. If you seriously put your wealth to work but spend inappropriately you will fall prey to regret and tongues will be loosed in reviling you. If you are tightfisted and do not make necessary expenditures you will be just as deprived of good things as a poor man, and additionally destiny and vicissitudes will bring about loss—like a pool that does not have outflow to match its inflow. Inevitably the water will spill over the edges or cause cracks, and all will be lost."

The merchant's sons listened to their father's advice and realized the benefits. The eldest brother went off to engage in commerce and traveled far and wide. He had two bulls. One was named Shanzaba, and the other was called Nandaba. Along the way there was a bog in which Shanzaba got stuck and scrambled out only with great difficulty. Too exhausted to go farther, he was left in the care of a man who was to feed him and bring

3

him to the merchant when he had regained his strength. The man stayed one day and then got tired and left Shanzaba, telling the merchant the bull had died.

Shanzaba grazed for a while and wandered around in search of pasture until he came to a meadow that had all sorts of plants and herbage. Shanzaba liked it; as has been said, "When you find what you like don't go any farther." As the proverb says, "When you come to a place with grass, dismount." When he had been there for a time and grown fat, he rejoiced in his ease and comfort and mooed loudly in exhilaration.

In the vicinity of that meadow was a lion, and there were many other beasts, all of whom obeyed the lion, who was young and good-looking but rather opinionated. He had never seen a cow or heard one moo. When he heard Shanzaba's mooing he was gripped by fear, but he did not want the other beasts to know he was afraid, so he stood still and did not budge.

Among the beasts were two jackals. One was named Kalila and the other was Dimna, and both were extremely clever. Dimna, who was the greedier and worldlier of the two, asked Kalila, "Why do you think the king is fixed in place and isn't moving?"

"What is it to you," replied Kalila, "and why do you ask? We enjoy ease at the king's gate and receive scraps. We are not of the class who are honored to converse with the king or whose words are listened to by royalty. Forget it, for anyone who meddles in what does not concern him will suffer the fate of the monkey."

"How was that?" asked Dimna.

The Monkey That Pulled Out the Wedge

A monkey saw a carpenter sitting on a plank, using two wedges to split it. When he pounded one wedge in he would take out the one he had driven in previously. The carpenter went to relieve himself, and the monkey sat on the end of the plank that had been split with his testicles dangling in the gap. Before he drove the second wedge in he pulled out the one that was there, and the two sides of the plank slammed shut, mashing his testicles so hard that he fainted. When the carpenter returned he beat him until he was dead. Thus it is said that carpentry is not a job for a monkey.

"I understand," said Dimna, "but when one seeks intimacy with kings it should not be in hopes of sustenance, for the belly can be filled anywhere and with anything. The benefits of intimacy with kings are elevation of station, acquisition of friends, and confounding of enemies. Contentment indicates low expectations and a lack of manliness. Anyone whose ambition does not go beyond a morsel is reckoned a beast—like a hungry dog that is happy with a bone and a crust of bread. When a lion sees a wild ass while hunting a rabbit, it leaves the rabbit and goes after the ass. When one achieves high status, even if it is as short-lived as a flower, the wise reckon it a long life filled with good achievements and renown, while he who is content to be obscure, even if it is as long-lasting as a cypress, is of no importance in the view of the successful."

"I hear what you say," said Kalila, "but consult your own intelligence and know that every class has its station, and we are not of the class that can aspire or attempt to achieve such heights."

"The ranks of the manly and those of high ambition are open to all and hotly contested," said Dimna. "Anyone who has a noble soul will get himself from a lowly position to a high one, while he whose mind is weak will sink from lofty position to obscurity. To ascend to high status has many benefits, while to sink from a position of power has few advantages. A heavy rock may be lifted from the ground and put on one's shoulder only with great difficulty, while it can be thrown onto the ground without much exertion. Anyone who does not agree with a high-minded individual in acquiring greatness is excused since the greater the demand, the fewer are those who are fit. We who are worthy of seeking high station are not satisfied with obscurity and lowliness."

"What plan have you thought up?" asked Kalila.

"I want to get a chance to show myself to the lion while he is confused and perplexed and advise him on a way out. By this means I will achieve intimacy and status," said Dimna.

"How do you know the lion is confused?" asked Kalila.

"With my own perspicacity I can see signs of it," said Dimna. "A wise man recognizes a quality by its external signs."

"How are you going to achieve intimacy with the lion?" asked Kalila. "You have never served kings and do not know how to do it."

"When a man is wise and capable," said Dimna, "he is not shy of leaping into action or bearing a great burden. An ambitious person who is

5

enlightened will not achieve little, and a wise person does not suffer from being alone or in exile."

"Kings do not always single out persons of excellence and virtue for honors," said Kalila, "but rather they give status to their intimates who occupy inherited positions and ranks and are devoid of all good qualities—like a grapevine, which does not go to the best and most productive tree but rather clings to whatever is nearest."

"The ruler's friends and their ancestors have not always held those positions," said Dimna. "They have acquired them over time with great effort. I seek the same, and therefore I will strive. He who joins a king's retinue will get his wish in the best possible manner provided he does the following: he must not mind being subjected to great tribulation or quaffing distasteful potions, he must quench the fire of wrath with the water of clemency, he must use an incantation of wisdom to lure the demon of passion into a bottle, he must not allow deceptive greed to overpower guiding wisdom, he must base his labor on honesty and acumen, and he must confront setbacks with calmness and resignation."

"Suppose you become intimate with the king," said Kalila. "How are you going to attract his favor and achieve high station?"

"If I can attain intimacy and learn his ways I will serve him loyally and focus my attention on carrying out his will, and I will avoid criticizing his deeds and actions. When he starts to do something that is correct and in the best interests of the kingdom I will make it seem good in his eyes and be eloquent in praising the benefits so that he will be more self-confident. If he initiates an action that would have bad results and would be harmful to the kingdom, after much reflection and contemplation I would tell him so in the gentlest of terms and with all humility and make him aware of the disastrous consequences in a way that other servants would not do. If an eloquent wise man wants to he can clothe the truth in a false garb and make falseness appear true. A clever painter can paint things that look three-dimensional even though they are flat, and he can make things appear flat when they are actually three-dimensional. When the king sees my skills he will be even eagerer to elevate me than I am to serve him."

"If you are resolved and determined to do this," said Kalila, "you must at least be aware that there is great danger. The wise say that only fools engage in three things: companionship with a ruler, testing poison, and telling secrets to women. The wise have likened a ruler to a high mountain on which are various fruits and mines but which is also home to lions, snakes, and other noxious animals that make going there difficult and tarrying there dreadful."

"It is true," said Dimna, "but he who avoids danger gets nowhere. One cannot engage in three things without lofty ambition and a strong constitution: working for rulers, commerce on the sea, and overcoming enemies. The wise say that there are two positions fit for a virtuous person: either to be honored in the service of successful kings or to be respected among contented ascetics."

"I hope you are successful in your endeavor," said Kalila, "although I am still opposed to the idea."

Dimna went off and greeted the lion. The lion asked his courtiers who he was. They told him that he was So-and-So, son of So-and-So.

"Oh, yes," he said, "I knew his father." Then he summoned Dimna forward and asked, "Where do you live?"

"I have taken up residence at the king's gate," he said, "and it is the direction in which I turn for all my needs and the focus of all my hopes. I am waiting for a job to come my way that I can accomplish with my wisdom and intelligence, for there are posts at a king's court for which underlings are necessary. No person, no matter how lowly, is devoid of the desire to repel harm and attract benefit, and even a dry twig tossed on the roadway may be of use, if only to scratch one's ear. How can a being be dismissed as useless when it has both benefit and harm and good and evil? As they say, if we cannot be made into a bouquet, at least we are good for kindling under a pot."

When the lion heard what Dimna said he was amazed and thought he would offer a piece of advice. Turning to his intimates, he said, "A skillful man with virtue, however obscure he may be and however many enemies he may have, will stand out among his peers for his intelligence and virtue, like a flame that rises up even though the kindler wants it to burn low." Dimna rejoiced at these words and knew that his charm had had an effect on the lion.

"It is incumbent upon a king's servants and members of his retinue to offer advice and make the king aware of their knowledge and understanding," said Dimna, "for unless a king knows his followers well and is aware of the limits of the acumen and loyalty of each he cannot derive benefit from their service or issue appropriate commands. So long as a seed lies hidden in the earth no one will tend it. Only when it has rent the veil of the earth and shown its face by turning the earth emerald green can it be known what it is, and consequently it will be tended and benefited from. Reliable men are useful in all respects, as is said, 'I am like the earth, and you are like the sun and the cloud. I will give forth flowers and tulips if you cultivate me.' Kings owe it to their subjects to promote each according to his skill, loyalty, and ability to advise and not to elevate or demote on a whim or to promote persons who are negligent in their tasks and devoid of skill over those who are competent and clever, for two things would be strange for kings to do: to wear a head ornament on the foot and to put a foot ornament on the head. To have a ruby or pearl set in lead or tin is not so much demeaning to the jewels as it is reprehensible for the person who has it done. Hordes of friends who are not farsighted and competent are harmful in and of themselves. Tasks are carried out by people of insight and understanding, not by crowds of henchmen and hangers-on. A person who has a ruby is not heavy-laden and can do anything he wants with it, while a person who has a rock in his purse is needlessly burdened and cannot do anything with it when need arises. A wise man does not demean a person of virtue even if he is obscure, for boughs may be raised from the dust and turned into saddles or bows and be fit for companionship with kings and nobles. It is not fitting for kings to neglect wise men simply because their ancestors were obscure and befriend the unskilled on account of their heredity when they have no skill. Rather kings' favor should be in proportion to the benefit a person will have for the kingdom, since if the unskilled are favored for their ancestors' service the kingdom will suffer and skilled people will remain undiscovered. No one is closer to humans than those of their own species, and when one of them falls ill they treat him with medicine that may be brought from far away. A mouse shares a house with humans, but when it becomes bothersome they drive it away or try to kill it. A hawk may be wild, but when it is needed it can be caught, however unwillingly, and it will sit on a king's arm."

When Dimna was finished talking the lion was even more amazed. Praising him greatly, he took to him. When he had a chance Dimna asked to speak to the lion in private and said, "For some time now I have seen the king staying in one place and not hunting or moving. What is the reason?"

The lion wanted to keep his fear hidden from Dimna, but just then Shanzaba mooed loudly, and the sound so shook the lion that he could not control himself and thus revealed his state to Dimna. "The cause is this sound you hear," said the lion. "I do not know from what direction it is coming, but I imagine its owner to be powerful in proportion to the sound. If that is the case, it would be unwise to remain here."

"Aside from this noise is the king frightened by anything else?" asked Dimna.

"No," he said.

"Then the king should not vacate his position or leave his home on this account, for it is said that the worst detriment to intelligence is boasting, the worst detriment to manliness is scoffing, and the worst detriment to a weak heart is a loud noise. It is shown in a fable that not every loud noise indicates a powerful body."

"How is that?" the lion asked.

The Fox That Tried to Eat a Drum

Once upon a time a fox went into a forest and saw a drum lying next to a tree. Every time the wind blew, a branch of the tree would hit the drum and cause a dreadful sound to reach the fox's ear. When the fox saw how enormous the body of the drum was and heard the terrible sound it made he greedily thought its innards would be as great as the sound. He strove to rip it open, but actually he found nothing but a greasy skin. Regretfully he said, "Now I realize that the larger the body and the more dreadful the sound, the less the benefit."

"I have told this fable so that the king may be enlightened and know that this sound should not trouble his mind," said Dimna.

The king found this comforting and ordered Dimna to go investigate. When Dimna was out of sight the lion reflected and, regretful at having sent him away, said to himself, "It was a bad idea to send him. A king should be very well informed of ten types of people before he sends one of them to an opponent or makes him an emissary and privy to secrets. The first is a person who has been tormented at a king's court without having committed a crime. The second is one who has suffered long, has been afflicted with poverty, and has been deprived of his possessions or status. The third is one who has been dismissed from his post. The fourth is a known troublemaker who plots sedition and does little good. The fifth is a criminal whose confederates are pardoned while he is punished, or they are punished and he receives an even harsher punishment. Sixth is someone who has done a good service with his peers and his peers are rewarded more. Seventh is one over whom a rival has been promoted. Eighth is one who is not trustworthy. Ninth is one who does something to the detriment of the king, thinking it beneficial to himself. Tenth is one who takes refuge with the king's enemy. This Dimna is farsighted and has long suffered deprivation at my court. If there is any spite lurking in his heart he may have treacherous thoughts and stir up sedition. He may find more favor with the enemy and prefer to serve him and share with him the secrets he has learned."

The lion was uneasy in these thoughts, getting up and sitting down restlessly and looking out, when suddenly Dimna appeared from afar. The lion sat down calmly. When Dimna joined him he asked, "What did you do?"

"I saw the bull whose voice the king heard," he said.

"How powerful is it?" he asked.

"I didn't see any splendor or magnificence that would indicate great power," he said. "When I got to him I spoke to him as an equal, and he did not evince any desire for humility or veneration. For my part I did not find him so awe-inspiring that great respect would be necessary."

"Nonetheless," said the lion, "that should not be attributed to weakness, and one should not be fooled, for a strong wind does not break a weak stalk while it can rip out mighty trees and fell strong buildings. The great recognize that it is not lordly to attack underlings, and unless an opponent is grand and noble a show of strength is not permissible. Everyone should be confronted according to his rank, for among the nobility equality of rank is of great importance. 'A hawk does not make a truce with locusts, and a lion does not go out to wound a jackal.'"

"The king should not attach any importance to it," said Dimna. "If so ordered I will go and bring him so the king may see what a submissive servant and obedient creature he is."

This pleased the king, and he ordered him to bring the bull. Dimna went and spoke to him without hesitation or indecision.

"The lion has sent me and ordered me to take you to him," said Dimna. "He has said that if you comply straightaway I am to offer you pardon for any shortcoming you may have committed in serving him. If you agree I will return immediately and report what has transpired."

"Who is this lion?" asked the bull.

"King of the beasts," said Dimna.

As soon as the bull heard the words "king of the beasts," he was afraid and said to Dimna, "If you assure me that I am safe from his wrath I will go with you." Dimna gave him assurance and reaffirmed what he had said, and they set out together in the direction of the lion.

When they were before him the lion asked the bull warmly, "When did you come to these parts, and what brought you here?" The bull told his story. The lion said, "Settle down here, for you will receive a full share of our compassion and bounty." The bull praised the lion and willingly entered the lion's service. The lion made him an intimate and was very kind to him. He also made an investigation into his condition and assessed the extent of his wisdom. After reflection, consultation, counsel, and auguries, he made him a confidant and privy to his secrets. The more experience he had of him, the more his confidence in his competence and understanding increased. Every day he rose in the king's opinion and received a greater share of the king's bounty until he surpassed all the army commanders and intimates.

When Dimna saw how intimate the lion had become with the bull and how he kept promoting him, jealousy and vengeful spite awoke in Dimna's heart and kept him awake. He went to Kalila and said, "Brother, do you see what a mistake I have made? I limited my ambitions to pleasing the lion and neglected to think of myself. I brought him this bull, who has been promoted to high station, and I have fallen from grace."

"The same thing happened to you that happened to the holy man," said Kalila.

"What was that?" asked Dimna.

The Holy Man's Adventures

A holy man was given a magnificent suit of clothing and a robe of honor by a king. A thief saw him wearing them and craved them, so he went up to him and said, "I want to accompany you and be initiated into the rites of your order." And he became a confidant of the holy man and lived comfortably until he got a chance to steal all the clothing. When the holy man saw his clothing gone he realized who had taken it and set out for the city in search of him.

Along the way he passed by two rams that were fighting, butting, and wounding each other with their horns. A fox was attracted and was lapping up their blood when suddenly the rams gored the fox and killed it.

The holy man reached the city by night and looked for a place to stay. He found the house of a madam who kept prostitutes. One of the girls was extremely beautiful and attractive. She had fallen in love with a good-looking youth, and of course he would not allow rivals to frequent her. The madam was fretting over her loss of income, and it was not long before she discovered the girl's secret and plotted to kill the youth. She had planned to do it on the very night the holy man came and was just waiting for her chance. She plied the two of them with strong drink until they both passed out. When both were asleep she put poison into a straw. One end of the straw she put in the youth's anus and the other end she put in her mouth to blow the poison into him. However, just as she took a breath the youth farted, forcing all the poison down her throat. She died on the spot, and the holy man witnessed it all.

When dawn lit the world the holy man freed himself from the degradation of those people and went out to find another place to stay. A cobbler welcomed him in as a guest and charged his wife to serve him well while he went off to visit some friends. The wife had a lover, and her go-between was the wife of a barber. She sent a message to her lover with the barber's wife telling him that her husband was not at home. The lover was just arriving that night when the cobbler returned drunk and saw him at the door. Since he had already harbored suspicions, he went in angrily, beat his wife, tied her to a post, and went to sleep. When everyone was asleep the barber's wife came and said, "Why are you keeping him waiting? If you are coming out, be quick about it. If not, tell him to come back another time."

"Sister," she said, "if you have any compassion, untie me and let me tie you up in my place. I'll apologize to my lover and return immediately. I will be obliged to you forever."

The barber's wife untied her, let herself be tied up, and sent her out. At this point the cobbler awoke and called out to her. The barber's wife was too afraid to reply lest he recognize her voice. He called out repeatedly, but she said nothing. The cobbler's anger increased, and he took a cobbler's knife and went to the post.

Cutting the woman's nose off, he handed it to her and told her to send it to her lover as a gift.

When the cobbler's wife returned and saw her go-between with her nose cut off she grieved and apologized. Then she untied her and tied herself back to the post. The barber's wife went home with her nose in her hand. All this the holy man saw and heard.

When the cobbler's wife had calmed down she lifted her hands in prayer and said, "O Lord, if you know that my husband has falsely accused me, forgive him and give me back my nose."

"You worthless witch," the cobbler said, "what's all this talk?"

"Get up, you tyrant," she replied, "and see how the Creator in his justice and mercy has given me back my nose in return for the cruelty I have suffered when it was clear that I was innocent. He did not let me remain mutilated and disgraced."

The cobbler got up, lit a lamp, and saw his wife whole and her nose intact. He immediately apologized, confessed his wrongdoing, and asked her forgiveness, promising never again to do such a thing without proof, not to harm a righteous woman on the say-so of evil informants, and never to do anything contrary to the will of a woman whose prayers were answered.

Meanwhile the barber's wife went home with her nose in her hand, wondering how she was going to explain it to her husband and neighbors. What was she to say if they asked? Just then the barber woke up and called out for his instruments because he was going to the house of a nobleman. The wife dallied for a while and then gave him only his razor. In the darkness of the night the barber threw it away, knocked his wife down, and yelled, "Your nose! Your nose!" The barber was utterly perplexed. The neighbors came running and blamed him.

When morning lit the sky the wife's relatives gathered and took the barber before the judge.

"For no obvious fault or known crime why did you mutilate this woman?" asked the judge.

Baffled, the barber had no excuse to offer. The judge sentenced him to retribution and punishment, but the holy man rose and said, "The judge must reflect on this case. The thief did not steal my clothes. The fox was not killed by the rams. The madam was not killed by poison. The barber did not cut off his wife's nose. We have all brought these things upon ourselves."

The judge let the barber go and turned to the holy man for an explanation. The holy man said, "If I had not been so desirous of having many disciples and a large following and not been deceived by the thief's drivel, he wouldn't have had an opportunity to steal. If the fox had not been so greedy and not licked up the blood it wouldn't have been harmed by the rams. If the madam had not tried to kill the young man she wouldn't have lost her life. If the barber's wife had not encouraged and abetted adultery she wouldn't have been mutilated."

"I have told this story," Kalila said, "that you may know that you have brought this misery upon yourself by being negligent of the consequences."

"It is as you say," said Dimna. "It was my own doing. Now, what do you see as a means of saving myself?"

"What do you propose?" Kalila asked.

"I think I may be able to reach this goal through subterfuge and cunning and try by whatever means possible to get rid of him. In the code of zeal neglect and shortcoming are not allowed, and if I am negligent I will be subjected to blame by the manly, and furthermore I will not be able to find a new position or get a promotion because I will be accused of greed and cupidity. There are five goals allowed by the intelligent in which any amount of wile and cunning are allowed: to regain past status and position, to avoid harm of which one has experience, to maintain a benefit one has, to get oneself out of a present calamity, and to attract benefit and ward off harm in the future. Since I am hopeful of regaining my position, the way to do it is to lie in wait until the bull departs this earth, for that would be the best thing for the lion since he has gone so far in preferring the bull that he can be accused of being addlebrained."

"I can find no fault in the lion for befriending and promoting the bull," said Kalila.

"He has gone too far," said Dimna. "He has been contemptuous of his other advisors to the point that they are complaining that they have been deprived of the benefits of his service. They say six things are disastrous for a king: deprivation, sedition, lust, reversal of fortune, ill temper, and ignorance. Deprivation means depriving oneself of well-wishers and leaving people of good counsel and experience in despair. Sedition means that unexpected battles and unplanned-for affairs happen and enemies' swords are drawn. Lust means a burning desire for women, hunting, singing, wine, and the like. Reversal of fortune means plague, drought, flood, fire, and such like. Ill temper means an excess of wrath and abhorrence and overdoing punishments. Ignorance means using appeasement when hostility would be more appropriate and engaging in dispute instead of cajolery."

"I see," said Kalila, "but how can you make an attempt on the bull's life? He is much stronger than you are and has more friends."

"You shouldn't worry about such things," said Dimna. "Things are not accomplished through strength and helpers alone. It is said that strategy comes before a show of bravery. That which can be done by strategy and cunning cannot be done by strength of arm. Have you not heard that the crow destroyed the snake by cunning?"

"How was that?" asked Kalila.

The Crow That Killed a Snake

Once upon a time a crow had its nest on top of a tree on a mountain. In the vicinity was a snake's hole. Every time the crow had a chick the snake would eat it. When this had gone on for a long time the crow grew desperate and complained to its friend the jackal, saying, "I think I will rid myself of this murderous tyrant."

"In what way are you going to do it?" asked the jackal.

"When the snake is asleep I will attack and pluck out its eyes so that in the future my dear children will be safe from its depredation," said the crow.

"This is not a wise plan," said the jackal. "A wise person attacks his enemy in a way that poses no danger. Beware lest you do like the heron that tried to kill the crab."

"How was that?" the crow asked.

The Heron That Schemed against the Crab

Once upon a time a heron lived beside a pond and caught fish according to need, passing his days in plenty. When the weakness of old age caught up with him and he could no longer fish he said

15

to himself, "Alas! Life has passed fleetingly and the only thing to come of it that would be of any use in old age is experience and practical knowledge. Now that I have no strength left, I must resort to cunning in order to obtain the sustenance on which life is based."

Then he sat down sadly on the edge of the pond. A crab saw him from afar, came over, and said, "You seem sad."

"Why should I not be?" said the heron. "I used to gain my livelihood by catching one or two fish, and I lived on that. It satisfied my hunger and did not decrease the number of fish significantly. Today two fishermen were passing by here, and one said to the other, 'There are a lot of fish in this pond. We should do something about it.' The other said, 'There are more in another pond. When we finish with them we can come back here.' If this is how things are I must bid farewell to life and suffer not only the pangs of hunger but also the bitterness of death."

The crab left and informed the fish. They all came to the heron and said, "He who is asked for advice should be trusted. We are consulting you, and a counselor should never withhold advice, even when an enemy asks, and especially when it concerns something from which he benefits. Your continued existence depends upon our procreation. What do you think is the right thing for us to do?"

The heron replied, "To combat the fishermen would be futile. I cannot advise trying to do so. However, I know of another pond in the vicinity the water of which is purer than lovers' tears and more glistening than the true dawn. Grains of sand can be seen on its bottom, and fish eggs can be seen on the top. If you move there you will be safe and enjoy comfort and plenty."

"That's a good idea," they all said, "but it won't be possible for us to get there without your help."

"I don't mind," the heron said, "but it will take time, and any moment now the fishermen will return and the opportunity will be lost."

The fish pleaded and implored, and it was decided. The heron then took several fish every day, and when he got to a hill in the area, he ate them. The others jostled each other in their haste to move as the heron looked upon their error and negligence, saying to himself, "This is what anyone deserves who is deceived by an enemy's blather and relies on a mean, ignoble creature."

When many days had passed the crab too wanted to move. The heron put him on his back and headed off in the direction of the hill that was the resting place of the fish. When the crab saw the fish bones from afar he realized what had happened and thought to himself, "When a wise person sees himself in imminent danger from an enemy, if he does not make some effort he will be complicit in his own death. If he makes an effort and is victorious he will gain renown; and if not, at least he will not be accused of lack of zeal, manliness, and courage and will be rewarded for his efforts with the label of martyr." So saying, he threw himself on the heron's neck and squeezed his throat so hard that the heron lost consciousness, fell from the sky, and went straight to hell.

The crab betook himself back to the remaining fish, consoling them on the loss of their friends and congratulating them on being alive as he explained what had happened. They all rejoiced and reckoned the death of the heron as a new lease on life.

✻ ✻ ✻ ✻

"I have told this story because many a person has been destroyed by his own machinations. I can, however, show you a way that will ensure your continued existence and the death of the snake if you can carry it out," the jackal said.

"One should not ignore the advice of friends," the crow said, "or go contrary to the opinions of the wise."

"Here's what you should do," the jackal said. "Fly up into the sky and cast your glance over the rooftops and fields until you spy a piece of jewelry you can snatch. Swoop down and pick it up. Keep flying low so that you are never out of the sight of people. When you are near the snake, drop the jewelry on it. The people will come looking for it. First they will deliver you of your enemy, and then they will take the jewelry."

The crow headed off to a village and saw a woman who had taken off her jewelry and put it on the edge of the roof while she made her ablutions. The crow snatched it away and threw it on the snake as the jackal had said. People came running after the crow and immediately smashed the head of the snake. Thus was the crow delivered.

"I have told this story that you may know that more can be done by cunning than by strength alone," said Dimna.

"How are you going to get to the bull by cunning when he combines brute strength with keen intelligence?" asked Kalila.

"It is so," said Dimna, "but he thinks he is safe from me. I will be able to catch him unawares, for an ambush of deception launched from a safe place is more effective, like the rabbit that destroyed the lion by deception."

"How was that?" asked Kalila.

The Rabbit That Outwitted the Lion

There was a meadow over which wafted perfumed breezes from paradise, the reflection of which illuminated the celestial sphere, and through every branch of which twinkled a thousand shining stars. In this meadow were many beasts living in comfort and plenty thanks to its greenery and water, yet on account of the proximity of a lion their pleasure was sullied. One day they gathered and all went to the lion, saying, "Every day, with much effort and exertion, you can hunt down one of us, and we are constantly in trepidation of you. We have thought up a plan that will assure you of leisure and mean safety for us. If you stop harassing us we will send you one of us every day."

The lion gave his consent, and some time passed. One day it was the rabbit's turn to go. He said to his friends, "If you delay in sending me I will deliver you from the cruelty of this tyrant."

"All right," they said.

The rabbit waited until the time for the lion's meal had passed. Then he crept very slowly toward the lion. He found the lion out of sorts because hunger had made him peevish and ready to break his word. When he saw the rabbit he cried out, "Where are you coming from, and what's wrong with the beasts?"

"They sent a rabbit with me," he said, "but along the way a lion took it from me. I told him it was for the king's meal, but he paid no attention and said, 'This hunting ground and its prey are better suited to me. My splendor and might are greater.' I hastened here to inform the king."

The lion got up and said, "Show him to me."

The rabbit led him to a large well, the water of which reflected things in perfect detail, and said, "He's in this well, and I'm afraid of him. If the king will take me in his embrace I'll show him to you."

The lion took him in his embrace and looked down into the well. Seeing his own reflection and that of the rabbit, he let the rabbit go, dove into the well, and drowned.

The rabbit went back to the beasts safe and sound. They asked about the lion. "I drowned him," the rabbit said, "and he is as deep under the earth as Corah's treasure." They all rejoiced and lived happily ever after in the meadow.

"If you can destroy the bull in a way that doesn't harm the lion, it should be all right according to the code of wisdom," said Kalila, "but if it doesn't turn out to be harmless to him, beware lest you inflict harm on him, for no wise person would harm his master for the sake of his own comfort."

They ended their conversation with these words, and Dimna stopped visiting the lion until one day when he got a chance to see him in private and went to him in abject despondency.

"I haven't seen you for days," the lion said. "I hope nothing is wrong."

"Oh, everything's all right," Dimna muttered as he shifted around.

"Has something happened?" the lion asked.

"Yes," he said.

"Tell me," the lion said.

"A time of leisure and privacy would be more appropriate," said Dimna.

"Now is a good time," said the lion. "Tell me quickly, for things do not brook delay, and a wise person of good fortune does not put off to the morrow what can be done today."

"One hesitates to begin a narrative that would be distasteful to the hearer," said Dimna, "unless he has full confidence in the hearer's intelligence and discrimination, and more especially when the benefits will accrue to the hearer and the teller cannot profit beyond repaying his obligation for patronage and giving advice. One may be permitted to do this because the king is so exceptional among kings for his intelligence and will of course listen with regal astuteness. It should also be known that I speak only out of compassion and honesty and have no ulterior motive. As is said, a scout does not lie to his own people. The continued existence of all the beasts depends upon the king, and a wise man must tell the truth. Anyone who withholds advice from a king, anyone who keeps his illness from a physician, and anyone who does not disclose his poverty to his friends betrays himself."

"Your complete trustworthiness is certain," said the lion. "Tell me what has happened, and it will be attributed to compassion and advice without the least suspicion or doubt."

"Shanzaba has met in private with the leaders of the army," Dimna began, "and won over each of them separately. He has said, 'I have tested the lion and know his strength and power and his acumen and cunning, and I have found major flaws and weakness in them.' The king has gone too far in elevating that treacherous ingrate and has made him equal to himself in issuing commands, which is one of the king's prerogatives. He has given him such free rein in ordering and prohibiting that the demon of sedition has laid an egg in his mind and the desire for disobedience has swelled in his head. They have said that when a king sees one of his servants equal to himself in dignity and wealth he should quickly let him go. Otherwise the king himself will be brought down. All in all, thoughts a king may have should not be entertained by others. I know that something must be done quickly before things get so bad that they will be beyond repair. It has been said that people are of two sorts, the foresighted and the incapable. The foresighted are also of two sorts.

"The first are those who recognize the evil in a thing before it happens. What others know at the end of affairs they know at the beginning, and they think first of the ends of things. 'The beginning of thought is the end of action.' Once a thing has taken shape, the negligent, the ignorant, the farsighted, and the intelligent are all the same. The Prophet has expressed this in these words, 'Things look alike in the future. Once they are in the past the ignorant know them as well as the intelligent do.' Since a person of acumen can foresee things he can always maintain control and get himself to shallow water before he is sucked into a whirlpool.

"Of the second sort are those who do not go to pieces when catastrophe strikes and do not let themselves experience fear and confusion. They are not blind to strategy and good choices.

"The incapable are those who are helpless, who hesitate to make a decision, who suffer confusion, and who are muddled in their thoughts and go to pieces and weep and wail when calamity strikes. Their ambition is limited to wishing and hoping for happiness.

"Appropriate to this classification is the story of the three fish."

"How is that?" asked the lion.

The Fates of the Three Fish

Once upon a time, in a pool far removed from the path of wayfarers, lived three fish. Two were foresighted, and one was incompetent. One day, by chance, two fishermen passed by and promised each other they would bring a net and catch all three fish. The fish heard them talking. The one who had the more foresight and had seen many vicissitudes in the cruel world and yet remained steadfast on the carpet of wisdom and experience set off and at once got out through the stream at the end of the pool. Just then the fishermen arrived and blocked both ends of the pool.

The second fish reflected, for he too was not devoid of wisdom or experience, and said to himself, "I have been negligent, and such is the fate of the negligent. Now is the time for cunning. However little benefit a ruse may have in a time of calamity, an intelligent person should never despair of the benefits of knowledge or delay in warding off the stratagems of enemies. This is a time for resolve and deceit." Then he pretended to be dead and floated on top of the water. The fisherman picked him up, and since he seemed dead they threw him away. With this trick he got into the stream and saved himself.

The one who had been totally negligent and in whom incapacity was apparent swam around, confused and bewildered and flailing left and right and up and down until he was caught.

"I have told this story so that it may be clear to the king that haste with regard to Shanzaba is necessary. A successful king is he who takes action before the opportunity is lost and brooks no delay in having his glittering sword annihilate the enemy and in having the blaze of his determination leave an opponent's home in smoke and ashes."

"Of course," said the lion, "but I don't think Shanzaba has any treacherous thoughts or would repay my patronage of him with ingratitude since so far I have done him nothing but good."

"That is true," said Dimna, "but the king's excessive kindness has opened the door for such ingratitude. A scheming snake-in-the-grass always gives good advice and appears loyal until he gets the status he hopes for. Then he wishes for other stations for which he is unworthy, and such ambition creates malevolence and treachery. Insincere service and advice are based on fear and hope: once such a person feels secure he will muddy the waters of beneficence and fan the flames of evil. The wise have said that a king should neither so withhold favor from his servants that they despair and turn to his enemies nor give them so much of his bounty that they grow rich and crave more. A king should adopt godly characteristics and follow the advice of revelation: 'There is no one thing but the storehouses thereof are in our hands; and we distribute not the same otherwise than in a determined measure' [Kor. 15:21] so that they may always pass their time between fear and hope and be neither tempted to boldness nor sunk in despair. 'Verily man becometh insolent, Because he seeth himself abound in riches' [Kor. 96:6f.]. The king must know that what is naturally crooked cannot be made straight and that a person who is innately evil cannot be forced to adopt good characteristics. 'Every vessel exudes what it contains.' No matter how much effort is exerted to rectify a scorpion by tying its tail up, when it is released it will revert to its nature and nothing can be done about it. He who does not listen to his counselors, however harsh and unkind their words may be, will experience regret in the end—like a patient who scoffs at his physician's advice and eats and drinks whatever he wants: every moment the disease will grow worse. Kings have a right to expect gratitude and advice from their servants, and the most compassionate underling is he who feels compelled to offer advice without regard for himself. The best action is that which has a good end, the best praise is that which comes from the tongues of the elite, the best friend is he who abstains from opposition and is always benevolent, the best trait is that which inclines to piety and chastity, and the richest of men is he who is never ungrateful and is not vexed by tribulation, for those two traits are in the nature of women, as the Prophet has said, 'When you women are hungry you grovel, and when you are sated you are ashamed.' No one who makes a bed of fire and has a viper for a pillow can sleep easily or comfortably. The benefit of having a sound mind and native intelligence is that when one sees enmity in a friend or ambition in a servant one can immediately fortify oneself and eschew him, and before an opponent has a chance to take a bite one can fix him a satisfying meal, for an enemy only gains strength from delay.

"The weakest of kings is he who is unmindful of consequences and disparages affairs of state. When an important affair arises and things get difficult he neglects foresight and precaution, and when an opportunity has been lost and he is overwhelmed by an enemy he blames his intimates. Among the dictates of ruling are that cracks must be repaired before an opponent gets a footing and an enemy becomes invincible, plans must be made according to wise policy, no attention should be paid to an enemy's deceit and hypocrisy, and determination must be reinforced by wisdom and assisted by good luck, for wealth without trade, knowledge without study, and kingdom without policy do not last."

"You have spoken quite sternly and forthrightly," said the lion, "and the words of an advisor should not be dismissed harshly or sharply but rather listened to with acceptance. It is obvious what Shanzaba can do and what trouble he can cause if he is an enemy. He would be a morsel for me, and while he subsists on grass I exist on meat. 'When could a deer look a lion in the face? How could a partridge gaze upon the countenance of a hawk?' However, I have granted him amnesty, and our association is based on that. How could treachery be permitted in the code of chivalry? How often have I praised him in front of everyone and spoken of his wisdom, honesty, loyalty, and trustworthiness? If I were to allow anything to the contrary I would be accused of breaking my word and of feeble-mindedness, and my promise would cease to carry weight."

"The king should not deceive himself by saying, 'He would be but a morsel for me,'" said Dimna. "If he cannot defend himself he will get friends and turn to cunning and deceit. I fear the beasts will join him because he has encouraged them all to turn on the king by making opposition seem right to them. He never entrusts this to others and takes it upon himself."

As Dimna's words had made an impression on the lion, he asked, "What do you think should be done?"

"When a tooth has an abscess the only remedy is to pull it out," replied Dimna. "The only way to get rid of food that the stomach refuses to digest and which results in nausea is by vomiting. Only by abandonment can one be delivered of an adversary who cannot be won over by kindness and whose obstinacy only increases with affection."

"Now I detest having him around," the lion said. "I will send someone to inform him that he may go wherever he likes."

Dimna realized that if this was disclosed to Shanzaba he would be able to prove his innocence straightaway and make his own lies and deceit known, so he said, "To do so would not be foresighted. Until a word is spoken options are open, but once something is expressed it cannot be retracted. No word that escapes the mouth and no arrow that flies from the bow can be either retracted or brought back. The dreadfulness of silence is a precious ornament for kings. 'Think evil of your brethren and entrust no secret to anyone.' It may be that when he recognizes the situation and sees that he has been discredited he will resort to force and do battle or prepare himself for such. The foresighted do not allow clandestine punishment for an obvious offense or obvious punishment for a clandestine offense."

"On the basis of mere suspicion and without clear certainty, to deprive my intimates and discharge them would be torment for me. It would be like cutting my own legs out from under myself," said the lion. "A king must reflect and be decisive in all things, especially in setting limits and inflicting punishments."

"It is the king's to command," said Dimna. "However, when this deceitful traitor comes you should be ready lest the opportunity be lost. If you look well you will see his disloyalty reflected in his ugly countenance, for the difference between the mien of friends and that of enemies is obvious and impossible to hide. How crooked he is inwardly is shown by how changeable and mercurial he is and how shiftily he looks left and right. He's preparing for war."

"It must be true," the lion said. "If anything is shown by these signs it is that all doubt has been removed."

Once Dimna had planted the seed of doubt in the lion's mind and knew that his seditious spark had taken, he wanted to see the bull and get away from the lion to be out of the way of suspicion. "Let me go see Shanzaba," he said, "and sniff out what's in his mind."

The lion gave him permission. Dimna went to Shanzaba with his head hanging low and looking sad.

Shanzaba welcomed him and said, "I haven't seen you for days. Have you been well?"

"How could a person who does not control his own fate be well?" asked Dimna. "Captive to the will of others, always in dread of my life, I do not take a single breath without fear and insecurity or say a word without unease and apprehension."

"What causes you such despair?" the bull asked.

"What has been destined," he said. "Who can vie with destiny? In this world who could achieve status and hold a goblet of the world's good things in his hand and not be intoxicated? How could one pursue one's lusts and not be exposed to ruin? How could one keep company with women and not be enchanted? How could one mingle with evil and seditious people and not fall prey to regret? How could one associate with a ruler and remain safe?"

"What you say indicates that perhaps you have been subjected to vilification by the king," said Shanzaba.

"Yes," he said, "I have been, but not on my own account. You know how close we have been in the past, and you remember the vows we made to each other back when the lion sent me to you. It is obvious that I have remained true to those promises, so it is impossible for me not to inform you of what has happened recently."

"Tell me, O compassionate and noble friend," said Shanzaba.

"I have heard from a trustworthy person that the lion has said, 'Shanzaba has grown quite fat, and there is no necessity for him. I will make a nice banquet of him for the beasts.' When I heard this I realized how tyrannical and overbearing he is. I came to warn you and discharge my chivalric duty. Now it would be in your interests to think up a plan and quickly use some ruse to save yourself."

When Shanzaba heard what Dimna was saying and remembered all the lion's promises, and since he believed implicitly in the lion, he said, "It cannot be that the lion suspects me of mutiny since no treacherous act has been perpetrated by me. It must be that others have lied and stirred him up against me, subjecting me to his wrath with their skulduggery and chicanery. There is a group of nasty persons in his service, masters of evil all and well versed in treachery and backstabbing. He has much experience of them and knows how to assess what they have to say about others. Of course the words of such evil people arouse suspicion of even the best people. Such experience can lead one astray, like the error of the duck.

The Duck That Saw the Reflection of a Star in the Water

They say a duck saw the reflection of a star in the water and thought it was a fish. He tried to catch it but got nothing. When he had tried many times and got no results he stopped trying. The next day every time he saw a fish he thought it was the same reflection and did not try to catch it. The result was that he went hungry all day.

"If the lion has been told something about me and believes it, it is because of his experience of others. The accusation of me must be due to their treachery. If that is not the reason and his hatred of me is baseless, then there is no remedy. When there is a cause for anger one can ask pardon and apologize, but what is done by chicanery and slander cannot be undone.

"I do not know, given all that has passed between myself and the lion, that I have not committed some fault since it is quite impossible for two people to be companions and to be together night and day, in good times and bad, in sadness and happiness, and to be so self-controlled that no slip ever happens. No one is exempt from error and mistake, and even when one is not accused of doing something intentionally there is great scope for transgression and connivance. No pardon or act of beneficence is so beautiful as pardon of a hideous crime. 'Opposites show the beauty of opposites.' If he attributes an error to me, I know only that I have sometimes opposed him in his opinions in his own best interests. Perhaps he attributes that to insolence and disrespect. I have never advised anything from which he did not derive benefit or advantage. Of course I have never said such things in public. I have always maintained deference for him and been as respectful as possible. Who could have expected that advice would be a cause for anger or that service would provoke enmity? Anyone who neglects an advisor's counsel, a physician's treatment, or a jurist's ruling in a doubtful case deprives himself of the benefits of correct opinion.

"If it is not because of that, it is possible that power has gone to his head and caused this. One failing in kings is that in their intoxication with power they listen to traitors agreeably and subject their counselors to wrath. The wise have said that to sink to the bottom of the sea in chains and to kiss a snake in drunkenness are both dangerous, but much more terrifying is intimate service to rulers.

"It may also be that my virtue has caused this hatred, for a horse has strength, but running tires it out, and the branches of a good fruit-bearing tree are broken by the weight of the fruit. The very beauty of a peacock's tail subjects it to having its feathers plucked out. The virtuous are always in peril of the envy of the dishonorable. The mean and ignoble are inimical to paragons, and since they are so numerous they can be overwhelming. A base person dislikes seeing a noble person, an ignorant man dislikes sitting with a learned person, and a fool dislikes conversing with a clever individual. The dishonorable so deprecate the virtuous that they represent to their masters everything the virtuous do as reprehensible, criminal, and treacherous, and the very virtue that should be a cause for happiness becomes a cause for misery.

"If the malevolent have attacked me and fate is in accord, it will be very difficult, for destiny can shut a raging lion up in a cage, put a viper in a basket, and mystify a wise man, and it can turn a heedless fool into a clever person, a brave person rushing headlong into a quivering coward, a fearful coward into an intrepid hero, a rich man into a poor beggar, and a poverty-stricken needy person into a wealthy one."

"What the lion is planning for you is not because of any of the things you have said," said Dimna. "It is his own infidelity and treachery that are making him do it, for he is an egotistical coward and a scheming traitor. At the beginning companionship with him means a sweet life, but the end is a bitter death."

"I have tasted the nectar," said Shanzaba. "Now it is time for the sting of the lancet. In truth it is fate that has brought me to this pass. Otherwise what business did I have being a lion's companion? I am food for him, and he has a craving for me. Fate, greed, and hope have brought me to this brink of disaster. No plan can help. A honeybee sits on a lotus, intoxicated by its perfume and aroma, but when it is time to fly away if the lotus's petals have closed it means the bee's death. He who is not content with mere sustenance from the world and seeks more is like a fly that is not content with beautiful meadows filled with herbage and green trees laden with blossoms and sits instead on the fluid dripping out of an elephant's ear. With one swift flap of the elephant's ear the fly is killed. Advising and serving one with whom you cannot vie is like sowing seed in brackish earth and hoping it will grow. It is like consulting the dead, whispering into the ear of a deaf person, and writing a riddle on flowing water."

"Enough talk," said Dimna. "You must come up with a plan."

"What plan could I make?" asked Shanzaba. "I know the lion's character and have much experience of it. He would not but wish me well, but his intimates have schemed to have me destroyed. If it is so it will not be easy for me, for when unjust schemers band together to attack someone they quickly achieve victory and bring him down—like the wolf, the crow, and the jackal that plotted against the camel and prevailed."

"How was that?" asked Dimna.

The Wolf, the Crow, and the Jackal That Conspired against the Camel

Once upon a time a crow, a wolf, and a jackal lived in service to a lion near a public road. A merchant's camel was left there and wandered into the jungle in search of pasture. When it came before the lion it saw no alternative to greeting it humbly and appeasing it. The lion asked if it intended to stay there.

"Whatever the king commands," the camel said.

"If you want to join me you will be comfortable and safe," the lion said. The camel was pleased and stayed in the jungle.

Some time passed. One day the lion went out in search of prey and encountered a raging elephant. A great battle took place between them. The lion returned wounded and moaning and could not hunt for days. As a consequence the wolf, the crow, and the jackal went without sustenance. The lion saw this and said, "Do you see any prey in the vicinity I can go out and hunt for you?"

They went into a corner and said to each other, "What's the use of having that camel in our midst? We are not friendly with it, and the king spends all his time with it. The lion should be persuaded to kill it. It will be a tasty morsel for him, and we will get something too."

"It cannot be done," the jackal said. "The lion has given it amnesty and taken it into his service. Anyone who encourages a king to break his word puts his own friends in jeopardy and invites disaster upon himself."

"That pledge can be broken," said the crow, "and the lion can be made to break his promise. You wait here until I return."

The crow went and stood before the lion. The lion asked, "Did you find anything?"

"When one is hungry one's eyes do not work," said the crow, "but there is another way. If the king allows it we will all enjoy plenty."

"Tell me," said the lion.

"This camel is a stranger in our midst," said the crow. "The king cannot derive any benefit from his being here."

The lion grew angry and said, "Your intimation reeks of disloyalty and ignobility. I have given the camel amnesty. How could I allow an act of cruelty?"

"I know about all that," the crow said, "but the wise have said that an individual should be sacrificed for the good of a household, a household should be sacrificed for the good of a tribe, and a tribe should be sacrificed for the good of a city, and a city should be sacrificed for the good of a king in danger. A way can be found to break a promise without the king's being labeled as treacherous while delivering himself from the hardship of poverty and fear of disaster." The lion hung his head.

The crow went back to his friends and said, "He raged and refused for a while, but in the end he calmed down and agreed. Now here's the plan. We will all go to the camel and remind him of the king and his injuries. We will say, 'We have spent our days happily in the shadow of this king's fortune and magnificence. Now that he is wounded, if we don't offer ourselves to him and sacrifice ourselves, we will be accused of ingratitude and will have no worth in the view of the virtuous. The right thing to do is for us all to go before him, thank him for his bounty, and tell him that we can do no more than offer ourselves to him. Each of us will say, "Today I will be the king's meal," and the others will object and give reasons why it should not be. In this way we will discharge our obligation, and no harm will come to us.'"

All these things they said to the long-necked camel and took the poor fool in. Then they went to the lion, and after they had praised and thanked him, the crow said, "Our comfort depends upon the king's life. Now that circumstances are exigent and the king is unable to obtain enough to stave off hunger, let him kill me."

"What would be the use of eating you?" the others said. "Who could be satiated by eating you?"

The jackal too offered himself, and they said, "Your meat is smelly and unpalatable. It is unsuitable for the king."

The wolf then spoke to the same purport, and they said, "Your meat causes swelling of the throat. It is as bad as lethal poison."

Now the camel offered his thanks and himself. The others unanimously agreed and said, "You are right. You are expressing the utmost of loyalty and compassion." And with this they all fell upon him and tore him to bits.

"I have told this story because the deceit of conspirators, especially when they act as one, is not without influence."

"How do you propose to defend yourself?" asked Dimna.

"There is no alternative to fighting and mounting a defense," he said. "If a person prays sincerely and gives alms his whole life he will not reap so much benefit as one hour spent in defending his life and possessions. 'He who is killed for the sake of his possessions is a martyr, and he who is killed fighting for his life is a martyr.' Since one can attain martyrdom by fighting for one's possessions, if no effort is made when push comes to shove, one will fall short of attaining that goal."

"A wise man does not rush into battle hastily," said Dimna. "And no one approves of running headlong into great danger voluntarily. So long as the possibility remains the wise recommend approaching the enemy with appeasement and mollification and prefer conciliation over contention. A weak enemy should not be underestimated, for when strength and force fail he may resort to trickery and skulduggery. The lion's overwhelming power is obvious and needs no elaboration. Anyone who underestimates an enemy and fails to do battle will be sorry, as the spirit of the sea was bested by the sandpiper."

"How was that?" asked Shanzaba.

The Plover That Threatened the Spirit of the Sea

It is said that there is a species of waterfowl called the plover. A pair of them lived on the shore. When it was time to lay eggs the female said, "You need to find a place where eggs can be laid."

The male said, "This is a good place. There is no need to move. Lay your eggs here."

"There is need for reflection," said the female. "If the sea were to churn up and carry our chicks away, how could you prevent it?"

"I do not suppose the spirit of the sea would be so bold as to underestimate us," said the male. "If he contemplates transgressing his borders one can seek retribution."

"It would be well to know oneself," said the female. "With what force and preparedness would you threaten the spirit of the sea with retribution? Cease this dictatorial stance and find a secure place for eggs, for he who does not listen to the words of counselors will suffer the fate of the turtle."

"How was that?" he said.

The Contentious Turtle and the Ducks

Once upon a time there were two ducks and a turtle living in a pond, and they lived as friends and neighbors. Suddenly the hand of treacherous fate intervened, and the water that was their source of livelihood decreased disastrously. When the ducks saw this they went to the turtle and said, "We have come to bid you farewell, O dear friend and companion."

The turtle wailed over being separated from them and shed many a tear, saying, "My friends, the decrease in water afflicts me greatly, for my livelihood depends upon it. Chivalry and good faith demand that you think up a plan to get me away."

"We would suffer greatly if we were separated from you," they said. "Wherever we may go, no matter in what plenty and bounty we may live, without you we would derive no pleasure from it, but you underestimate the advice of friends and are not constant in what is in your own best interests for the present and the future. If you want us to carry you, it will be necessary, when we have taken you up and are flying in the air with you, no matter how people look upon us and regardless of what they say, that you not contend with them and absolutely not open your mouth."

"I will do as you say," said the turtle. "Do what you must in chivalry. I will keep my mouth shut and suffer in silence."

The ducks brought a stick, and the turtle closed his mouth tightly around it. Then the ducks took either end of the stick in their mouths and lifted him up.

When they were high in the air people were astonished at the sight and came running from all directions, saying, "Look! Ducks carrying a turtle!"

The turtle held himself in for a time, but in the end he couldn't restrain himself and said, "To hell with you!"

No sooner did he open his mouth than he fell. The ducks cried out, "Well-wishers give advice. The fortunate heed it."

The turtle said, "This is all madness. When the temperament of destiny turns bilious and it looks threateningly in a person's direction, no intelligent person would even dream of defending himself."

* * * *

The male plover said, "I have listened to your tale. Be calm and fear not."

The female laid her eggs, and the sea swelled and carried off their children. When the female saw that she said in alarm, "I knew you couldn't gamble with the sea. You in your ignorance have lost our children and rained down fire on me. At least think of something to do!"

The male plover replied, saying, "Speak rationally. I will do as I said and take retribution on the spirit of the sea."

At once he went to the other birds, assembled the leaders of every species, and told them what had happened. "If we do not join hands and support each other in requiting this, the spirit of the sea will grow bolder and you will all be taken unawares," he said.

The birds all went to the phoenix and told him what had happened. They warned him that if he did not take revenge he could no longer be the king of the birds. The phoenix shook himself and stepped forward energetically. The birds resolved to help and assist him, determined to get their revenge. The spirit of the sea, who had previous experience of the phoenix and the other birds, gave the plover back his children.

✤ ✤ ✤ ✤ ✤ ✤

"I have narrated this tale that you may know that no enemy should be underestimated."

"I do not want to initiate war," said Shanzaba, "but there is no way to avoid defending myself."

"When you see him sitting up straight, puffed out, and thumping his tail on the ground, those will be signs of danger," said Dimna.

"If these signs are seen, there will be no doubt of his hostile intentions," said Shanzaba.

Dimna went back to Kalila, smiling with satisfaction.

"How far have you gotten?" asked Kalila.

"Success looks assured," he replied.

Then they both went to the lion, and they happened to arrive at the same time as the bull. When the lion saw the bull he stood up, growled, and coiled his tail like a snake. Shanzaba, knowing he was going to attack, said to himself, "A ruler's servant suffers fear and trepidation like someone who shares a house with a snake or sleeps with a lion, for even if a snake is asleep and a lion is not seen, in the end one will rear its head and the other will open its jaws." With this thought in mind he got ready to fight. When the lion saw him charge into battle he sprang, the two grappled, and blood flowed on both sides.

Seeing this, Kalila turned to Dimna and said, "Look, you fool, upon the disastrous consequences of your chicanery."

"What disastrous consequences?" asked Dimna.

"Harm to the lion and his breaking his word, the destruction of the bull and his loss of blood, and the loss of unity in the army," said Kalila, "as well as your inability to do what you claimed, that is, to get this done peaceably. You have brought things to this pass! The most ignorant of men is he who needlessly involves his master in battle. When the wise have the upper hand they back away from confrontation like a crab and avoid waking sedition and involving themselves in danger. When a minister encourages a king to prefer battle over a peaceful solution it proves his stupidity and foolishness and furnishes ample proof of his imbecility and treachery. It is well known that good sense takes precedence over bravery, for things can be achieved by good sense that cannot be done by the sword, and where good sense is lacking bravery is useless, just as a simpleminded dimwit will be mute in conversation and not try to be eloquent. I always knew that you were self-satisfied, arrogant, and blinded by your lust for power in this world, which is as deceitful as a ghoul and as seductive as a mirage, but I hesitated to tell you and waited for you to wake up from your slumber of negligence. Now that things have come to this pass it is time for me to speak of your perfect ignorance, foolishness, and wantonness and to recount to you some of the faults of your mind and hideous actions. What I say will only be a drop in the bucket. It is said that nothing is so dangerous for a king as having a minister whose words outweigh his actions. You are like that, and your words outweigh your skill. The lion was taken in by your talk. It is said that little benefit can be derived from words without action, an exterior devoid of interior, the wealth of an unwise person, the friendship of a faithless person, knowledge without rectitude, alms without intent, and life without security. Though a king be just and benign, when his minister is cruel and malevolent, all benefits of the king's justice and compassion are cut off from the subjects, like beautiful, pure water in which they see a crocodile—no one will enter the water or put his hand or foot into it no matter how thirsty he may be.

"Competent servants should be adornments to kings. You don't want anyone else to have a chance to serve the king and think he should rely on you alone. It is the height of folly to seek benefit for oneself in harming others, to have expectations of sincere friends without being loyal or taking pains, to expect reward in the hereafter for hypocrisy in your worship, to make love to women harshly and roughly, or to think you can acquire knowledge with ease and comfort. There is no use in saying all this, since I know that it will make no impression on you. My talking to you is like the man who said to the bird, 'Don't bother trying to mend something that can't be mended.'"

"How was that?" Dimna asked.

The Bird That Tried to Advise Monkeys

Once upon a time a group of monkeys lived on a mountain. When the king of the planets went off into the west and the world was covered in darkness the north wind launched an attack on the monkeys. The poor things, shivering from the cold, were looking for refuge when they spied a firefly and thought it was a fire. They heaped kindling on it and blew on it. A bird called out from a tree opposite and said, "That isn't fire." Of course they paid no attention to it.

Just then a man arrived and said to the bird, "Don't bother. They won't believe you, and you are giving yourself unnecessary trouble. To attempt to reform such persons is like testing a sword on a stone or hiding sugar under water." The bird did not listen to him and flew down from the tree to make the monkeys understand about the firefly. They grabbed it and ripped its head off.

"You are just the same. You will never accept advice or listen to counselors. You will persist in your dictatorial inclination and will regret your chicanery and deviousness only when they no longer benefit you and wisdom finally whispers into your ear that you have been on the wrong track. Only then will you suffer regret, as did the clever partner—but only when it was too late."

"How was that?" asked Dimna.

The Two Partners and the Betrayed Trust

There were two partners. One was clever and the other foolish. They went off to trade. Along the way they found some gold in a valley. They said, "There is much unearned profit in the world. We should be content with this and turn back." When they were near a town they were about to divide the gold when the one with a claim to cleverness said, "Why should we divide it? Let's take as much as we need for our expenses and hide the rest. Every once in a while we will come and take what we need."

This was agreed upon, so they took a goodly amount, buried the rest under a tree, and went into the town. The next day the clever one went out and took the remaining gold. Some days passed and the gullible one needed some money. He went to his partner and said, "Let's go get some of our buried treasure. I need some money." They went together and found no gold. Pretending to be astonished, the clever one yelled and screamed and grabbed the gullible one, saying, "You took it! No one else knew about it."

The poor fellow swore he hadn't taken it. Of course it was to no avail. His partner took him to court and made a claim for the gold, telling the whole story.

"Do you have any proof?" asked the judge.

"The tree under which it was buried will bear witness that this traitor took it and deprived me," said the clever partner. The judge was amazed by this claim, and after much discussion he stipulated that the next day he would go and hear the case under the tree and decide according to the tree's testimony.

The clever one went home and said to his father, "The affair of the gold depends upon your complicity and steadfastness. Relying on you, I have said that the tree will testify. If you agree we'll take the gold and more besides."

"What can I do?" he asked.

"The tree is hollow enough for one or two persons to hide inside," he said. "Tonight you will go and get into the tree. Tomorrow when the judge comes you will give the necessary testimony."

"My son," said the old man, "many is the ruse that has rebounded on its perpetrator. Beware lest your scheme be like that of the frog."

"How was that?" he asked.

The Frog, the Crab, and the Weasel

A frog lived near a snake. Every time the frog had a baby the snake would eat it. The frog was friendly with a crab. He went to it and said, "Brother, think up something, for I have a powerful enemy to whom I can offer no resistance, and I cannot move from here. It is a beautiful spot, set with emeralds and enamel and edged with coral and amber."

The crab said, "The only way to overcome a puissant enemy is by deceit. There is a weasel in a certain place. Go catch a few fish, kill them, and lay them out from the weasel's lair to the snake's hole. The weasel will eat them one by one, and when he gets to the snake he will deliver you of his cruelty." By this ruse the frog had the snake destroyed.

A few days passed. The weasel, having grown accustomed to having fish, wanted more, and being habituated to something is worse than being in love. He went out looking for fish and didn't find any. So he ate all the frog's children instead.

* * * *

"I have told you this story that you may know that many a deception has brought disaster on its perpetrator."

"Father," he said, "cut it short. You go on too long. This thing will yield much benefit with only a little effort."

The father was persuaded by greed for money and love of his son to ignore the dictates of religion and virtue and commit an act contrary to the law.

The next day the judge went out, and many people came to watch. The judge faced the tree and asked about the gold. He heard a voice say, "The gullible one took it." The judge was astonished. He went up to the tree, realizing that there was someone inside it, and ordered a lot of firewood brought and piled up around the tree. Then he had it lit. The old man tolerated it for a while, but when he was near death he asked for mercy. The judge had him taken out and persuaded him to tell him the truth so that the gullible partner's innocence was shown and the son's treachery was proven. The old man passed out of this world as a martyr and was pardoned. The son, after being punished and reprimanded severely, carried his dead father home on his back. The gullible partner got the gold thanks to his truthfulness and honesty and departed.

"I have told this story that you may know that the consequences of deceit are dire and that the end of treachery is dishonor. You, Dimna, are too evil, greedy, and weak in judgment for words to express or for anyone to imagine. The result of your chicanery and deceit for your master is as you see, but the final disaster will come to you. You are as two-faced as a rose, for anyone who befriends you gets scratched. You are as fork-tongued as a snake, but a snake is better than you because venom drips from both sides of your tongue.

"Rightly has it been said that water in a stream is sweet until it reaches the sea and that the people in a household are righteous until an evil demon joins them. The compassion of brotherliness and friendship remains as long as a two-faced, fork-tongued snake-in-the-grass does not find a way in. I was always afraid of being with you, for I remember what the wise say, that you should avoid evil people even if they are friends and relatives, for allowing a dissolute person near is like training a snake: no matter how much trouble a snake charmer goes to, one day the snake will bite him. One should rather befriend a reasonable person, for although some of his qualities may not be pleasing outwardly, one can adopt his qualities of reason and wisdom and avoid what is displeasing. Beware of befriending an ignorant person. As his conduct can only be reprehensible, what benefit can be derived from mingling with such a one? In his ignorance he only becomes more wayward.

"You are one of those from whom one should flee a thousand leagues on account of your evil nature and crooked character. How could one entertain any hope of fidelity or generosity from you when you have treated in this fashion a king who honored you, elevated you, made you respected and grand, and gave you power over others? Those who befriend you are like the merchant who said, 'In a land in which mice can eat a hundred maunds of iron, why should it be strange for a hawk to carry off a boy of ten maunds?'"

"How was that?" asked Dimna.

The Iron-Eating Mice

Once upon a time a merchant who had some commodities wanted to go on a trip. He deposited a hundred maunds of iron in the house of a friend and departed. When he returned the friend had sold the iron and pocketed the proceeds. One day the merchant went to get his iron, but the man said, "I put your iron in the cellar and failed to take precaution. By the time I became aware of it mice had eaten it all."

"Oh, sure," the merchant said, "mice love iron, and their teeth are more than capable of gnawing it!"

The false friend, satisfied that the merchant had given up on the iron, said, "Be my guest today."

"I'll come back tomorrow," said the merchant, who went out and carried off one of the friend's sons. When the boy was searched for and heralded through the town the merchant said, "I saw a hawk carry the boy off."

The false friend cried out, "Why do you speak nonsense? How could a hawk carry off a child?"

The merchant laughed and said, "In a city in which mice can eat a hundred maunds of iron a hawk can carry off a child."

The friend realized what was up and said, "Mice didn't eat your iron. I have it. Give me back my son and take the price of your iron."

"I have told this story that you may know that since you have done this to the king others can have no expectation of fidelity from you. Nothing is more wasted than friendship with a person who lags behind on the field of generosity and can only hang his head when fidelity is mentioned. Similarly wasted are beneficence to a person who ignores obligations and gratitude, giving counsel to one who turns a deaf ear to all advice, and telling secrets to a person who is a snitch and an informant.

"It is as clear to me as the sun in the sky that one should avoid your evil conduct and betrayal, for friendship with evil people brings misery while mingling with the good is a recipe for happiness. It is like a morning breeze: if it wafts over fragrant herbs it carries the scent to the nose, but if it blows over a cesspool it carries that odor. Clearly these words are displeasing to you, for the truth is bitter and unwelcome to the ears of the hearer."

By the time their conversation reached this point the lion had finished with the bull, having killed it. When he saw the bull lying in a pool of blood and his rage subsided he reflected and said to himself, "Poor Shanzaba. He had so much intelligence, perspicacity, and gallantry. I am not sure I did the right thing. Were they truthful in what they told me about him, or were they treading the path of treachery?"

As signs of regret were obvious and unmistakable in the lion, Dimna cut short his conversation with Kalila and went to him, saying, "Why are you worried? How could there be a better time for rejoicing or a day more fortunate than this? The king should be strutting in victory and triumph with his enemy wallowing in failure and abasement. Success has dawned, and the day of strife is over."

"Every time I remember my friendship with Shanzaba and his service, knowledge, and competence I am overcome with regret and sadness. He was truly the mainstay of my army, the kingpin of my followers, and a thorn in the side of my enemies," the lion said.

"The king should have no regrets over that ungrateful traitor," said Dimna, "but should rather rejoice over his victory and triumph. It should be reckoned as a monument that will be recorded on the pages of history. In wisdom it is not proper to spare someone from whom one cannot be secure. For the king's enemies there is no prison like the grave and no whip like the sword. Wise rulers make intimates of persons with whom they have little intimacy on account of their skill and loyalty, and they drive away persons they love on account of their ignorance and treachery.

It is like taking bitter, unpalatable medicine: it is taken for its benefit, not because one likes it. A finger may be an ornament to the hand and an implement that can open and close, but when a viper bites it it is cut off for the sake of the rest of the body, and the momentary pain is a source of comfort."

The lion was somewhat comforted by these words, but in the long run providence had its revenge for Shanzaba, and Dimna was discredited when his slander and calumny became known to the lion and he was put to a miserable death. As a sapling of action and a seed of speech are planted and nourished so do they bear fruit.

The consequences of deceit and treachery have always been blameworthy, and the results of malevolence have always been unpropitious. Anyone who steps onto that path or stretches forth his hand in that direction will suffer pain and be laid low.

"Injustice brings down its perpetrators, and the pastures of tyranny are bitter."

Chapter Two

The Trial of Dimna

The Raja said to the Brahman, "I have heard how the scheming informant cloaked certainty with suspicion so that the lion's reputation was sullied and he was branded with the infamy of breaking his word and how enmity took the place of friendship and abhorrence the place of intimacy due to the actions of the king's minister. Now, if you will, tell me the end of Dimna and how he justified himself to the lion and the beasts. The king must have consulted his own mind and become suspicious of Dimna. How did he make amends, and how did he become aware of Dimna's treachery? What was Dimna's justification, how did he seek to save himself, and in what way was an inquest held?"

"Murder will out," said the Brahman. Awakening sedition is never auspicious for any reason. I have read in histories and legends that when the lion finished with the bull he regretted his hastiness. Every time he remembered all his indebtedness to the bull and all his past actions he was pained all the more by thoughts of his having been his best friend and dearest follower. He wanted to speak of him and hear him spoken of constantly. To this end he met privately with each of the beasts and asked them to tell him stories of the bull.

Once the leopard was with him until late into the night, and as he was returning home he passed by Kalila and Dimna's house. Kalila was regaling Dimna with all that he had done to the bull. The leopard stopped and listened. Kalila had reached the point at which he was saying, "You did a dreadful deed. You found an opening for treachery and backstabbing and perpetrated a massive betrayal on the king. You can never be safe because at any moment you may suffer the consequences. Not one of the beasts will ever forgive you or help you escape. All will be unanimous in wanting you killed or mutilated. I do not need you as a neighbor. Away with you! Never come to me again!"

Dimna said, "'If I detach my heart from you and take my love from you, upon whom shall I bestow that love and to whom shall I take that heart?' There is nothing to be done about the past. Get these gloomy thoughts out of your mind and be happy. An enemy has been overthrown, the world is open to us, and the skies of hope are clear. I was not unaware of the evil of my betrayal in the code of chivalry and honesty, but I was overcome by greed and envy."

When the leopard heard this he went to the lion's mother and made her promise to keep secret what he was going to tell her. After she promised he related to her what he had heard and reported in full Kalila's sermons and Dimna's confession. The next day the lion's mother went to see her son and found him grieving. When she asked the reason he said, "Killing Shanzaba and the memory of everything he did for me. The more I try to get the memory of him out of my mind, when I contemplate the best interests of the kingdom and think of a compassionate, sincere, and knowledgeable advisor, the more I think of him and his good character."

The lion's mother said, "The king's words indicate that his heart is telling him that Shanzaba was innocent, and this is causing him dismay. It is weighing on his mind that he took action without certainty and clear proof. If the king had thought about what he was being told and had been able to maintain self-control and consider it dispassionately, the truth would have been known, for there is no beacon in the darkness of doubt like the king's discerning and enlightened mind. A king's perspicacity can discover what is in the mind of the celestial sphere and the secrets of the unseen world."

"I thought much about the bull," the lion said, "and was anxious to accuse him of treachery so that I would be excused by others for killing him. Now the more I think about him, the better I think of him and the more I regret having killed him. The poor thing was too enlightened and conducted himself too well for an accusation by the envious to be right, for the wishes of the unwise to have taken root in his mind, or for him to have contemplated opposing me. Neither was anything due him neglected that would have provoked enmity or contention. I want to have an inquest into this affair and am going to insist on it, however useless it may be and despite the fact that I have left no room for redress. Nonetheless, recognizing where wrong and right are is not without great benefit. If you know or have heard anything, tell me."

"I have heard something," she said, "but it is not possible to reveal it, for one of your intimates has sworn me to secrecy. The wise have warned sternly against disclosing secrets. Otherwise all would be told."

"The dicta of the wise have many different aspects and interpretations," said the lion. "They think it right to apply them according to circumstances. To keep secrets about persons under suspicion is to abet them. It may be that the person who told you wanted to absolve himself of the responsibility of telling it and put it upon you. Reflect well and do whatever you think best."

"This view is correct," she said, "but to disclose the secret has two obvious drawbacks. The first is the enmity of the person who has relied on me, and the second is the mistrust of others, who will never tell me anything again or make me a confidante to any secret."

"You are perfectly correct," said the lion, "and I would not want to make you unwillingly do something wrong in order to acquit myself of responsibility for this error. If you do not want to name the person or disclose his secret, at least tell me in general."

"What the wise say about the excellence of forgiveness and benevolence is well known," said the lion's mother, "but that only applies to crimes the effects of which are not widely detrimental. When the harm is seen to be widespread and touches upon the king, when it provokes boldness in other troublemakers, when it allows enemies to gain strength, and when it is seen as a license for misconduct and corruption, there is no longer any room for forgiveness or disregard of evil, and it must be dealt with. That Dimna, who persuaded the king to do it, is a scheming snake-in-the-grass and a seditious troublemaker."

"I knew it," the lion said to his mother.

He went off and thought about it, and then he dispatched messengers to summon the army and sent word for his mother to come. Then he had Dimna brought in. Turning away from him, he was lost in thought. When Dimna saw that he was facing calamity he turned to one of the intimates and whispered, "Has something happened? Why is the king worried? Why have you been assembled?"

"The king is considering whether to let you live or not," the lion's mother said. "Since your treachery has been discovered and the lie you told about his champion and counselor has been revealed you shouldn't be left alive for even a moment."

"The ancients have left no piece of wisdom unsaid about the vicissitudes of the world that the moderns could add to," said Dimna. "It was said long ago that all plans are subject to destiny, and the more a wise man tries to avoid it and protect himself, the nearer he comes to a snare of catastrophe. To seek safety in advising the king and happiness in keeping company with evil people is like writing on water and entrusting winnowed chaff to the wind. Anyone who is a loyal advisor in service to a king is in greater danger because both the king's friends and his enemies oppose him. The friends oppose him because they are envious and compete for the status he enjoys, and the enemies oppose him for the sincere advice he gives on affairs of the kingdom. This is why the really wise take refuge in safety, turn their backs on the fleeting world, renounce its pleasures and lusts, and choose solitude over mingling with people and worship of the Creator over service to the created, for in service to divine majesty there is no such thing as error or mistake, and it cannot be imagined that good could be rewarded with evil. According to the law of the Creator, judgment must be given with absolute justice. Affairs of people differ markedly, and happenstance is more important than merit. Sometimes the disloyal are rewarded as though they were loyal, and sometimes counselors are taken to task as though they were criminals. Kings are subject to whim. Mistakes are apparent in their actions, and good and evil are alike to them. A successful king is he whose actions are nearer to correctness and farther from harshness, who neither patronizes out of need nor torments out of fear. The most pleasing characteristic of kings is a desire to do right and to empower good servants. The king well knows—and none of those present will fail to testify—that between the bull and me there was no contention, tension, ancient enmity, or hereditary animosity that would cause any friction. I did not think that he had either ill or good intentions toward me that would have engendered envy or hatred. I gave the king advice and discharged my obligation by doing so. He saw the truth of my claim and proof of it and acted in accordance with his own views. Many treacherous and inimical persons have been afraid of me. Of course they will connive and cry out unanimously against me. But I never thought that the result of my advice and service would be that the king would be pained by my existence."

When the king heard Dimna's words he said, "He should be turned over to the judges for a trial, for in all justice punishment cannot be meted out without clear proof."

"What judge is fairer or more just than the king's own impartial mind?" Dimna said. "No verdict he gives can be objected to or gainsaid. The king knows that there is nothing like deliberation for resolving doubt and increasing insight. I am confident that if a trial is held I will be safe from the king's wrath and my innocence and the truth of my allegation will be proven. However, much effort must be exerted in the investigation of me, for fire cannot be brought out of stone without great effort. If I thought I was guilty of a crime I would not be so insistent, but I am confident that an inquest will reveal my loyalty. If I were involved in this affair there were plenty of opportunities to escape and I would not have continued to serve at the king's court and sit around waiting for calamity to strike. I expect the king to turn this affair over to an honest and impartial person and order him to report his findings every day. The king will consider the evidence until I am cleared of all suspicion, for the very thing that made killing the bull just in the king's eyes will keep him from doing the same to me.

"For what reason would I think of such treachery? I possess neither stature nor station that I would fail to be worshipful or entertain notions of grandeur. Being a servant of the king, in the end I share in his justice and there is no way I can be deprived of it or have my hopes of it cut off during my lifetime or after my death."

One of those present said, "What Dimna says is not in veneration of the king. He wants to ward off calamity from himself."

"Who is worthier to advise me than myself?" said Dimna. "Anyone who fails himself in time of need and does not strive to protect himself can have no hopes of others. Your words indicate your lack of understanding and great ignorance. Beware lest you think that these justifications will cloud the king's mind. When he reflects and applies his regal discrimination to your skulduggery you will be disgraced and your spite revealed, for in one night he can do what would take a lifetime and with one indication he can defeat massive armies."

"Given your past deceit and treachery," the lion's mother said, "I am not surprised that you have a ready supply of adages and sermons for every situation."

"A sermon is appropriate when it is accepted," said Dimna, "and an adage is timely when it is listened to."

"Traitor," said the lion's mother, "you still hope to save yourself through chicanery and deceit."

"If a person rewards good with evil," said Dimna, "I at least kept my promise and was faithful to my word. The king knows that no traitor would dare to speak in his presence and that if he allows such with regard to me the detriment would redound on him. It has been said that anyone who rushes into something and neglects the benefits of reflection and deliberation will suffer the fate of the woman who was so eager she couldn't tell the difference between her lover and his slave."

"How was that?" asked the lion.

The Lover and His Slave

It is related that there was a merchant in Kashmir named Hamir. He had a beautiful wife the likes of whom had never been seen. She had cheeks as radiant as a day of victory and tresses as twisted and endless as a night of separation. A master painter who put all others to shame was their neighbor, and he was having an affair with the merchant's wife. One day the wife said to him, "Every time you go to so much trouble to come here it takes so much time for you to call out and throw a stone. Why don't you use your skill to make something that will be a sign for me?"

"I will make a sheet of two colors," he said. "The white will glisten like stars shining on water, and the black will shine like curly ebony hair on the necks of Turks. When you see it you can quickly come out."

A servant of his heard these words. The painter made the sheet, and some time passed. One day the painter went out on business and was gone for a long time. The servant borrowed the sheet from the painter's daughter and deceived the merchant's wife with it and went in to her. After satisfying his lust he returned the sheet. When the painter came and wanted to see his beloved he threw the sheet over his shoulder and went there. The woman ran out to him and said, "My beloved, you have just left. I hope nothing has happened that you have returned so soon."

The man realized what had happened. He chastised his daughter soundly and burned the sheet.

"I have told this story that the king may know that one should not be hasty. Truly one should recognize that I am not saying these things in fear of punishment or death, for death, although it is an unsought-for sleep and rest, will certainly occur and cannot be escaped. If I had a thousand lives and knew that the loss of them would benefit the king and that he was so inclined, I would instantly give them all and know that my happiness in this world and the next lay therein, but the king is obligated to look to the consequences of this affair, for kingship without followers is not possible, and to attack competent servants for a false notion is not without detriment. It is not every day that a competent servant can be found who is reliable and worthy of patronage."

When the lion's mother saw that Dimna's words were being listened to agreeably, she became suspicious and thought the lion might believe his gilded treachery and honeyed lies, for he was truly eloquent and silver-tongued and was justly proud of his articulateness. Turning to the lion, she said, "Silence implies consent. Thus is it said that remaining silent is tantamount to agreeing." So saying, she arose angrily.

The lion ordered Dimna to be bound and turned over to the judges to be imprisoned until they could investigate his case.

After that the lion's mother came back and said, "I always used to hear talk of Dimna's charlatanism, but now it has been confirmed by the lies he tells and the justifications he comes up with to wriggle out of it. If the king lets him speak he will save himself with one word. His death will be a great relief to the king and the army if you are quick about it and do not give him any respite."

"Kings' intimates are envious, contentious, and suspicious," said the lion, "and they lie in wait for one another day and night. The greater an intimate's virtue, the more he is attacked and the more he is the object of malevolence and envy. Dimna's station of intimacy was hard for the army to take. I don't know whether they have united in this affair to advise me or whether it is out of enmity toward him. I do not want to be so hasty with regard to him that I harm myself for the benefit of others. Without having a thorough investigation I cannot consider myself absolved of having him killed, for following one's lusts and falling prey to passion cloud correct opinions and right strategy. If I undermine people of virtue and competence on suspicion of treachery, my wrath will quickly subside, but I will regret it."

When Dimna was taken to prison and placed in heavy chains, Kalila was moved by brotherly compassion to sneak in to see him. As soon as he saw him tears rolled down his cheeks and he said, "O brother, how can I see you in such misery and affliction? What enjoyment can I have in life after this? Now that things have come to this pass, if I speak sternly to you, you won't mind. I saw it all unfold and gave you advice, but you paid no attention. The most unwelcome thing to you is advice. If in times of need and safety I had neglected to give you advice, today I would be your partner in crime. However, you gave in to your own self-satisfaction and reliance on your own opinion. I told you what the wise say, that a schemer dies before his time, and by dying they do not mean a cessation of life but torment that spoils life such as you have fallen prey to. Death would be preferable. Rightly have they said that a man's destruction lies between his jaws."

"You always said what was right and advised me well," said Dimna, "but concupiscence and craving high position clouded my judgment and rendered your advice worthless in my mind—like a sick person avid for food even though he knows it is to his detriment. He pays no attention to advice and eats according to his lust. To live happily and without opponents, to pass one's days free of worry and in safety, is another thing altogether. Wherever there is great ambition there is no escaping pain and expectation of dreadful harm. I know that I have planted the seed of this calamity, and anyone who plants something will of course reap what he has sown even if he regrets it and knows that he has planted a poisonous plant. Today it is time to harvest the fruits of my own actions and words. What makes it worse is the fear that you may be accused along with me on account of our past friendship. God forbid you be tortured into revealing what you know of my secrets. Then I would be under two burdens. One would be the burden of my own pain and the shame for what you suffer on my account, and the other would be that I would have no more hope of salvation since there is no doubt of your truthfulness, and when you bear witness for strangers there is no doubt about your doing the same for me, with whom you shared such a friendship. You see my condition today. Now is the time for compassion and kindness."

"I understand what you are saying," said Kalila. "The wise have said that no one can bear up under torture and will say anything, true or false, to make it stop. I know of no ruse that can help you. Now that you are in this state you might as well confess your crime, own up to what you have done, and save yourself in the afterlife by repenting, for there is no doubt that you are going to perish."

"Let me think about it," said Dimna, "and I'll do what needs to be done together with you."

Kalila left in pain and sadness, his heart heavy with worries. He lay down on his bed and tossed and turned until he stopped breathing.

Imprisoned with Dimna was a beast, and he was sleeping nearby, but he woke up while Kalila and Dimna were talking and heard everything they said and remembered it, but he said nothing.

The next day the lion's mother repeated what she had said before, that merely imprisoning evildoers was equivalent to killing good people and that anyone who lets a miscreant live shares in his evil. The lion ordered the judges to be quick to decide on Dimna's case and make his treachery known to elite and commoner alike. He also repeated his order that they report their proceedings every day.

The judges assembled and gathered the elite and the commoners. The judge's advocate turned to those present and said, "The king has commanded that all care be taken in Dimna's case and in investigating the charge made against him so that no doubt remain and the verdict you give be in full compliance with justice and in no way attributable to currying favor with or intimidation by the king. Every one of you must say what you know of his guilt for three purposes. First, to assist in justice and to speak the truth are of the utmost importance in religion and virtue. Second, when one traitor is punished, all wayward persons will be chastised. Third, the comfort and benefit of all will be assured by punishing persons who engage in chicanery and corruption and by ending their means of doing so."

When this speech ended, all those present fell silent. No one said anything, for their certainty was not apparent. No one thought it right for anything to be said on mere suspicion or wanted a verdict to be given or blood shed based on his testimony.

When Dimna saw that, he said, "If I were guilty I would be glad of your silence, but I am innocent. He who cannot be proven guilty of a crime cannot be touched. In the view of the wise and honest he is acquitted. Everyone must speak of what he knows about my case and speak honestly and truthfully. There is accountability for every word either in the short run or in the long run, and this will be a verdict of life or death. Anyone who condemns me on suspicion or doubt without irrefutable proof will be like the man who claimed to be a physician without any medical knowledge, ability to diagnose, or skill in medicines or treatment."

"How was that?" asked the judges.

The Quack Physician

In a certain city in Iraq there was a skilled physician, renowned for his treatments, known for his knowledge of medicines and causes, and of vast experience. Destiny, as is its custom to take back its gifts and snatch away precious things, struck him down and deprived him of his sight, and gradually he lost his vision. A shameless ignoramus, seeing the field empty, began to claim to be a physician and gained some renown.

The king of the city had a daughter he had married to his nephew. She was having difficulty giving birth, and the wise old physician was called in. He asked about her pain, and when he heard the answer and diagnosed the cause he prescribed a medicine called *zamahran*. "It will have to be made," they said.

"My eyes are weak," he replied. "You will have to do it."

Now the quack stepped forward and said, "It's a job for me. I know how to do it." The king called him forth and told him to go into the storehouse and get the ingredients. He went in without any knowledge or expertise. By chance a bag of lethal poison fell into his hands, and his mixed it in with the other ingredients and gave it to the young woman. No sooner did she drink it than she gave up the ghost. In grief over his daughter the king gave the quack a draft of the same poison. He drank it and died on the spot.

"I have told this story that you may know that acting on ignorance and doubt may have disastrous consequences."

One of those present said, "It would be better not to ask either the commoners or the elite how deceitful or corrupt he is. The best person to ask would be himself, for the signs of crookedness can be seen in the ugliness of his face."

"What are those signs?" asked the judge. "They must be told because not everyone will know."

"The wise have said that if one has a wide brow, if his right eye is smaller than the left and constantly twitches, if his nose is inclined to the right, if he has three hairs growing from every pore in his body, and if his gaze is always toward the ground, such a person's impure being is a compendium of corruption and deceit and a source of degeneracy and treachery. All these signs are found in him," he said.

"In verdicts rendered by people there may be suspicion of favoritism and hypocrisy," said Dimna. "Only God's verdict is absolutely correct, and no error or mistake can be imagined in it. If such signs as you have mentioned can determine justice and truth, and if they can be used to distinguish truth from falsehood, then people have no need of proof for anything, and no one need be praised for doing good or punished for doing evil because no one can get rid of these marks. Reward for good and retribution for evil are both null and void. If, God forbid, I have done what they say I have done, these traits made me do it, and since it was not possible to get rid of them I should not be punished, for they were created along with me. Since there was no escaping them, how can a verdict be given? You have at least made clear your own ignorance and blind traditionalism, and you have interfered unnecessarily with your incomprehensible speech."

When Dimna gave this reply those present fell silent and said nothing. The judge ordered him taken back to prison.

Kalila had a friend named Rozbih. He went to Dimna to inform him of Kalila's death. Dimna grieved, sighing from the bottom of his heart and shedding tears.

"Alas for a compassionate friend and brother of good counsel to whom I ran when I was in trouble," he said. "I took refuge in his counsel and advice. His heart was a storehouse of his friends' secrets that the world would never know. Now what comfort can I have in life and what is the use of living longer? Were it not for the fact that I take consolation from this affliction in your friendship, I would kill myself now. Thank goodness you are recompense for all losses, and your life consoles me for the loss brought on by his death. Today you are for me that same brother that Kalila was. Give me your hand and accept me as a brother."

Rozbih agreed and said, "I am under a great obligation to you. All persons of gallantry, wisdom, and experience would be proud to call you friend. I only wish I could get you released and were able to do something worthy."

They took each other by the hand and swore friendship. Then Dimna said, "In a certain place there is buried treasure belonging to Kalila and me. If you will take the trouble to bring it you will be thanked for your efforts."

Rozbih went to where he indicated and brought it. Dimna took his share and gave Kalila's share to Rozbih, charging him to stay near the king to sniff out what was happening and report it to him. Rozbih did this until the day of Dimna's death.

The next day the judges took their verdict to the lion and presented it. The lion took it and opened it. Then he summoned his mother. When she read the verdict she was perturbed and said, "If I speak sternly it will not please the king, and if I do not, I will be remiss in compassion and advice."

"In giving advice compassion is not necessary," said the lion. "Whatever you have to say will be acceptable, and it will not be subject to doubt."

"The king cannot distinguish between falsehood and truth," she said, "and does not recognize what benefits him from what is detrimental. If given a chance Dimna will stir up sedition that the king will be powerless to counter." So saying, she got up in anger and left.

The next day Dimna was brought out, and the judges assembled and sat in the presence of the public. The judge's advocate repeated what he had said on the first day. When nobody said anything the chief judge turned to Dimna and said, "Although those present are befriending you by their silence, all minds are set against you for your treachery. When you are so labeled what is the use of keeping you alive in our midst? It would be better for you to confess your guilt and save yourself in the afterlife with remorse. At least then you will have two things in your favor to be recorded in history. First, confession of your crime for salvation in the hereafter and choosing the eternal world over this fleeting one. Second, renown for your eloquence in these questions and answers and the various justifications you have given. Know truly that to die with a good name is preferable to living in infamy."

"The judge cannot condemn me on the basis of his suspicion and that of those present without clear proof and evidence. Suspicion does not at all allow one to dispense with facts. Even if you have suspicions and everyone else is convinced of my guilt, I am the best judge of my own actions. To keep my certainty hidden because others have doubts is far from wise or honest. Concerning the suspicion you harbor that, God forbid, I may have caused someone's blood to be shed there are different opinions and beliefs differ, but if I bring about my own death for no good reason, how could I be excused for doing that? No one has the right over me that I have over myself. Therefore how could I allow for myself what I would not in all chivalry allow for the least person? Enough of this talk. If it is advice, you'll have to find better advice to give, and if it is a trick, to persist in it after it has been exposed is not the way of the wise. It is the job of judges to render a verdict, and avoidance of error is praiseworthy. You have always been truthful and fair, but in this case you have taken to driveling on about how miserable and misfortunate I am and set aside all pretense to certainty and caution. You have rendered your verdict according to the insinuations of self-interested parties and your own baseless suspicions. Anyone who gives testimony about something of which he knows nothing will suffer the fate of the scheming gamekeeper."

"How was that?" asked the judge.

The Scheming Gamekeeper

There was a local ruler of some renown who had a wife named Baharoë. She had a face as beautiful as the moon, cheeks like roses, and skin like silver. Not only was she extremely beautiful but she was also very pious and virtuous. Her actions were pleasing, she was charming, and she was very kind. The ruler also had a shameless slave who kept the falcons. His gaze fell upon the virtuous wife, and he tried to get to her, but she paid him no attention. Despairing of her, he wanted to do her harm by plotting to expose her to shame. He got two parrots from a bird catcher and taught one of them to say, "I saw the gatekeeper in the master's clothing sleeping with the mistress." He taught the other to say, "I at least am saying nothing." Within a week he had taught them to say these things. Then one day when the ruler was drinking with his friends the slave brought the birds in and set them down in front of him. They repeated what they had been taught to say. As it was in the language of Balkh, the ruler didn't know what it meant, but he did like the sound of their voices and found them attractive. He turned the birds over to his wife to care for.

Some time passed. A group of people from Balkh were guests of the ruler. When they had finished their meal they sat drinking. The ruler called for the birdcage, and as usual they said their two speeches. The guests hung their heads and exchanged glances. Finally they asked the ruler if he knew what the birds were saying.

"No," he said, "I do not, but their voices are charming."

One of the men of Balkh who held a position of authority explained the meaning to him and took his hand from the wine, excusing himself by saying, "In our city it is not customary to eat or drink anything in the house of a man whose wife is a profligate."

While this was going on the slave said, "I too have seen them many times and can bear witness."

The ruler was astonished and ordered his wife to be killed. However, she sent a message saying, "Haste is the work of the devil, and the wise and experienced consider deliberation and reflection necessary, especially when blood is going to be shed, as the Koran says: 'O true believers, if a wicked man come unto you with a tale, inquire strictly into the truth thereof' [Kor. 49:6]. Retribution for my actions is necessary, and when the truth has been ascertained, if I deserve death, I will submit instantly. At least allow that the people of Balkh be asked if the birds know anything of the language of Balkh other than those two phrases. If they do not then you may be certain that the shameless gamekeeper has coached them, for when he could not have his way with me and my virtue prevented him from having his way, he came up with this plot. If the birds can say anything else in that language know that I am guilty and my blood is licit."

The ruler took all precaution and established that his wife was innocent, so he retracted his order for her death and commanded that the falconer be brought in. He came back with a falcon on his arm, ready to serve.

The wife asked, "Did you see me do what you said?"

"Yes, I did," he replied. With this the falcon on his arm flew into his face and pecked his eyes out.

"This is the reward for eyes that thought they saw what could not have been seen," she said, "and you deserve it in the Creator's justice and mercy."

"I have told this story that it may be known that to proceed in haste based on suspicion is inauspicious and futile and has disastrous consequences in this world."

All of these proceedings they wrote down and sent to the lion. He showed them to his mother. When she had apprised herself of the contents she said, "Long live the king. The only benefit all my efforts in this affair have had is that that accursed one has been disgraced. Today his chicanery and deceit are focused on destroying the king and causing an upheaval in affairs of state. The consequences will be worse than what he perpetrated on a loyal minister and counseling champion."

These words made a great impression on the lion, and he thought long and hard about it all. Then he said to his mother, "Tell me from whom you heard the truth so that I will have a justification for putting Dimna to death."

"It would be difficult for me to disclose the secret of a person who relied on me, and killing Dimna would give me no reason to rejoice. How could I permit myself to disclose a secret that has been entrusted to me? However, I will ask that person. If I am given permission I will reveal it."

She left the lion and summoned the leopard and said, "The various forms of patronage and preference the king has given you are well known. The distinction you enjoy is too obvious to need elaboration." Then she said, "You need to discharge the obligation you owe him for the good things you enjoy. People of virtue consider it obligatory to assist one who has suffered injustice by disclosing proof in a case of life and death, for anyone who withholds evidence of a murder will be condemning himself on the day of judgment." And she recited to him convincing arguments of this sort.

"If I had a thousand lives I would sacrifice them all in an instant for the king," the leopard said, "and I still would not have discharged the least of my obligations to him and would still consider myself defective in being a good servant. The reason I refrained from giving testimony was to avoid being suspected by the king. Now that things have come to this pass I must not neglect the best interests of the kingdom and will do what is commanded." He then told the king of the conversation between Kalila and Dimna as he had heard it, and he testified before the assembly of the beasts. When that became general knowledge the other beast who had heard their conversation in prison sent a messenger to say, "I too have testimony." The lion ordered him brought, and he bore witness to what had transpired in prison between Kalila and Dimna.

"Why didn't you speak up on the first day?" he was asked.

"A sound verdict cannot be given on the basis of one witness," he said. "I cannot allow animals to be tormented without benefit. With two witnesses Dimna's sentence of death is justifiable."

The lion ordered Dimna to be bound and held under surveillance. Food was withheld from him and he was held under duress until he died of hunger and thirst. Such is the consequence of chicanery and the end of dishonesty.

Chapter Three

The Benefits of True Friendship

The Raja said to the Brahman, "I have now heard the tale of two friends who were estranged from each other by the machinations of a snake-in-the-grass and whose friendship turned to such enmity that an innocent person was killed. Now tell me a story of true friends and how they enjoyed the fruits of that friendship."

The Brahman said, "For the wise nothing outweighs true friends, for in days of comfort good companionship is expected of them, and during trials and tribulations it is expected that they will help one another. One example is the story of the dove, the mouse, the crow, the turtle, and the gazelle."

"How was that?" asked the Raja.

The Dove, the Mouse, the Crow, the Turtle, and the Gazelle

Once upon a time in Kashmir there was a pleasant hunting ground and lush meadow so beautiful that a peacock's tail would look like a crow's feathers by comparison. There was much game to be had there, and hunters frequented it. A crow had its nest in a large tree. He was perched, looking left and right, when suddenly he spied an evil-looking hunter in rough garb with a net over his shoulder and a staff in his hand headed toward the tree. The crow was afraid and said to itself, "This man is coming here for some reason. He may be after me or somebody else. I will keep watch and see what happens."

The hunter opened his net, sprinkled some grain, and lay in wait. After a while a flock of doves came led by their queen, a dove called Mutawwaqa. When they saw the grain they alighted, unaware of the danger, and were all caught in the net. The hunter, delighted, approached to catch them, and the doves all panicked, each trying to save itself.

"This is no time for strife," said Mutawwaqa. "We should all consider it more important to save our friends than to save ourselves.

We should cooperate in using our strength to lift the net, for therein lies our salvation." In obedience the doves lifted the net and flew off. The hunter ran after them, hoping they would tire and come down. The crow thought to himself, "Let me go after them and find out how this ends, for I cannot be safe from such an event, and one can use experience as a weapon to ward off vicissitudes."

When Mutawwaqa saw that the hunter was following them, she said to her friends, "This vengeful man is earnest in pursuing us. Unless we can get out of his sight he will never stop. We should fly to villages and forests to block his view of us, and then he will give up. Nearby there is a mouse who is a friend of mine. I will ask him to cut these bonds." The doves did as she suggested and flew away, and the hunter was left behind. The crow followed along to find out what would happen to them.

Upon reaching the mouse's home Mutawwaqa ordered the doves to alight. The mouse, whose name was Zabra, was very wise and experienced in the ways of the world. He had made a hundred holes to escape misfortune and had connected them all by passageways.

Mutawwaqa cried out, saying, "Come out!"

"Who is it?" asked Zabra. When she told him her name he recognized her and came out at once.

When he saw her ensnared he wept and said, "My dear friend and companion, who did this to you?"

"Good and evil are both determined by destiny," she said. "Whatever is fated will eventually happen, and there is no avoiding it. Fate has done this to me. It tempted my friends and me with grain and blinded us to the trap into which we would fall. Those who are stronger and mightier than I cannot vie with the dictates of destiny. When heaven so decrees the sun turns dark and the moon turns black. The will of the Creator brings fish from under the water to the surface and pulls birds down from the air. It is that same will that lets an incompetent person achieve his goal and prevents a wise man from reaching his."

When the mouse heard this he started gnawing the bonds that held Mutawwaqa, but she said, "First free my friends." The mouse paid no attention. "My friend," she said, "it would be better to begin by cutting my companions' bonds."

"You repeat this," the mouse said. "Have you no thought for yourself? Do you not know your own worth?"

"You should not blame me for this," she said. "I have taken on responsibility for these doves, and therefore I have an obligation to them. They repay me by obeying me, and it is due to their cooperation that I escaped the clutches of the hunter. I must fulfill my obligations as leader. I fear that if you begin by freeing me you will tire, and some of them will be left in bondage. If I am left ensnared, even if you grow weary you will not neglect me."

The mouse said, "Such is the custom of people of nobility. It is because of such qualities that their loyalty to and affection for you grow stronger and their trust in your leadership increases." So saying, he cut all their bonds, and Mutawwaqa and her friends were freed.

When the crow saw the mouse helping by cutting the bonds he was desirous of becoming friends with him and said to himself, "I can never be safe from what happened to the doves, and I cannot do without such a friend." Approaching the mouse's hole, he cried out.

"Who is it?" the mouse asked.

"It is I, the crow," he said and told him how he had followed the doves and learned of the mouse's good efforts on their behalf. Then he said, "Now that I have realized how virtuous and chivalrous you are and seen how lucky the doves were to have you as a friend, I am determined to become friends with you."

"There can be no friendship between you and me," said the mouse. "Wise men do not think it prudent to seek something that is impossible. No wise person would try to sail a boat across dry land or to ride a horse across the sea. How could there be friendship between you and me? I would be a tasty morsel for you, and I can never be secure from your designs."

"Think well," said the crow. "How could I benefit by harming you? How could I be sated by eating you? Indeed, the continuation of your race and securing your friendship would save me from turns of fate. It is not chivalrous of you to reject me when I have come from afar seeking your friendship. Virtue can never remain concealed even when it is not very apparent. It is like the scent of musk, which can never be hidden no matter how hard you try to hide it. In the end it escapes and perfumes the air. It is unworthy of your good character to turn me away in despair and deprive me of your friendship."

"There is no enmity like instinctual enmity," said the mouse, "for it never ends short of the extinction of one of the two. Such enmity is of two sorts. The first is like that of lions and elephants. They can never meet without hostility, but victory is not assured to one, and defeat is not slated to the other: sometimes the lion triumphs, and sometimes the elephant is victorious. This sort of enmity is not so deep-seated that it cannot be rooted out or dealt with by trickery and deceit. The second is the enmity between mice and cats and between crows and kites. Where one side has murderous intentions, how can there ever be a truce without the other side imagining what past experience has taught it? This sort of enmity is stronger and grows more powerful every day. The passage of time cannot diminish it, for harm and misery are slated to one side, and comfort and benefit are reaped by the other. When true enmity is thus it is certain that there can be no truce, for at the slightest provocation the trust will be ruptured and each will revert to type. To be deceived into thinking peace possible is unwise. Water, even if it sits in a pot long enough for its smell and taste to change, will still be able to quench fire. The only way to treat an enemy is like a snake charmer, who keeps his snake in a basket. How can a wise person ever be comfortable with a clever enemy?"

"Hearing words born of wisdom is not devoid of benefit," said the crow, "but it would befit your generosity and gallantry more to believe me and not worry. Forget the notion that we cannot be friends. Generosity demands that every path to good be followed. The wise say that friendship between affectionate and affable persons is quickly formed and hard to end, like a vessel of pure gold, which is hard to break and soon mended, while friendship between evil schemers is hard to form and quickly ended, like an earthenware pot, which is easily broken and can never be mended. A generous person, on one day's acquaintance, becomes a compassionate friend and brother, while from a base person, no matter how long-standing the friendship may be, one can expect no kindness unless there are ulterior motives. The signs of your generosity are obvious, and I am in need of your friendship. I will not leave, and I will neither eat nor drink anything until you make me a friend."

"I willingly accept your friendship," said the mouse. "My initial rejection of you was so that, should you ever betray me, I could at least say that I was absolved and you would not be able to say that you found me an easy target. Otherwise, in my religion it is not allowed to deny a request, especially when the asker has voluntarily sought my friendship." With this he came out and stood at the entrance to his hole.

"What is keeping you from coming out into the open and getting used to seeing me?" asked the crow. "Do you have any lingering doubt?"

The mouse replied, "When people seek out a confidant and spend precious moments of their lives in conversation, once the benefits accrue to them they become true friends and brothers. Those who are nice for momentary gain are like hunters who spread grain for their own benefit, not to feed birds. He is a better friend who is willing to sacrifice his life for a friend than one who merely sacrifices his money. The fact remains that accepting you as a friend puts my life in danger. I do have confidence in you; however, you have friends whose natures are opposed to me, as is yours, and they may not be so willing as you to befriend me. I fear one of them may see me and attack."

The crow said, "True friends are friendly to their friends' friends and inimical to their enemies. Today the bond of friendship between you and me has been so cemented that only someone who does not harm you can be my friend. There will be no danger, for I will break with anyone who does not take your part. It is the custom of gardeners to rip out any weed they see growing among their plants."

The mouse was heartened by what the crow said, and they became fast friends. When a few days had passed the mouse said, "If you were to settle here and bring your wife and children, it would be a kindness. It is a very pleasant spot."

"So it is," said the crow, "and there is no disputing its pleasantness, but I know of a meadow surrounded by blossoms and flowers where my friend the turtle lives and there is more than enough for me to eat. This place is next to a highway, and we may be bothered by wayfarers. If you like we can go and spend our days there in plenty and security."

The mouse said, "What could I desire more than to be in your company and live near you? My story is long and contains many marvels, which I will relate to you when we are at leisure."

The crow took the mouse by the tail and headed off. When they got there the turtle saw them from afar and dove fearfully into the water. The crow set the mouse down gently on the ground and called to the turtle. As the turtle came lumbering, he asked, "Where are you coming from, and what's up?" The crow told him everything that happened from the time he went after the doves and saw the mouse save them and how this had moved him to become friends with the mouse. When the turtle heard all this he said to the mouse, "It is our good fortune that you have been brought here, and you are most welcome to these parts." After these niceties the crow said to the mouse, "Would you be so kind as to relate what you promised so that the turtle may also hear? His friendly feelings toward you will be no less than mine."

The mouse began by saying, "I was born and raised in an ascetic's hut in the city of Marut. The ascetic had no wife, and every day someone would bring him a basket of food from the home of one of his disciples. He would eat some and put the rest away for the evening. I would wait for an opportunity, and when he went out I would eat my fill and toss the rest to the other mice. The ascetic was stymied, but he thought up a trick and hung the basket up high. Of course it didn't work, and he couldn't keep me away from it. This continued until one night when he had a guest. When they had eaten the ascetic asked, 'Where do you come from and where are you going?' He was a world traveler who had seen much in his day, and he related many strange things he had seen in the world. As he was talking, every once in a while the ascetic would clap his hands to shoo the mice away.

"The guest grew angry and said, 'I'm talking and you keep clapping your hands. Are you making fun of me?'

"The ascetic apologized and said, 'No, I'm clapping my hands to scare the mice away. They eat everything I store up.'

"'Are they all so bold?' the guest asked.

"'No,' the ascetic said, 'one in particular is bolder than the rest.'

"'There must be a reason for its boldness,' the guest said. 'It is like the man who said, "There must be a reason this woman is selling husked sesame for unhusked sesame."'

"'How was that?' the ascetic asked.

The Woman Who Sold Sesame for Sesame

One night in a certain city I stopped at the house of an acquaintance of mine. When we had had our evening meal he gave me a nightshirt and went to his wife, and I could hear them talking because there was only a reed mat separating me from them. He was saying to his wife, "Tomorrow I want to invite a group of people for a party since a dear friend has come."

The wife objected, saying, "How can you invite people when there isn't enough in the house for your family? Will you never think of the morrow or have a care for your children?"

"But," the man said, "if you have a chance to do good and spend money, there can be no regrets, for hoarding is inauspicious and does not end well—just like the wolf."

"How was that?" the wife asked.

How the Greedy Wolf Died Eating a Bowstring

One day a hunter went out hunting. He killed a gazelle and was headed home when a boar attacked him. The hunter drew an arrow and shot the boar, but it had inflicted a mortal wound on him, and they both died. A hungry wolf came by, saw the man, the gazelle, and the boar, and rejoiced, saying to himself, "This is a time to take advantage of a good opportunity to store up some victuals, for if I neglect to do so I will be accused of imprudence and of being ignorant and improvident. It would be in my best interests to make do for today with the bowstring and store the fresh meat somewhere for leaner days." And as he began to eat the bowstring, the bow snapped, hitting him on the neck, and he died on the spot.

✚ ✚ ✚

"I have related this story so that you may know that the desire to store things up can be unlucky," the man said.

"You are right," the woman said. "I have some sesame seed and rice in the house. Tomorrow I'll fix a meal that will suffice for six or seven people. Invite whomever you like." The next day she husked the sesame and put it in the sun to dry. To her husband she said, "Drive the birds away while this is drying." And when she went off to do something else the man fell asleep, and while he was asleep the dog licked the seeds. The woman saw this and did not want to use them, so she took them to the market and sold them for an equal amount of unhusked sesame. I was in the market to see it and heard somebody say, "There must be a reason this woman is selling husked sesame for unhusked."

* * * *

" 'Therefore it occurs to me that there must similarly be a cause for this mouse's being so bold. Bring me an ax so that I can open his hole and see what he has stored there that makes him so audacious.' Immediately an ax was brought. At that time I was in another hole, but I could hear what was going on. I had a thousand dinars in my hole. I don't know who put it there, but I used to wallow in it and rejoice, and every time I thought about it I would get excited. The guest dug up the floor until he found the money. Giving it to the ascetic, he said, 'He won't bother you any longer.' When I heard this my heart sank, and I knew I would have to move from my hole. Not many days passed before I detected that I had lost status among the mice and that the high esteem in which they had held me was severely diminished, and they even began to lord it over me. When I did not leap onto the basket as they expected they turned away from me and said, 'He's finished. Soon he will have to submit to us.' They all abandoned me and joined my enemies, and they spoke of my faults, made up stories deprecating me, and no longer had anything good to say about me.

"It is well known that anyone who loses his wealth is scorned by his people. I therefore said to myself, 'He who has no wealth has no family or friends, anyone who is impecunious will fail at everything, and none of his desires will come to anything—just like rain in the heat of summer that comes to naught in valleys: neither does it get to the sea nor does it join any stream. Rightly has it been said that he who has no brother is alone, he who has no children fades quickly from memory, and he who has no money will fail to use his mind and intelligence to make something of himself in this world and the next. When one is in need friends scatter, woes gather, and one is demeaned by everyone. It often happens that, in order to feed oneself and one's family, one is forced to make one's livelihood by

immoral means, and that deprives one of any reward in the hereafter and ensures one's everlasting misery. Truly a tree that grows
in brackish earth and suffers damage from all sides is luckier than
a poor man who is dependent on others, for the humiliation of
poverty is difficult. It is said that the measure of a man's dignity is
his ability to be independent of others. Poverty is the source of all
afflictions: it engenders hostility in other people, it robs one of one's
dignity and manliness, and it saps one's strength and zeal. Anyone
so afflicted has no recourse because he has been stripped of his dignity. When one's dignity has been taken away one is despised and
subjected to taunts, all happiness in one's heart withers, and one's
mind is submerged in grief. One subjected to such trials is blamed
no matter what he says or does. All his plans go awry. All who used
to reckon him trustworthy now accuse him, the good opinion of
his friends is reversed, and he is blamed for the faults of others. All
words and expressions that are praise for a rich person are censure
for a poor man. If a poor man is bold it is attributed to foolishness.
If he is generous he is called a spendthrift and squanderer. If he
exhibits clemency he is said to be weak. If he tries to be dignified he
appears lethargic. If he is eloquent he is called garrulous. If he takes
refuge in silence they say he is taciturn. Death is better than poverty
and having to beg from people. It is easier to put one's arm into
a dragon's maw and to snatch a morsel from a lion's mouth than
to ask a base, stingy man for a favor. It is said that if one falls into
illness with no hope of recovery, or into an estrangement in which
no reconciliation can be imagined, or into an exile from which one
cannot expect to return and in which one cannot remain, or into
poverty that leads to begging, one's life is truly death, and death
would be a comfort. It often happens that shame keeps one from
revealing one's inability and need, and necessity forces one to stretch
one's hand out to other people's possessions even though throughout one's life one avoided doing such things. The wise have said it
is better to be mute than to tell a lie, better to be tongue-tied than
to be eloquent in cursing, and better to be poor than to be rich by
dishonest acquisition.'

"When the ascetic and his guest removed the gold from my hole
and divided it between themselves, I saw the ascetic drop his share
into a purse and put it under his pillow. I determined to get some

of it back—perhaps some of my status would return and my friends and brothers would be inclined to associate with me again. When he was asleep I went out, but the guest was awake and struck me with his staff. I limped back to my hole and lay down, waiting for the pain to subside. Once again greed stirred me up, and I went out again. The guest was waiting and landed such a blow on my head that I passed out. I got back to my hole only with great difficulty and told myself that truly that pain had soured all the riches of the world to me. My discouragement had reached such proportions that if it were put on the back of the celestial sphere it would stop turning and if it fell on a mountain it would spin like the firmament. I came to the conclusion that the cause of all calamities and afflictions was greed and that it caused all the pain suffered by the people of the world, for covetousness held the reins and drove them. It is easier for a covetous person to endure the terrors and dangers of travel for the sake of monetary gain than it is for a generous person to extend his hand to acquire money. One can learn from experience that acceptance of one's fate and contentment constitute true riches. The wise have said that you should be content with your lot and not blame others for being stingy. There is no knowledge like a good plan, no abstinence like abstaining from dishonest acquisition, no quality like good character, and no riches like contentment. An affliction it is impossible to ward off is better borne with resignation. It has also been said that the greatest possessions are mercy and compassion, the basis of friendship is benevolence toward one's companions, and the origin of intelligence is the ability to distinguish between what can be and what cannot be. Gradually I became content and submitted willingly to my fate. Necessarily I moved from the ascetic's house into the field and the dove became my friend. Friendship with her led me to friendship with the crow, and he told me about your kindness. Hearing of your good qualities engendered friendship for you as though I had seen you. Since he was coming to you I wanted to accompany him and meet you and seek your companionship, for loneliness is difficult and there is no joy in the world like that of companionship with friends. The pain of separation is a heavy burden no one can tolerate, and desire for reunion is a palatable potion no one can resist. From all these experiences it should be clear that an intelligent person should be content with enough of the chattel of this world to meet his basic needs, which are very few, only food and shelter, for if the whole world were given to one individual he could only benefit by having all his needs met, and everything left over he would desire to share with others. Now I am here with you and am proud to call you a friend, and I hope that I will occupy the same position with you."

When the mouse finished his narrative, the turtle responded kindly, saying, "I have heard what you said, and everything you said was good. The proofs of your gallantry and nobility are clear, but I see that you are sad in your loss of status. Do not allow your mind to dwell on it, for good speech achieves beauty when it is coupled with good action. When an ill person recognizes the need for treatment, if he does not act on it there is no benefit in the knowledge. One's knowledge should be put into practice to derive benefit from the fruits of one's mind, and one should not grieve over lack of wealth. A virtuous person, even if he has few material possessions, is always welcome—like a lion, whose awesomeness is never diminished even if it is in chains or in a cage—while a rich person of low mind appears despicable—like a dog, which is abject everywhere even if it wears a jewel-studded collar. Do not allow regret to weigh on your mind, for wherever an intelligent man goes he can rely on his intelligence. One should always be thankful, and there is no adornment during times of affliction like the adornment of patience. The Prophet said, 'The best things humans have been given are a thankful tongue, a patient body, and a mindful heart.' One must have patience and strive to keep one's heart mindful, for when these are done happiness will come to you like water flowing downhill and ducks coming to water, for all sorts of excellent things are in store for persons of insight that never await hesitant and indolent people and flee from them like lustful young women from impotent old men. Do not be sad and say you used to have wealth that was lost, for wealth and all the goods of this world are impermanent. When you toss a ball into the air, you cannot attach any importance to its rising or falling. The wise have said that there are several things that have no permanence: the shadow of a cloud, the friendship of evil people, the love of women, false praise, and great wealth. It is unworthy of an intelligent person to rejoice over having great wealth or to grieve over having little. One should consider one's wealth as that by which one attains a skill and that by which one stores up good action, for it is certain that neither of these can be taken away and that no vicissitudes can touch them. To have provisions for the afterlife is also important because death can only come without warning, and no one is given a respite or a certain period of life. It is clear that you do not need my advice and know well how to distinguish between what is beneficial and what is harmful, but I did want to give you your due. Now you are our brother, and all commiseration possible will be given to you."

When the crow heard the turtle's kind words to the mouse he said, "You have gladdened me, as you always do. Be proud of your generosity and live happily. The person who most deserves to be happy is he to whom the way is paved for friends, under whose compassionate protection brethren and friends spend their days, whose door is always open to them, and who is ready to grant their requests and fulfill their needs. As the Prophet has said, 'The best of you are those with the best character, whose refuges are well trodden, who are companionable and sociable.' If a generous person needs help it is the generous who will provide it—like an elephant stuck in the mud: only other elephants can get it out. An intelligent man always strives to acquire honor and to leave behind a good name, and if he must face danger, or even lose his life, he will not shirk because to do so means he will have sacrificed the eternal for the transitory and purchased little at great cost. A person of praiseworthy characteristics is he around whom many asylum seekers gather in safety and at whose door grateful beggars crowd. A person who passes his days in ignominy and enmity with people is not mentioned among those who are truly alive."

The crow was in the midst of this speech when from afar a gazelle could be seen running. They supposed someone was after it. The turtle dove into the water, the crow flew to a tree, and the mouse disappeared into a hole. The gazelle approached the edge of the water, took a sip, and stood trembling. When the crow saw this he flew up to see if anyone was chasing the gazelle. Looking in all directions, he saw no one. He then called to the turtle to come out of the water, and the mouse also came out.

When the turtle saw the gazelle's consternation, for he was looking at the water and not drinking, he said, "If you are thirsty, drink and do not be afraid. There is nothing to fear." The gazelle stepped forward, and the turtle welcomed him warmly and asked how he was and where he was coming from.

"I live in these meadows," he said, "and hunters are always chasing me. Today I saw an old man I thought must be a hunter, so I fled here."

"Do not fear," the turtle said, "for no hunters have been seen in these parts. We welcome you as a friend. There are grazing grounds nearby."

The gazelle was glad to join them and settled in that meadow. There was a reed bed where they used to repair together and play and recount their adventures. One day the crow, the mouse, and the turtle met and waited for the gazelle, but he did not come. They began to worry, and, as friends do, they imagined all sorts of catastrophes. The mouse and the turtle said to the crow, "Look down on the area and see if you see any trace of the gazelle." When the crow flew up he saw the gazelle caught in a trap. Immediately he came back and informed his friends. The crow and the turtle said to the mouse, "In this event you are our only hope, for we can do nothing."

The mouse ran to the gazelle and said, "O compassionate brother, how have you fallen for this with all your sagacity and cleverness?"

"What is the use of cleverness in the face of destiny, which one cannot see or know when it will strike?" the gazelle said.

Just then the turtle arrived, and the gazelle said to him, "O brother, your coming here is harder for me than this affliction because if a hunter comes and the mouse has broken my bonds, I can run faster than the hunter can, the crow can fly away, and the mouse can flee into a hole, but you can neither flee nor offer any resistance. Why did you come?"

"How could I not come?" the turtle asked. "How could I have stood by and done nothing? What pleasure is there in a life spent in separation from one's friends? Who would consider that a life? One consolation in affliction is seeing and talking with brothers. Do not worry, for soon you will be freed and this difficulty will be resolved. In any case one should be thankful, for if there were any mortal danger it would be impossible to imagine any way of dealing with it."

The turtle had scarcely uttered these words when a hunter appeared from afar. As the mouse finished gnawing the rope the gazelle leapt away, the crow flew off, and the mouse scurried into a hole. The hunter, seeing the rope that had been around the gazelle's leg cut, was perplexed. He looked left and right, and suddenly his gaze landed on the turtle. Seizing him, he bound him tightly and left. At once the friends gathered and discussed the turtle's fate. It was clear that he was in the clutches of disaster.

"Will malevolent fate never smile?" asked the mouse. "Rightly has the sage said that people are always fine until they stumble, and once the floodgates of catastrophe are opened torrents of affliction pour down. When one clings for safety to one branch, disasters pour down from another, and at every step one falls into another snare. What affliction is worse than separation from friends? Ill luck constantly hounds me. Just as it separated me from my family, children, and property, it has snatched from me a friend in whose companionship I lived. His affection was not out of expectation of reward but was so based on generosity, intelligence, fidelity, and virtue that it could not be ruptured by any vicissitude. Were it not for the fact that I am accustomed to these pains and used to these disasters, how would life be possible? Woe is me, caught in the clutches of calamity, a prisoner to the vicissitudes of the world, bound to changing conditions. Afflictions gather on me, and the good things of life are as impermanent as the rising and setting of the stars: when one rises another sets. Grief over separation is like a wound: as soon as it starts to heal another is inflicted on top of it, both pains coalesce, and there is no longer any hope of recovery. The pains inflicted by the world are assuaged by the sight of friends, but what consolation can there be from one far away?"

The crow and the gazelle said, "No matter how eloquent your lament is it won't help the turtle. You would do better to think of a way to rescue him. It is said that brave and courageous men are assessed on the day of battle, honest men are appraised when they engage in commerce, wives and children are tested in times of poverty, and friends and brothers are judged in times of affliction."

"Here's what should be done," the mouse said to the gazelle. "You go show yourself to the hunter and appear to be wounded. The crow will alight on you as though he means to attack you.

When the hunter spies you he will of course have designs on you. He will leave the turtle with his belongings and go toward you. When he is near limp away from him, and do it slowly so he won't give up on you. I will come from the other direction and free the turtle while you are limping off."

Thus they did. The hunter went after the gazelle, and when he returned and saw that the sack in which the turtle had been was open, he thought about how the gazelle's bonds had been broken, how the gazelle had come back looking wounded, how the crow had alighted on it, and how the turtle's bonds had been cut. Gripped by fear, he thought the area must be infested by fairies and sorcerers and he should get away as fast as he could.

The gazelle, the crow, and the turtle went home safe and sound and lived happily ever after.

This has been the story of cooperation among friends in good times and bad and the steadfastness they exhibited in the face of vicissitudes. Thanks to their loyalty and sincerity they were rescued from the brink of several disasters.

A wise man should reflect on these stories, for the friendship among weak animals, when their hearts are pure and they work hand in hand to ward off danger, can yield good results. If intelligent people form such a friendship, what can they not achieve?

Chapter Four

The Consequences of Failing to Beware of Enemies

"I have heard your tale of cooperative friends and compassionate brethren," the Raja said to the Brahman. "Now tell me a story of an enemy by whom one should not be deceived even if he exercises the utmost of pleading and humility to disguise what lurks in his heart."

"A wise man should pay no attention to the words of an enemy," the Brahman said, "and the more kindness you see from a clever enemy, the more you should be suspicious of him and avoid him. If you are negligent and expose yourself he will ambush you. Once it is too late to check him regret will do you no good, and what the crows did to the owls will happen to you."

"What was that?" asked the Raja.

The Owls and the Crows

The story goes that on a high mountain there was a huge tree with many branches and leaves in which lived around a thousand crows. The crows had a king whose orders they all obeyed. One night the king of the owls came out and launched a surprise attack on his enemies the crows, returning victorious and triumphant.

The next day the king of the crows assembled his army and said, "You see how the owls attacked so boldly. Today there are among you some who are dead or wounded and others who have lost their feathers or gotten their wings broken. Worse than this is their audacity and their knowledge of our home. I do not doubt that they will come again soon and repeat their attack. Reflect and see what should be done."

Among the crows were five known for their intelligence and wisdom, and the crows depended upon them for advice and counsel during times of trouble. The king valued their advice and never failed to heed their counsel. He asked one of them, "What do you think should be done?"

He replied, "As the wise have said before our time, when one is unable to resist an enemy one should abandon one's family, possessions, and homeland and flee, for there is great danger in waging war, especially when one is defeated. To engage in it without reflection is like sleeping in the path of a torrent. To rely on one's strength and to be deceived by one's power and bravery are most imprudent, for a sword has two edges and destiny is blind: it neither recognizes nor values the brave, and it cannot be relied upon."

The king turned to the second and asked, "What do you think?"

"What he says about fleeing and abandoning one's home I would never say. How can it be wise to give in to such humiliation at the first blow? It would be better to assemble our forces and go out to battle. A successful king is he who has high aspirations and whose might quells sedition. The best plan would be to set watchers at our vulnerable places. If they attack we will be ready and prepared to do battle until we either are victorious or have a good reason to retreat. On the day of battle kings should not be concerned with ultimate consequences: they should think that neither the present nor the future poses danger."

The king said to the next advisor, "What is your view?"

"I do not know what they are talking about," he said. "It would be best to send spies to investigate the situation of the enemy. We should see if they are inclined to make a truce and be content with tribute from us. If possible, we should make peace and accept to pay tribute to be safe and secure from their might, for it is a wise move for a king to use his wealth as a shield for his kingdom and subjects when an enemy is exceptionally dominant and there is fear that one's subjects will be exposed to destruction. To risk one's kingdom is not a wise or prudent thing to do."

The king asked the fourth advisor to tell him what he would advise.

"To bid farewell to one's home and to suffer exile seem preferable to risking one's honor at auction and humbling ourselves before an enemy who has always been inferior to us," he said. "Even if we accept their impositions and bear the expense, they will not be satisfied and will try to exterminate us. It has been said that you should approach an enemy only enough to satisfy your need and no more, for you will be demeaned and the enemy will grow bolder. It is like a stick held on end in the sun: if it is bent slightly the shadow will lengthen, but if it is bent too much the shadow will decrease. They will never be content with our tribute. We should forbear and do battle, for however much wise persons avoid war, avoidance of it in a manner to which death would be preferable is not praiseworthy."

The king asked the fifth advisor whether he thought war, truce, or exile was better.

"It would not become us to make war so long as we can find another way of dealing with them because they are more daring than we are in battle and much stronger. No wise man should underestimate his enemy because then he falls into self-deception, and anyone who is self-deceived is lost. Before this event I feared them and was afraid of what I had seen of them even if they were not planning to attack us, for a cautious person can never be too secure from his enemies. When they are near he should worry about a surprise attack, and when they are distant he should fear their return, in retreat he should fear their ambush, and if he is alone he should fear their deceit. The wisest of men is he who avoids war when he can and there is no necessity for it, for in war there are expenses and risk of life while in other ways there is only risk of possessions and goods. It would be improper for the king to decide on doing battle with the owls because anyone who contends with an elephant will be trampled."

"If you are averse to war," the king said, "then what do you advise?"

"In such a situation one should reflect, weigh the pros and cons, and look well left and right, for with advisors kings achieve goals not possible through massive supplies and soldiers, and kings' views are enlightened by consultation with counselors, like the water of the sea that grows fed by streams.

"A wise man should not neglect to assess his own strength or to take into account the deceit of enemies, and he should consult trustworthy and reliable counselors, for if anyone neglects to ask for advice it will not be long before everything fortune has given him will be lost. Good things are not to be had by lineage and beauty but rather by intelligence and heeding the advice of the experienced. The fortune of one who is enlightened by native intelligence and heeds advice is always full, like shadow in a well and not like the light of the moon, which wanes and can be eclipsed. Mars' hand will polish the weapons of his triumph, and Mercury's pen will scribe writs of his good fortune. Today the king is adorned with intelligence. Since I have been consulted in this matter I have some things to say in public and others to say in private. As much as I reject war I also reject humiliation and the shame of paying tribute, for time is long and has only just begun. Does the hawk obey the sparrow? Does the lion bow to the fox? A noble person wants a long life in order to perpetuate the memory of his good deeds. If one is unfortunate enough to fall into such tribulation and shame, would he not prefer a short life? Would he not reckon the stricture of the grave as an unassailable refuge? I do not think it right for the king to exhibit helplessness, for it would only be a preamble to destruction and loss of kingdom and life. Anyone who gives in to such a thing will have closed the doors to happiness upon himself and set up stumbling blocks of perplexity for himself.

"For the rest of what I have to say we need privacy. Determination is the basis of victory and triumph and the mainstay of fortune and happiness, and the beginning of determination is consultation. In this consultation the king has held and made his servants privy to, the need for determination and steadfastness, as well as wisdom and gravity, is most apparent.

"It is well known that consultation means asking for opinions, and the correct opinion can only be achieved through an exchange of views and guarding secrets. Kings may share their secrets with counselors and ambassadors. However, treacherous persons may be eavesdropping, and they may tell what they hear to others. A secret kept from such persons is safe from becoming common knowledge. Guarding one's secrets has two obvious benefits. First, if a plan succeeds, victory is assured; and second, if destiny is not felicitous, one's well-being will still be undamaged. Kings must have trustworthy counselors and honest treasurers to whom they reveal their secrets and whom they ask for help in implementing their designs, for a king, even if he is cleverer than his minister and is superior to him in all respects, can still benefit from an advisor's opinion, like the light of a lamp that depends upon oil and a fire that depends upon kindling. Anyone who has good ideas and the assistance of intelligent men will both achieve victory and bind the hands of danger. When God told the Prophet to consult he did so not to get help in his views, which were reinforced by divine inspiration through Gabriel. No, he was told to do so in order to communicate the benefits of consultation so that the people of the world would adopt that characteristic. It is incumbent upon servants to agree with their lord in what is right when he has a plan, but if his determination inclines to error, they must state the reasons and do so kindly and gently. Any minister or counselor who does not respect his lord and is unreliable in advising the right thing must be considered an enemy. To make plans with such a person is like a man who recites an incantation to send a demon after somebody else, but since he does not recite the incantation properly the demon falls on him.

"The king does not need to hear these things, for with his determination he has thrown dust in the eyes of monarchs and with his might and policies he has stationed watchers and guards so that he is safe and secure from calamity and sedition.

"When a king keeps his secrets closely guarded, when he has a competent minister, when he has put dread into the hearts of the common people, when his magnificence prevents any dissemination of his secrets, when he knows that it is necessary to reward persons of good action and loyal service and to punish transgressors and those whose service falls short, and when he is appreciative of his servants, then he is worthy of having his kingship last forever, safe from the vicissitudes of time.

"It is certain that all people want and try to acquire happiness and wealth, but getting them depends upon determination and steadfastness of resolve. Kings' secrets are various: some cannot be shared with two persons, and others can be disclosed to a number of people. This secret is one that only two heads and four ears can be privy to."

The king went to one side to speak privately. "What was the cause of the enmity between us and the owls?" he asked.

"It was something a crow said," he said.

"What was that?" the king asked.

The Birds That Wanted to Make the Owl Their Prince

A group of birds assembled and agreed to make the owl their prince. They were discussing this when a crow appeared from afar. One of the birds said, "Let's wait until the crow comes and we can consult him, for he is one of us and until the elite of every species are unanimous there can be no agreement." When the crow joined them the birds informed him of the situation and asked his opinion.

"If all the noble birds were killed and the peacock, the hawk, the eagle, and other leaders were lost, the birds should live without a king rather than being subjected to following the owl or losing their dignity by submitting to his will," the crow said. "He is hideous in appearance and ill-omened. He possesses little intelligence and much obtuseness, is prone to anger, and lacks compassion. In addition to all these things he avoids the light of day and the warmth of the sun. Furthermore he has a sharp temper and is shameless and impossible to get along with. Forget about this bad idea and look to your best interests—like the rabbit that made himself a messenger of the moon and performed a great deed."

"How was that?" the birds asked.

The Rabbit That Made Himself a Messenger of the Moon

In a country belonging to elephants there was such a drought that all the springs dried up. The elephants were driven by thirst to complain to their king. The king sent elephants out in all directions to look for water, and they complied with all urgency. Finally they located a spring called the Spring of the Moon that was flowing with abundant water. The king of the elephants and all his retinue went there to drink, but it was in the land of the rabbits, which were of course worried about being harmed by the elephants since they could be easily trampled, and many of them were trod underfoot. The next day they all went to their king and said, "The king knows how we are suffering from the elephants. Quickly tell us what to do, for hour by hour more are coming and they will tread the rest of us underfoot."

The king said, "He among you who is the cleverest and most intelligent should come forth so that we may consult, for it is imprudent to decide on action before consultation."

One of the most intelligent of the rabbits, whose name was Piroz, stepped forward, and the king recognized him for his native intelligence and good opinion.

"Let the king send me as a messenger and appoint an honest person over me on whose knowledge I can speak and act," he said.

"There can be no doubt of your honesty or trustworthiness," said the king. "We believe what you say. You should go and do what you think best, for a king's messenger is his tongue, and anyone who wants to know what is in a person's mind should look to his messenger, for if virtue is seen in his actions it indicates the king's discrimination in choosing him, and if he makes a mistake the tongues of revilers will be loosed against him. The wise have stressed the importance of sending the wisest and most eloquent person as a messenger. He should be able to speak as sharply as a sword to communicate the might of a king, but both cutting and mending are required since every communication that begins sharply should end softly and persuasively."

Piroz set out when the moon was full, and when he came to where the elephants were he thought to himself, "To approach the elephants could mean my destruction even if they do not intend it, for if someone picks up a viper, even if it does not bite him, the smallest drop of its venom will kill him. Service to kings has the same risk, for even if a person is very cautious and proves his reliability and trustworthiness, his enemies may bad-mouth him and cast him in the guise of a traitor, and he can never escape retribution. I should go up on a hill and deliver my message from afar." Thus he did. Calling out to the king of the elephants, he said, "I am a messenger from the moon, and a messenger is not to be blamed for what he says. Even if the message is harsh, it should be listened to attentively."

"What is your message?" the king of the elephants asked.

"The moon says that anyone who is superior in strength and, falling prey to self-deception, wants to demean others will be dishonored and destroyed. You, who think yourselves superior to other animals, have fallen prey to a great deception. You have gone so far as to bring your troops to a spring sacred to me and muddied its water. I give you fair warning with this message. If you stay in your own place and cease what you are doing, well and good. Otherwise I will come, pluck your eyes out, and put you to death in the most horrible fashion. If you have any doubt of this message, come now and see me in the spring." The king of the elephants, amazed by this speech, went to the spring and saw the reflection of the moon in the water.

"Take a bit of water with your trunk," said the messenger, "wash your face, and prostrate yourself." When the elephant's trunk touched the water it rippled, and the elephant thought the moon was moving.

"Did your king move because I touched the water with my trunk?" it asked Piroz, quivering with fear.

"Yes, it did," said Piroz. "Be quick and prostrate yourself."

The elephant obeyed and agreed not to go there anymore and not to let other elephants go either.

☩ ☩ ☩

"I have told this tale so that you may know that in every one of your species you will find a clever individual who can lead you and ward off your enemies. This would be much better than demeaning yourselves by making the owl your king." In this manner the crow used his deceit and treachery by saying, "There is no fault in kings worse than deceit and breach of promise, for kings are the shadows of the Creator, and without the sun of their justice the world would be dark. Their commands rule the blood, the families, the lives, and the possessions of their subjects. Anyone who is afflicted by a treacherous ruler will be like the partridge and the hare who consulted the fasting cat."

"How was that?" the birds asked.

The Partridge and the Hare Take Their Case to the Cat

A partridge and I were neighbors and lived together with friendly relations. Once he went away and was gone for a long time. I thought he must have died. After a period of time a hare came and occupied his dwelling. I did not contest this. Some time passed and the partridge returned. When he found the hare in his house, he said, "Vacate the premises. This house is mine."

"I am in possession," the hare replied. "If you have a right to it, prove it."

"It's mine, and I have deeds," the partridge said.

"Then we need an impartial judge to listen to both our claims and render a fair decision," said the hare.

"There is an ascetic cat who lives on the riverbank," said the partridge. "He fasts by day and prays by night. He never sheds blood or harms any creature. He only breaks his fast with water and plants. We will not find a more impartial judge. Let us go to him to decide between us."

They both agreed, and I went after them to watch and see how the fasting cat would decide the case. When the cat saw them it reared up on its hind legs and faced the prayer niche to the astonishment of the hare. They waited until the cat had finished praying and then greeted him humbly, asking him to render a judgment between them and end the dispute over the house in a just manner.

"State the case," he said. When he had heard it he said, "Old age has come upon me, and my senses are defective. Such is the effect of the vicissitudes of time: it makes young men old and cripples old men. Come closer and speak louder."

They went closer to him and repeated their cases. "I understand," said the cat. "Before I render judgment I will give you some advice. If you listen well the fruits of it will benefit you greatly. If you don't, it won't be my fault. The fact is that you are both seeking your rights, and a person in the right must be considered victorious even if the judgment goes contrary to his desire. A false claimant must be considered vanquished even if the judgment goes in accordance with his wishes. The people of this world actually possess nothing, no chattel, no wealth, other than good deeds they can store up for the hereafter. An intelligent person should not strive to acquire transitory goods: he should focus his attention on seeking lasting good. Life and status in the world are as fleeting as clouds in summer. Wealth is no better than pebbles. If you spend it, it comes to an end, and if you hoard it, there is no difference between it and rocks or potsherds. Love of the world is like a viper from which you can never be safe and for which no sack can be made to contain it safely. You should consider others as precious as your own life, and you should hate for others what you hate for yourself."

With such advice he charmed them until they felt safe and went further forward. In one fell swoop the cat grabbed them both and killed them. Such was the result of the fasting cat's asceticism and rectitude!

✝ ✝ ✝

"The owl's hypocrisy and treachery are no less, and what has been said is only a drop in the bucket. Beware lest you decide on the owl, for when the royal crown is defiled by the owl's hideous mien and reprehensible conduct, the sun and moon will cast stones at that crown."

The birds at once decided not to follow the owl, and the owl, left sad and dejected, said to the crow, "You have wreaked your vengeance on me. There is now an enmity between you and me that time will not diminish. I don't know whether you were repaying me for something in the past or whether you just felt compelled to act in such a *benign* fashion! Know that if a tree is cut down, in the end it will sprout branches from its roots and grow back to what it was. A sword wound can be treated and will heal. When an arrow sticks in someone it can be pulled out. Wounds caused by words never heal, no shaft of words that pierces the heart can ever be pulled out, and the pain lasts forever. Every hurt has a remedy: for fire there is water, for poison there is antidote, for grief there is forbearance, and for love there is separation; but the fire of spite is infinite. All the oceans could wash over it and it still would not die. The roots of the enmity between our species go deep, and its branches rise high into the sky." So saying, the owl departed dejectedly.

The crow regretted what he had said and thought to himself, "I have made a dreadful mistake. I have created a vindictive enemy for myself and others of my species. In no way was I worthier than the other birds to offer advice, and those who were my superiors kept silent. Although they knew the owl's faults better than I did, they thought better of the consequences. Even worse, it was said face-to-face, and doubtless that makes the spite and desire for vengeance even stronger. Although a wise man may have all confidence in his own strength, he should not needlessly expose himself to hostility and contention. One should not drink poison just because one has all sorts of antidotes and medicine. Virtue lies in good action and not merely in good words because in the end the effect of a good deed will be seen through experience to be much better. Again, he whose words outweigh his actions can clothe bad things in rhetoric and make them look good, but in the end they lead to blame and censure. I am that talker lacking action who does not look to the ends of things. Otherwise I should have eschewed such stupidity. Had I possessed wisdom I would have first consulted with others and only after much thought would I have spoken cautiously and suggestively, for to have meddled spontaneously in such a great affair was extremely unwise. Anyone who plunges into action without consulting wise advisors is reckoned among the nefarious and is labeled as ignorant, as the Prophet said, 'The worst of my community is the loner who is satisfied with his own opinion, hypocritical in his actions, and contentious.' I did not need to expose myself to such hostility and make such an enemy."

Thus did intelligence speak to the crow as it whispered into his ear the proverb, "The chatterbox is like someone who gathers kindling at night." Blaming himself, he flew away.

✳ ✳ ✳ ✳

"This was the beginning of the enmity between us and the owls."

"I understand," said the king, "and therein lie many benefits. Tell me now what we should do to give us peace of mind and save our army."

"With regard to leaving war aside, not wanting to give tribute, and avoiding exile, what has been said has been said, but I hope we may escape through a ruse, for many have achieved triumph through machinations that could not have been achieved through mere strength and overwhelming numbers—like those who got a sheep from the ascetic through deceit."

"How was that?" asked the king.

Three Charlatans Fool an Ascetic

An ascetic bought a sheep to sacrifice. Along the way a group of charlatans saw him, set their sights on the sheep, and agreed to fool him so they could get it.

One of them went up to him and said, "Where are you taking this dog?"

Another said, "He must be going hunting to have a dog along."

The third joined in and said, "This man is dressed like an ascetic, but he doesn't look like one, for ascetics don't play with dogs, and they know the necessity of keeping their clothes free of defilement by dogs."

And they kept saying such things until doubt arose in the ascetic's mind and he thought to himself that maybe the man who sold him the sheep was a sorcerer who had enchanted him. In short, he left the sheep and went away, and the charlatans took the sheep.

* * * *

"I have told this story for it to be clear that we must base our actions on deceit and trickery, for then victory will be assured. I think the king should pretend in public to be angry with me and order me to be beaten bloody and left under a tree. The king and the army will go off and wait for me to come. When I have worked my deceit I will come and inform the king." The king so ordered and then took his army off to the place he had named.

That night the owls came back, but they did not find the crows. They also did not see the one who had put himself through so much and was waiting in ambush to work his treachery. Fearing that the owls would retreat and his efforts would be wasted, he writhed around and cried out feebly so the owls would hear him and inform their king. The king and several other owls came to him and asked, "Who are you? Where are the crows?"

He told them his name and his father's name and said, "My condition indicates that I cannot be the repository of what you ask about the crows."

"This is the minister of the king of the crows," the king said, "and the sharer of his secrets and advisor. It must be learned why this has happened to him."

"My lord suspected me," the crow said.

"For what reason?" the king asked.

"When you made that surprise attack the king summoned us and told us to advise him what to do. I, who was one of his intimates, said, 'We do not have the ability to oppose the owls, for they are much bolder in battle and stronger than we are. My opinion is that we should send a messenger and ask for a truce. If we receive a positive response, well and good; otherwise we should disperse into cities, for battle favors them while truce is more convenient for us. We must be humble, for a strong and bold enemy can only be placated by humility. Do you not see that a stalk springs up in a strong wind only by bending gently in every direction?' The crows got angry and accused me of taking the part of the owls. The king refused to take my advice and had me tortured, as you see. I could see that they were determined to make war."

When the king of the owls heard what the crow said he asked one of his ministers what he thought should be done with the crow.

"There is no need to worry about him," he said. "The face of the earth should be cleansed of his defilement as soon as possible, for therein lie our comfort and benefit to escape his plots. The crows will reckon his death a great loss. It has been said that anyone who lets an opportunity slip by will not get another, and regret avails naught. Anyone who sees an enemy weak and alone and does not rid himself of him will not get another opportunity. When an enemy escapes the brink of death he will gain strength and reinforce himself to find an opportunity to cause trouble. Beware lest the king be seduced by his words, for to rely on unproven friends—not to mention deceitful enemies—is imprudent. The Prophet has said, 'Trust people slowly.'"

The king asked another minister, "What do you think?"

"I cannot advise killing him," he said, "for a weak and helpless enemy is worthy of compassion, and the wise seek out such a one to prove to the people of the world their nobility through pardon and beneficence. One who seeks amnesty should be spared to prove his worthiness of it. Some things make people kind to enemies—like the thief who made the merchant's wife tremble for her husband even though it was unintentional."

"How was that?" the king asked.

The Old Merchant and His Young Wife

There was a merchant who was very rich but ugly and dull, and he had a wife with a face like an angel and tresses as black as a register of evil deeds. The merchant desired her greatly, but she abhorred him and shrank from him. Every day the man grew more smitten with her until one night a thief came into their house. The merchant was asleep, but the wife, frightened by the thief, clutched her husband tightly. He woke up and said, "What is this compassion, and what have I done to deserve such favor?"

When he saw the thief he said, "My good fellow, take whatever you want. It's yours because thanks to you my wife is being kind to me."

* * * *

The king asked the third minister what he thought.

"It would be better to leave him alive," he said, "and give him a reward so that he may advise the king and save us. A wise man counts it as a victory when he has separated his enemies one from another and sowed dissension among them, for disagreement among opponents is a cause for ease of mind, like the disagreement between the thief and the demon over the holy man."

"How was that?" asked the king.

The Holy Man, the Thief, and the Demon

A holy man got a milking cow from a disciple and was headed home. A thief saw him and lay in wait to steal the cow. A demon in human guise joined him. The thief asked him who he was.

"I am a demon," he said, "and I am following that holy man so that when I get a chance I can kill him. Tell me about yourself."

"I am a rogue," he said. "I'm thinking I'll steal the holy man's cow."

So they fell in together and followed the holy man to his cell. They got there at night. The holy man went into his cell, having tied up the cow with enough to eat.

The thief thought, "If the demon tries to kill him before I steal the cow he may wake up and cry out. People will come and it won't be possible to steal the cow."

The demon thought, "If the thief gets away with the cow and doors are opened, the holy man will wake up and it won't be possible to kill him." He then said to the thief, "Give me time to kill the man. Then take the cow."

The thief answered, "It would be better for you to wait until I have gotten away with the cow. Then you can kill him."

This disagreement between them continued until the thief cried out to the holy man, "This is a demon, and he wants to kill you."

And the demon yelled, "This thief is going to steal your cow."

The holy man woke up, people came, and both of them ran away. Thus were the holy man's life and property saved by a disagreement between enemies.

✲ ✲ ✲ ✲

When the third minister finished telling this story the first minister, who had advised killing the crow, said, "I think that this crow has enchanted you with deceit, and you are going to throw caution to the winds. I stress, you should wake from your slumber of heedlessness, take the cotton out of your ears, and reflect on the consequences of this action, for the wise base their actions in dealing with enemies on a foundation of correctness and neither listen to the words of opponents nor are seduced by lies. The negligent pay no attention to this advice and are swayed by a little flattery, and they leave aside ancient feuds and hereditary enmity. Not bothering to investigate the truth, they believe enemies' lies and are easily won over to a truce. Little do they know that making peace with an enemy is like waging war with a friend. They are like the carpenter who was deceived by his unfaithful wife."

"How was that?" the king asked.

The Unfaithful Wife and Her Foolish Husband

There was a carpenter in the land of Serendip who had a wife like a fox in her promises and like a lioness in coquettishness. She had a face as bright as the thought of Islam in the heart of an infidel and tresses as black as a seed of doubt in the mind of a believer. In truth he was so smitten by her that he could not bear to have her out of his sight for even a moment. A neighbor's gaze fell upon her, and for a time they enjoyed friendly relations. However, her in-laws found out about it and informed the carpenter. He wanted to be certain and then do something about it.

"I am going to the countryside," he said to his wife. "The distance is not more than a league, but I'll be gone for several days. Fix me some provisions." She prepared them at once. The carpenter said goodbye to his wife, ordering her to keep the door closed as a precaution and to keep watch over their possessions lest anything happen during his absence.

When he was gone the wife sent word to her lover and fixed a time for a rendezvous. The carpenter returned unexpectedly and found his wife's lover there. He waited for a moment until they had gone into the bedroom, and then the poor fellow crept under the bed so he could see what was going on. The wife spied his foot and realized that catastrophe had struck.

"Ask me in a loud voice whether I love you more or my husband," she said to her lover. When he asked her she said, "Why are you asking? There is no need for you to do so." When he persisted, the wife said, "Such things may happen to women by mistake or out of lust, and they take friends for whose worth and lineage they care nothing and to whose bad character and blameworthy customs they attach no importance. When passion has cooled they are no more than other strangers. A husband, however, is like a father, brother, and friend, and unworthy is the woman who does not hold her husband a thousand times dearer than her own life and who would not give her life for his comfort and pleasure."

When the carpenter heard this he felt compassion in his heart and said to himself, "The fault is mine for having doubted her. The poor thing longs for me and burns with passion for me. If a forlorn person makes a mistake one should not attach much importance to it. No one is immune to error. I have tormented myself uselessly. Now at least I will not interrupt their pleasure and dishonor her in front of this man." And so he remained under the bed until night fell.

The other man left, and the carpenter came out and sat on the bed. The wife pretended to be asleep. He roused her gently and said, "Were it not for your modesty I would have hurt that man and taught a lesson to other home-wreckers, but since I know how much you love me and long for me, if you engage in such illicit behavior it is by mistake, not by intention. I should curry favor with that fellow and be mindful of your modesty. Be of good cheer and do not fear. Pardon me for having thought ill of you and having entertained all sorts of suspicions." The woman was clement, and the anger on both sides subsided.

✳ ✳ ✳ ✳

"I have told this story lest you be deceived like the carpenter and have what you see before your own eyes charmed away by sleight of hand and chicanery. Any enemy who is too far away to attack will seek to get nearer and offer advice. He will worm his way into your confidence with false friendship and flattery, and when he has learned your secrets and finds an opportunity he will inflict any wound he can as swiftly as lightning and will fall upon you as certainly as destiny. I have experience of the crows and know how farsighted, perspicacious, and clever they are. As soon as I saw this accursed one and heard his words the depth of their intrigue was obvious."

The king of the owls disregarded his suggestion, ordered the crow to be taken along with all honor, and issued an edict for everyone to hold him in high esteem.

The minister who wanted to have him killed said, "If you don't kill the crow, at least live with him as an enemy, and do not think even for the blink of an eye that you are safe from his treachery and plots, for the only reason he has come among us is to make trouble." The king rejected this advice and scoffed at the words of his peerless counselor.

The crow lived in the king's service with all respect and omitted no observance of service and obedience. He was compassionate toward his friends and peers and showed respect for everyone according to his station. Every day he was held in higher regard by the king and his followers. The trust of the king and his subjects in his loyalty and advice also increased, and he was regarded as a confidant in everything and consulted on all affairs. One day during a private gathering he said, "The king of the crows injured me for no reason and had me tortured without guilt. How can I sleep and eat without extracting revenge on him? It has been said that retribution is a necessary concomitant of nature. I have thought much about it. I have realized that as long as I am in the form of a crow I cannot get my wish. I have heard from the learned that if a wronged man is at the mercy of an opponent and knows that he is going to die at the hands of an unjust ruler, when he is about to enter the fire and make a burnt offering of himself, any prayer he utters will be granted. If the king agrees, let him order me to be burned, and at the very moment the fire reaches me I will ask the Creator to turn me into an owl. Perhaps by that means I will be able to get to that tyrant and soothe my burning heart."

The owl who advised killing him happened to be present, and he said, " 'If you are not as twisted as a hyacinth and as blackhearted as a tulip, don't be two-faced and ten-tongued like a rose and a lily.' You, treacherous one, are as outwardly beautiful and inwardly hideous as a beautiful, aromatic potion laced with poison. If your filthy, vile body were burned time and again and oceans washed over it, your impure essence and blameworthy conduct would never change. The crookedness of your mind cannot be rectified by water or fire. It is part of your very being, however you may be and in whatever form you take. If you became a peacock or a phoenix your desire to be with crows would never change—just like the mouse that was offered the sun, the cloud, the wind, and the mountain in marriage and that rejected all of them to embrace a mouse of her own kind."

"How was that?" asked the king.

The Mouse That Was Offered the Sun, the Cloud, the Wind, and the Mountain in Marriage

A holy man was sitting by a stream, and a kite dropped a baby mouse in front of him. The holy man had compassion on it, picked it up, wrapped it in leaves, and took it home. Then he thought that it might be trouble for his household and destructive, so he prayed to the Deity, and it was turned into a girl so beautiful that the radiance of her cheeks would drive away shadows from a well and the blackness of her tresses would put the spots on the moon to shame. Then he took her to one of his disciples and asked him to raise her. The disciple did as his master asked and raised the girl with kindness. When her days of childhood were over the holy man said, "Daughter, you are grown and need a husband. Choose whom you will of humans and fairies and I will give you to him."

The girl said, "I want a strong and powerful husband who can acquire all sorts of strength and glory."

"Would you want the sun?" he asked.

"Yes," she said.

The holy man said to the sun, "This girl is beautiful and well-formed. I want her to be under your protection, for she has asked for a strong and powerful husband."

"I will show you someone stronger than myself," said the sun. "He can cover my light and deprive the people of the world of the beauty of my countenance. It is the cloud."

The holy man went at once to the cloud and repeated his offer.

"The wind is stronger than I am," it said. "It can take me anywhere it wants. Next to him I am but a plaything."

The holy man went to the wind and repeated his offer.

"Absolute strength belongs to the mountain," he said. "He calls me light-headed and dusty-footed. He considers my constant movement a defect. He is constant and immobile, and my effect on him is no more than a whisper in a deaf ear."

The holy man made his offer to the mountain.

"The mouse is more puissant than I am," said the mountain. "He can gnaw into me and make his home in my heart, and I cannot even think of getting rid of him."

"He is right," the girl said. "He will be my husband."

The holy man made his offer to the mouse.

"My mate must be of my own species," said the mouse.

"Pray for me to turn into a mouse," said the girl.

The holy man lifted his hands in prayer and asked the Deity, and his prayer was granted. He gave them to each other and departed.

✳ ✳ ✳ ✳

"You are just like this, and your actions, deceitful traitor, are of the same sort."

The king of the owls, as it always is with those slated for misfortune, did not listen to this advice and refused to consider the consequences. Every day the crow would tell amusing stories and amazing tales and so made his way into the owls' confidence that he learned their most closely held secrets.

All of a sudden, he absconded and went back to the crows. When the king of the crows saw him he asked what had transpired.

" 'Rejoice, for fate is obedient and time submits to your command,' " he said. "Thanks to Your Majesty's good fortune I have achieved what had to be done."

"We will follow your advice," said the king. "Tell us what to do that we may give the order."

"All the owls are on a mountain, and they spend their days in a cave. There is much firewood in the vicinity. Let the king of crows have some of it carried to the mouth of the cave. In the camp of some shepherds who graze their flocks nearby there is fire. I will bring some embers from that fire and put them under the firewood. When the king gives the order the crows will fan them with their wings. Once the fire has caught, any of the owls that come out will be burned, and any who remain in the cave will die from the smoke."

Off they went to execute this plan, and all the owls were burned. The crows achieved a major victory and returned triumphant. The king and his army were effusive in thanking the crow for his efforts. He praised the king and said, "Everything that happened was due to the king's good fortune. I saw signs of this victory on the day they launched their attack."

One day during consultation the king asked him, "How were you able to abide being with them for so long? Nobles are seldom able to tolerate being with the base."

"It is so," he replied, "but a wise man does not avoid difficulties when it comes to his lord's pleasure and will eagerly embrace any trial that comes his way. A man of determination does not give way to distress at every failure and difficulty. When one is involved in a great labor and important mission and one's life, tribe, kingdom, and territory are at stake, if it is necessary to demean oneself and suffer humiliation to exterminate the enemy, when it is certain that the end result will be victory and triumph, a wise man will attach little importance to what he has to suffer. The author of the law has said that the touchstone of an affair is its end results."

"Tell us something of the owls' perspicacity and knowledge," said the king.

"I saw no clever person among them," he said, "except for the one who advised killing me, but they belittled his opinion and refused to accept his advice. Little did they suspect that I, who had advanced to a high position among them and was thought to have some intelligence, would betray them. It never occurred to them. Neither did they listen to good advice nor did they keep their secrets from me. It is said that kings should exercise the utmost of precaution in keeping their secrets, most especially from desperate friends and fearful enemies."

"It appears to me that the cause for the owls' destruction was their hubris and the bad opinions of their ministers," said the king.

"It is as the king says," he replied. "Few are they who achieve victory without falling prey to hubris. Few are they who relish the company of women without being disgraced. Few are they who overeat without falling ill. Few are they who trust ministers of bad opinion and remain safe. It has been said that the arrogant should not lust for praise, the wicked should not look for many friends, the ill-bred should not think of nobility, the miserly should not expect to be charitable, the greedy should not presume to be innocent, and a negligent tyrant who has ministers with bad opinions should not imagine that his kingship will last or his subjects will be righteous."

"You have undergone a difficult trial and humbled yourself before your enemies against your will," said the king.

"Anyone who suffers pain with expectations of benefit must first rid himself of misplaced zeal and embarrassment, for only he can be called manly who, when he is determined to carry out a task, is first and foremost willing to risk his life and then steps into the field. The king will have heard of the snake that willingly served a frog when he saw that it was in his best interests to do so."

"How was that?" asked the king.

The Snake That Served the Frog

It is related that a snake had grown so old and weak that he was unable to hunt. He wondered what to do since life without sustenance was impossible and without strength he could not hunt. He said to himself, "Youth cannot be regained, and old age does not last. To expect fidelity from time and to hope for kindness from fate are desires that would never occur to a wise person, for to look for dryness in water or coldness in fire is a fancy that can only result in disappointment. The past cannot be brought back, but it is important to plan for the future. From youth one does acquire experience from which one's livelihood can be gained for the rest of one's life. I must put fancies out of my head and resign myself to being harmless. I must not be bothered by censure that comes my way, for the world contains both good things and bad."

So saying, he went to the edge of a spring where there were many frogs, and they had a successful king whose word was obeyed. Making himself look dejected, he cast himself down. A frog asked him why he was so sad.

"Who is worthier of dismay than I?" he said. "My means of livelihood used to be catching frogs, but today I am so afflicted that even if I do catch one I cannot hold on to it."

The frog went to inform his king of this good news. The king asked the snake, "How did this affliction come upon you?"

"I went after a frog," he said, "but it got away and hid itself in a holy man's house. I went in after it. The house was dark and the holy man's son was there. I bit his toe thinking it was the frog. He died on the spot. In a rage over his son the holy man chased me and cursed me, saying, 'I ask my deity to bring you low and make you carry frogs. You will not be able to eat a frog unless the king of the frogs gives you one in alms.' I have therefore come here to serve you and submit to my destiny."

This pleased the king of the frogs and, imagining it a great honor for himself, he got on the snake and swelled with pride.

After a while the snake said, "Long live the king. I must have sustenance to remain alive and carry out this service."

"Yes," said the king of the frogs, "it is necessary." And the king assigned the snake an emolument of two frogs a day. He ate them and passed his days. Since he recognized the benefit to himself in that humiliation, he did not consider it blameworthy.

✳ ✳ ✳ ✳

"If I forbore it was because the destruction of an enemy and the good of the tribe were involved. An enemy can be overcome sooner with kindness than with conflict and arrogance. Thus it is that it has been said that wisdom is better than manliness, for when one person, no matter how strong and courageous he is, goes into battle he can take down ten, or at most twenty, persons, but one man with great wisdom can bring down a kingdom and confound a massive army. Fire, with all its power, can burn only as much of a tree as is above ground. Water, with all its gentleness, can rip out the largest tree by the roots so that it can never grow again. The Prophet said, 'Gentleness was never in anything without adorning it, and harshness was never in anything without marring it.' There are four things a little of which must be reckoned as much: fire, illness, enmity, and debt. All of this was accomplished thanks to the king's foresight and fortune.

"It has been said that if two persons seek something and are both up to it, he will succeed who is superior in manliness. If they are equal in that, he who is the more determined will succeed. If they are equal in that, he who has more friends and helpers will win. If they are equal in that too, he who is the luckier will come out on top.

"The wise say that anyone who opposes a king who is assured of victory and safe from defeat invites his own death, especially when that king is aware of the subtleties and obscurities of affairs, does not confuse gentleness and harshness, wrath and contentment, or haste and hesitation, and can discriminate between today and tomorrow, can plan for the future from initial actions, and knows how to make up for losses. Never will he fail to exercise clemency and appeasement or ignore the code of might and wise policy. Today no king rules a country and safeguards his roads without first exercising precaution and determination. One cannot train one's servants or encourage the arts and crafts without being smiled upon by fortune and being willing to sacrifice oneself for one's subjects."

"The success of this mission and the overthrow of our enemies are due to your wise counsel," said the king. "In everything in which I relied upon your advice the results have been obvious. No one who entrusts the reins to a minister of good counsel will ever suffer misfortune. What is most astonishing is that for a long time you lived among enemies and never said a word about being suspected."

"I took the king's good character as my example," he said, "and copied his finest traits, knowing that the success of my mission lay in following his good example, for the king combines nobility with good planning and splendor and magnificence with awesomeness and courage."

"From among my servants at court I have found only you who combine eloquent speech with good action," said the king, "and were able to achieve such a great thing by exercising determination and steadfastness so that God granted us this victory. I have not been able to enjoy food or drink or to rest or sleep for worry. No one who is afflicted with an overpowering enemy can rest until he is delivered. The wise have said, 'Until a sick person regains his health he cannot enjoy food, and until a porter lays down his heavy burden he cannot rest.' Until people are secure from an overwhelming enemy, be it a thousand years, the burning in their breasts cannot be quenched. Now you must tell how you found the conduct of the owls' king in battle and banquet."

"I found everything he did to be based on inappropriate conceit, arrogance, pride, and hubris, and with all this his weakness was apparent. He lacked discernment and had no acumen. All of his followers were of the same ilk except for the one who advised killing me."

"What traits in him seemed good to you and more clearly indicated his intelligence?" the king asked.

"First, his advice to kill me. Second, he withheld no advice from his master even when he knew that it would not be well received and would result in anger and distaste. Even then he remained obedient and never engaged in severity or disrespect. He spoke calmly and gently and most worthily maintained respect for his lord. If he saw an error in his master's actions he would couch his warning in parables to avoid provoking his anger, and the parables contained palatable messages. Since he related the flaws of others in his stories and confessed to his own mistakes in them there was no occasion for him to be taken to task. One day I heard him say to the king, 'A ruler enjoys high and lofty station that cannot be reached by striving or wishing. It is attained only by chance and good luck. When one has it one should cherish it and make every effort to keep it and protect it. It would therefore be appropriate for there to be little negligence or underestimation of affairs, for the permanence of a kingdom and good fortune are not possible without great determination, perfect justice, good counsel, and sharp swords.' However, no attention was paid to his words, and his advice was not taken. Neither did they benefit from his intelligence and perspicacity nor did he escape calamity through his own wisdom and sagacity. Rightly have they said that he who is disobeyed sees nothing but loss. The Commander of the Faithful Ali has said, 'He who is not obeyed has no opinion.'"

This has been the story of being wary of treacherous plots and the deceits of enemies even if it involves great humiliation and debasement, for one lone crow, with all his weakness, was able to defeat a powerful opponent and numerous enemies because of their lack of judgment and little understanding. Otherwise he could never have accomplished his goal and could not even have dreamt of that victory. A wise man should learn from this example and realize that one should never trust an enemy or underestimate an opponent no matter how weak he may appear. The most beneficial store one can have and the most profitable trade one can engage in is the winning of good friends and worthy helpers. If one has those two one can keep one's friends devoted and thankful and rid oneself of treacherous enemies and deceitful opponents and enjoy happiness in this world and the next.

Chapter Five

The Monkey and the Turtle

The Raja said, "I have heard the story of securing oneself from the deceit of enemies and how avoidance of it is necessary. Now tell me a story of one who strives hard to get something and after getting it loses it through negligence."

"It is easier to get something than it is to keep it," said the Brahman, "for many precious things have been acquired by happenstance and good luck without any effort, but keeping them can only be done with foresight and good planning. Anyone who walks in the field of wisdom devoid of foresight will soon lose what he has acquired and be left with regret, like the turtle who trapped the monkey without much effort and then lost him through gullibility."

"How was that?" asked the Raja.

The Monkey and the Turtle

There were many monkeys on an island, and they had a king named Kardanah who reigned in great splendor with good policy, effective command, and all-encompassing justice. When his days of youth, which is the springtime of life and the season of gaiety, had passed, the weakness of old age appeared and made its effects apparent in his bodily strength and sharpness of vision, for it is the custom of time to change the freshness of youth into the withering of old age and to let the debasement of poverty overwhelm the glory of wealth. Time shows itself to the people of the world in the garb of a bride, outwardly beautifully adorned to attract all hearts and minds. Her external adornment fools the unwise, and her empty splendor deceives the greedy so that they all fall into her trap, unaware of how ugly she is inside, how deceptive her outward show is, how base her nature is, and how false her promises are. A wise man should pay no attention to any of these things and not set his heart on the search for fleeting prestige. He should turn his attention to acquiring everlasting good because status and the life of this world are impermanent. If he acquires any possessions he will have to leave them at the brink of the grave for sharp-toothed dogs to fall upon.

In short, Kardanah's old age and weakness became known, and dread of him decreased markedly. One of his relatives, a young man in the bloom of youth, arrived. Auspicious signs were visible on his brow, good fortune was obvious in his movements and actions, and he was seen as worthy of the kingship. He curried favor with the army and so endeared himself to the subjects that all befriended him and were glad to obey him. The old king was removed and forced to turn over the reins of power to the young man. The poor old king, forced into exile, betook himself to the seashore, where there was a thick forest with much fruit. He chose a fig tree overlooking the water and contented himself with what sustenance he could derive from its fruits while he laid up provisions for the afterlife in repentance, contrition, and acts of worship.

A turtle used to come and sit under the tree and rest in the shade. One day the monkey picked a fig and tossed it into the water. He liked the sound and felt exhilarated, so he kept throwing figs into the water and enjoying the sound. The turtle imagined he was throwing them to him, and this engendered friendly feeling toward him. "Without any prior acquaintanceship he is doing me this kindness," he thought to himself. "If a cause for affection were added, who knows what favors he might not do and what great benefits might not accrue from his friendship?" Therefore he called out to the monkey and proposed becoming friends. When he received a favorable reply they found that each of them had a great inclination for the other, and they became fast and inseparable friends.

Some time passed. Now, since the turtle had been away from home for a long time, his wife became worried and anxious and took her plight to a friend.

"If you don't blame me and berate me," the friend said, "I will inform you of what is going on."

"Sister," she replied, "how could there be any doubt of what you say? How could I imagine berating you for your advice?"

"He has formed an attachment to a monkey," she said, "and given his heart and soul to him. He consoles himself in your absence with affection for him and quenches the fire of longing for you with the water of union with him. There is no use in grieving. Think up a plan to end it."

They sat and connived together, knowing that nothing was more imperative than a plan to destroy the monkey. At the friend's suggestion the wife pretended to be ill and sent for her husband.

The turtle took his leave of the monkey, telling him he was going home to see his wife and children. When he got there he found his wife ill. He addressed her kindly and affectionately, but of course she turned her back on him without offering any explanation. Then he asked her friend and nurse why she was suffering in silence.

"How could a sick person who has despaired of medicine and has no hope of treatment speak?" she said.

When he heard this he was alarmed. "What medicine is it that cannot be found in these parts or acquired somehow?" he asked. "Tell me quickly that I may go on a quest and search for it far and wide. If I have to lay down my life for it I am ready."

"Treatment for such a female complaint is a matter for women," she said, "and the only remedy for it is a monkey's heart."

"Where can one get such a thing?" he asked.

"Just so," she said. "That is why we have summoned you lest you be deprived of her final farewell, for the poor thing has no hope of recovery."

The turtle was greatly distressed, but however much he pondered how to address the problem he found no solution. Then he thought of his friend and said to himself, "If I were to betray him and ignore all our past friendship and oaths I would not have an iota of manliness or gallantry, but if I am true to my word and do not stain myself with betrayal, my wife, who is the mainstay of my household, will be beyond hope." He reflected on these thoughts and hesitated for a time, but in the end love for his wife triumphed and he decided to get the medicine as fidelity to his friend was outweighed in the balance. The Prophet said, "Love for a thing blinds and deafens you." He realized, however, that unless he could entice the monkey to his island there was no way he could get what he was after.

With this thought in mind he went back to the monkey. The monkey was delighted to see him again, for he had been miserable during his absence, and as soon as he saw him he was consoled and asked warmly about his children and clan.

The turtle replied, "I missed you so much that I could take no delight in seeing them, and every time I thought of your loneliness and your being cut off from your comrades life was soured to me. Now I have every expectation that you will grace my home with your presence so that my friendship with you may be known to all and my relatives and kinfolk may take pride. They will set before you food they have prepared in hopes of repaying some of your kindness."

"Do not concern yourself with such things," the monkey said. "You should not think that my friendship for you elevates you in any way, for I am much more in need of your friendship since I am far from my clan, land, servants, and retinue, and I did not abandon kingship and kingdom by choice, however much the realm of contentment is more permanent and association without contention is more enjoyable. Had I had any inkling of this comfort before, and had I tasted its pleasures and sweetness, I would never have sullied myself with that kingship, which conferred so much trouble and so little benefit. Were it not for the fact that God placed a new obligation on me with your friendship and affection and has given me the gift of love for you in such a place of exile, who could have delivered me from the clutches of deprivation and tribulation as you did? Therefore your kindness toward me is the greater. You have no need to make such elaborate preparations or to go to such trouble, for between people of virtue loyalty is important and nothing more has any weight. All sorts of animals sit together to enjoy food and drink, and when they have finished they part company. Friends, though separated by the distance between the horizons, are consoled and comforted by the memory of each other, delight in the thought of reunion, and go to sleep hoping to dream of each other. Thieves do not break into houses together because they are friends. They do it because they are willing to go to a lot of trouble to get something. If a person who walks a tightrope is not accompanied by his friends, in no way can it be attributed to enmity, but since they see no benefit in it they think it best not to make a futile attempt. If you want me to visit your family, you'd best know that it is impossible for me to cross the sea."

"I will carry you on my back to that island, where you will have safety, security, and plenty," said the turtle.

In short, he talked him into it. The turtle took the monkey on his back and set out for his home. When they got to the middle of the water he thought about the evil he had in mind. "The things the wise have warned against the most are infidelity and treachery," he thought to himself, "especially with regard to friends and for the sake of women, who cannot be imagined ever being true to their word and of whom no fidelity can be expected. It has been said that the assay of gold can be determined by fire, the strength of a pack animal can be measured by a heavy load, and the honesty of men can be discerned by commerce, but never can knowledge encompass the lengths to which women will go and how unfaithful to their word they can be."

As he stopped and debated thus with himself signs of hesitancy became apparent in him. The monkey began to have suspicions. As the Prophet said, "An intelligent man sees with his heart what an ignorant one cannot see with his eyes."

"Why are you worried?" he asked. "Has carrying me tired you out?"

"What are you talking about?" said the turtle. "What makes you think I'm worried?"

"It is apparent that you are debating with yourself and wondering what to do," said the monkey.

"You're right," said the turtle. "I am thinking that this is the first time you are going to such trouble. My wife is ill, and something is sure to be lacking. I will not be able to host and honor you as I wish."

"Since your friendship is assured," said the monkey, "and your desire for my happiness is known, it would be more appropriate to our companionship and intimacy for you not to go to such trouble. What I know of your friendship is beyond your needing to regale and feast me. Put your mind at rest and don't worry."

The turtle proceeded. Once again he stopped and had the same thoughts as before. The monkey's suspicion increased, and he said to himself, "When suspicion of a friend arises in one's mind one should take precaution and remain calm. If the suspicion proves true one can remain safe from malevolence and stratagem. If the doubt is misplaced no harm can come of being vigilant. The mind is fickle, and one cannot know at any given moment whether it is inclined to good or to evil." Then he said to the turtle, "Why do you seem lost in thought and worry?"

"It is so," replied the turtle. "Thoughts of my wife's illness and distress worry me."

"In all friendship you should tell me of your concerns," said the monkey. "We should see what the cause is and how to deal with what you seem unable to resolve."

"The physicians have prescribed a medicine that cannot be obtained," said the turtle.

"What is it?" he asked.

"A monkey's heart," he said.

And there, in the midst of the water, the world turned dark before his eyes and he said to himself, "Greed and cupidity have brought me to this pass. I am not the first person to be taken in by hypocrites. An arrow of calamity has been shot from a bow of ignorance and waywardness into my heart, and now I know of nothing that can assist me other than a ruse. As soon as I am on that island, if I refuse to turn over my heart, I will die of hunger or be imprisoned. If I try to escape by throwing myself into the water I will drown."

"I know how to treat your wife," he said. "It is simple. The wise have said that it is not good to withhold something others seek for good purposes, for kings to deny something that would be for the benefit of all, or to refuse friends something that would be a comfort to them. I know the place your wife holds in your heart, and in all friendship it would not be right for me to withhold for any reason medicine that would cure her. If I were to hesitate, how could I be excused by people of virtue? I know what is wrong with her, for it often happens to our women, and we give them our hearts, for only a little pain is involved, and that is negligible next to the comfort it gives us and the cure it brings them. If you had told me I would have brought my heart, and it would have been easy for me to do so since it would have cured your wife and I wouldn't have missed it. I cannot imagine ever needing my heart for the rest of my life since I am in a place where nothing is harder for me than the company of my heart. It has been burdened with much care and wells up all the time with grief, and my only wish is to get rid of it. If I didn't have it I would regret separation from my people and worry about my homeland less, and I would be free of those anxieties and thoughts for a while."

"Why did you leave your heart behind?" asked the turtle.

"It is the custom of monkeys, when they go visiting friends and want to spend the day with them in good cheer and don't want their cares to infect their happiness, not to take their hearts along since they are seats of tribulation and grief and it is not in the owner's power to fix them on sadness or happiness. Any moment they may sour a good time and disrupt enjoyment. Since I was going to your house I wanted you to be glad to have me there. Now I'm sorry to hear of your wife's illness and not to have brought my heart with me. You may forgive me, but your people will think badly of me and say that with all our past friendship I have failed to do this one little thing and have neglected to comfort you with something that would not hurt me."

The turtle immediately turned back, confident that he was going to get what he wanted. When he delivered the monkey to the water's edge the monkey scrambled up into a tree. The turtle waited for a while and then called out. The monkey laughed and said, "I have reached the end of my life and have had much experience of the world. My eyes have been opened to its good and evil, and now that time has taken back what it gave and I have seen misfortune, I can still distinguish between good and bad. Enough of this talk! Never again boast of fidelity. If a person claims all gallantry and boasts of manliness he should emerge honorably when put to the test. All sorts of wood may look alike, and if color and beauty are sought few could compete with aloes. However, when fire is wanted aloes will be set aside and pine will be used for heating. Do not imagine that I'm like the donkey that the fox said had no heart or ears."

"How was that?" asked the turtle.

The Donkey without Ears or Heart

It is related that a lion got the mange and grew so weak that he couldn't move, and hunting was impossible. There was a fox in his service that ate scraps from his table. One day the fox said, "Is the king not going to treat this disease?"

"I am troubled by that very thought," said the lion. "If medicine were available I wouldn't hesitate, but they say the only remedy is the heart and ears of a donkey, and they are impossible to get."

"If the king so orders," said the fox, "it will be done without delay and miraculously produced. The king's fur has fallen out and his glory and splendor are somewhat diminished. He cannot go out of the forest lest his majesty suffer indignity. Nearby is a spring in which a washerman washes clothes every day. A donkey that carries the clothes spends all day grazing in the meadow. I'll trick it into coming. The king should vow to eat only the heart and ears and give the rest away." The king so vowed.

The fox went to the donkey and started talking to it. Then he asked, "Why do you look so lean, thin, and sickly?"

"This washerman makes me work nonstop," the donkey said, "and only occasionally does he tend to me. Of course he doesn't worry about fodder and has no thought that I need rest."

"Salvation is at hand," said the fox. "Why should you labor under such conditions?"

"Such is my reputation," said the donkey, "and no matter where I go I can't escape hard labor. I am not alone in this calamity, for all like me suffer the same fate."

"If you follow me I'll take you to a meadow where the ground sparkles like jewels and the air is as fragrant as musk," said the fox. "Previously I led a donkey there, and today he lives in comfort and safety."

When the donkey heard this, temptation got the better of him and he said, "I will do as you say. I know you are acting out of friendship, sympathy, and compassion."

The fox led the donkey to the lion. The lion attacked him and wounded him, but not seriously, and the donkey escaped.

The fox was somewhat astonished by the lion's weakness and said, "Without benefit or need it is not a good idea to hurt animals. Since it wasn't possible to get it, now what could be worse than my master's inability to take down a skinny donkey?"

The lion was offended by these words and thought, "If I ignore him I'll be accused of feeble-mindedness and irresolution. If I admit my lack of strength I'll be labeled a weakling." Finally he said, "Nothing kings do should be questioned by their subjects.

Not everyone can understand their reasoning. Do not question me. Instead, think up some ruse by which you can get the donkey back. Assure him of your friendship and loyalty, and you will enjoy favor and patronage over your peers."

The fox went back to the donkey, who asked, "Why did you take me there?"

"It's no use," said the fox. "Your period of pain and affliction is still not over. It is impossible to combat destiny and fate. Otherwise, you would not have taken fright and run away. If the lion stretched his paw out to you it was out of yearning, and desire for your friendship made him hasty. If you had stayed you would have seen much kindness and I would have been commended for leading you there." And he kept charming him with such words until he seduced him and took him back.

The donkey had never seen a lion before and thought he was a donkey. The lion treated him kindly and won him over, and then he leapt on him and killed him.

"I'm going to wash," he said to the fox. "Then I'll eat the heart and ears, which will cure this disease."

As soon as he was out of sight the fox ate the donkey's heart and ears. When the lion came back he asked, "Where are the heart and ears?"

"Long live the king," the fox replied. "If he had had a heart and ears, one of which is the seat of the mind and the other the organ of hearing, after having experienced the king's ferocity he would not have listened to or been deceived by my lies and would not have come to the edge of the grave on his own feet."

✳ ✳ ✳ ✳

"I have told this story that you may realize that I am not without heart and ears. There is no ruse you have not tried, but I have outsmarted you with my intelligence and cunning and endeavored until the dark path turned bright and difficulty became easy. Do you still think I'll come back? There is little use in entertaining futile notions."

"I confess what I have done and am sorry," said the turtle. "Now you harbor in your heart a grudge against me that not all the kindness in the world can make up for. The brand of malevolence, baseness, and regret will never be erased from my forehead, and there is no use in being sorry and repenting. I must accustom myself to being separated from you." With these words he turned and departed sadly.

This has been a story of one who gained friendship or wealth and then regretted foolishly letting it slip away. Beating one's head against a wall does no good. Those of intelligence and awareness should submit this chapter to their own wisdom and experience and realize that one should hold dear whatever one has acquired, be it friends, wealth, or anything else, and beware of losing or squandering it, for nothing that is lost can ever be regained by wishing, and remorse is to no avail.

Chapter Six

The Ascetic and the Weasel

The Raja said to the Brahman, "I have heard the story of a person who, having had something in his grasp, failed to keep it and suffered remorse. Now tell me a story of someone who was too hasty in his actions and was negligent in planning and foresight. What happened to him in the end?"

The Brahman said, "He who does not base his actions on foresight and clemency will suffer censure and regret in the end. The most praiseworthy quality God has given human beings is clemency because its benefits are widespread and can include all people. The Prophet said, 'You can never extend your wealth to all people, so extend to them your good qualities.' If a person exhibits all noble traits and good characteristics and outstrips all his peers in them, when harshness and hard-heartedness are added, they mask all virtues and hatred is engendered. 'If thou hadst been severe, and hard-hearted, they had surely separated themselves from about thee' [Kor. 3:159]. It is said of Abraham that he was full of pity and compassionate because a clement person is beloved and all hearts are inclined to him. Mu'awiya said, 'It is necessary for a Hashimite to be generous, for an Umayyad to be clement, for a Makhzumi to be arrogant, and for a Zubayri to be brave.' When these words reached Hasan he said, 'He wants Hashimites to be generous so they will be poor, he wants Makhzumis to be arrogant so that people will hate them and consider them enemies, he wants Zubayris to be proud of their bravery, hurl themselves into battle, and perform laborious feats so that they will be killed and people will be rid of them, and he wants the clan of Umayya, who are his kinfolk, to be spoken of for their clemency and harmlessness so that they will be loved by the people and people will be inclined to be friendly and faithful to them.'

"The quality of clemency cannot be acquired except by firm resolve and calmness of nature, as the Prophet has said, 'There is no clement person without gravity.' Haste is not a pleasing quality and does not accord with the conduct of people of wisdom. 'Haste is of the devil.' Appropriate here is the story of the ascetic who failed to have insight and stained his hands with innocent blood by killing an innocent weasel."

"How was that?" asked the Raja.

The Ascetic and the Weasel

It has been related that an ascetic married a chaste woman whose cheeks shone like the dawn and whose tresses mirrored the dark night, and he was very anxious to have a child. When some time passed and it did not happen, he lost hope. After he had despaired God had mercy on him and his wife got pregnant. The old man rejoiced and wanted to talk about it day and night. One day he said to his wife, "Very soon now you will have a son. I will give him a good name and will instruct him in the rites of my order and train him well. In a short time he will be fit for religious service and ready to receive heavenly grace. He will attain renown and have children in whom we will take delight."

"How do you know I will have a son?" the wife asked. "It is possible that I may not have a child at all, and if I do have one it may not be a boy. If the Creator does grant this blessing life may not be propitious. In all this there are many possibilities, and you are ignorantly building castles in the air. All your talk is just like the hermit who spilled honey and oil all over his face and hair."

"How was that?" asked the ascetic.

The Hermit Who Spilled the Honey and Oil

There was a hermit who lived near a merchant who sold honey and oil. Every day the merchant would send a bit of his commodities for the hermit's sustenance. He would consume some and put the rest in a pot he had hanging in a corner of his house. Gradually the pot was filled. One day he looked at it and thought, "If I can sell this honey and oil for ten dirhems I can buy five head of sheep. Every month another five will be born, and soon I will have flocks that will enrich me. I will be able to furnish a household and get a wife from a good family. Of course I will have a son. I will give him a good name and teach him well. When he is grown if he disobeys me I will chastise him with this staff."

The thought was so powerful that he waved his staff and accidentally hit the pot. It broke, and the honey and oil all poured down on his face.

* * * *

"I have told this story that you may know that to say something without certitude is reprehensible and brings regret in the end."

The ascetic was chastened by these words and ceased mentioning it. When the pregnancy was over, indeed a good-looking boy was born. They rejoiced and gave what they had vowed. When the wife's confinement was over she wanted to go to the bath, so she entrusted the child to the father and left. An hour passed, and the king's messenger came to summon the ascetic. Delay was impossible. There was a weasel in the house on which they relied, so he left the child with the weasel and departed. While he was gone a snake slithered over to the cradle to kill the child. The weasel killed the snake and saved the child.[1]

When the ascetic returned, the weasel ran to him covered in blood. The ascetic thought it was the blood of his son and fainted. When he came to he beat the weasel with his staff and crushed its head. Entering the house, he found his son safe and sound and saw the snake torn to pieces. Heartsick, he beat his head against the wall and tore at his breast, saying, "Would that this child had never been born and I had never grown to love it, for then this innocent blood would not have been shed! What calamity could be worse? I have killed my own pet for no reason and covered myself with regret. Was this the thanks to God for giving me a child in my old age? Anyone who is negligent in giving thanks and appreciating a good thing will have his name entered in the register of the sinful, and all mention of him will be erased from the record of the thankful."

He was lost in these thoughts when his wife returned from the bath and saw what had happened. She comforted him in his grief, and they discussed it for a while. Then she said to the ascetic, "Remember this, for anyone who is hasty in his actions and fails to exercise gravity and calmness should be forewarned by this story and learn from this experience."

1. Since mongooses are not commonly known in Arab and Persian lands a weasel is substituted in the Arabic (*ibn 'irs*) and the Persian (*rāsū*), but since weasels are not domestic animals and do not kill snakes, it should be kept in mind that in Indian versions the animal is a mongoose.

This has been a story of a person who rushed into something without foresight. An intelligent person should follow these examples and polish the mirror of his mind with the dictates of the wise. In all regards he should deliberate and think ahead and avoid haste and foolishness, for then fortune will smile upon him constantly and felicity will come his way.

Chapter Seven

The Cat and the Mouse

The Raja said, "I have heard the story of a person without forethought and contemplation who cast himself into a sea of confusion and remorse and fell into a snare of loss and regret. Now tell me a story of someone so beset by enemies left and right and fore and aft that he is on the brink of death and destruction, but then he sees a way out by being benign and kind and by making himself agreeable. He escapes to safety and keeps his word to the enemy. If such a thing is not possible how can peace be achieved?"

The Brahman said, "Usually friendship and enmity are not permanent and are caused by some turn of fate. They are like springtime clouds: sometimes they rain and sometimes the sun shines through them, and they have no great permanence. Women's agreeability, a ruler's intimacy, a madman's kindness, and an adolescent's beauty all have the same quality and should not be counted on for permanence. Many is the friendship that has flourished in all kindness and unity and lasted for a long time when suddenly the evil eye strikes and it is changed to enmity and grievance, and many an ancient enmity and hereditary hatred have disappeared with one kind act and turned into firm friendship and affection. An enlightened person of intelligence will put the Prophet's words into practice in both cases: 'Love your friend gently, for one day he may be your enemy. Hate your enemy gently, for one day he may be your friend.' Do not neglect to accommodate your enemy and do not give up hope of friendship with him; do not rely totally on every friend or have confidence in his fidelity, and do not ever think you are safe from the machinations of fate. A foresighted person will consider an enemy's request for a truce to be a golden opportunity since it may ward off harm and have benefits for all the reasons stated. Anyone who keeps all these things in mind and watches out for his own best interests will sooner gain his objective and have good fortune and felicity. A good example is the story of the cat and the mouse."

"How was that?" asked the Raja.

The Cat and the Mouse

It has been related that in a certain city there was a tree, and beneath the tree was a mouse's hole. Nearby was a cat's home. Hunters often frequented the area, and one day a hunter laid a trap and the cat got caught. The mouse came out of his hole in search of a morsel and looked around cautiously before proceeding. Suddenly his gaze fell upon the cat. Since the cat was caught he rejoiced, but just then he looked back and saw a weasel lying in ambush for him. Then he looked up at the tree and saw an owl ready to pounce on him. Frightened, he said to himself, "If I go back the weasel will jump on me. If I stay where I am the owl will swoop down. I can't go forward because the cat is in the way." Then he thought to himself, "With all these looming disasters I shouldn't lose heart. I have no refuge better than intelligence, and nothing will help me more than wisdom. He who is strong of mind does not allow himself to be alarmed in any situation or let fear and confusion into his mind, for tribulations suffered by the perspicacious do not rise to the level of clouding the intellect, and comfort is never so firmly established in their minds that they are overwhelmed by arrogance and neglect cunning. Inside they are like a sea the bottom of which cannot be reached and the depth of which cannot be known: anything thrown into it sinks and disappears without a trace. No plan would be more convenient for me than to make peace with the cat, for he is trapped in adversity and will not be able to get out without my help. He may listen to my words wisely, apply the discernment of the astute, realize that I am trustworthy, and know that he is not being deceived with trickery and guile and accept a truce with me in hopes of gaining my assistance. With honesty and cooperation we may both be saved."

Therefore he went to the cat and asked how he was.

"Trapped in misery and affliction," he said.

"'Had I not abandoned lying because it is a sin I would have abandoned it because it is a matter of honor.' Have you ever heard anything other than the truth from me? I have always rejoiced over your consternation and considered your failure to be tantamount to my own success. I have focused all my attention on anything that causes detriment to you, but today I am your partner in affliction and see that my own salvation depends on yours. For that reason

I am being kind. You will recognize that I am telling the truth and am contemplating no treachery. You can see the weasel stalking me and the owl up in the tree. Both are going to attack me, and they are both enemies of yours. If I get close to you they will turn their gazes from me. Now, if you assure me of my safety and swear to it, I will come to you. I will get what I want, and when I gnaw your bonds you will be free. Remember this and be assured of my conduct, for no one is more deprived of attaining happiness than two persons: the first is he who does not trust anyone or have confidence in the sayings of the wise, and the second is he whose word others refuse to believe and the wise do not trust. I will keep my word. Accept my offer of kindness and do not delay, for the intelligent do not recommend delay in action. Be glad that I am alive, for I am happy that you are since the salvation of each of us depends upon the life of the other, like a ship that reaches the shore through the efforts of its captain, and the captain is saved by means of the ship. My truthfulness will be proven by putting it to the test, and it is more obvious than the sun in the sky that if my promise falls short of action my deed will be preferable to my word."

When the cat heard the mouse's words and saw that they contained truth he was glad and said, "Your words seem true. I accept this truce according to the command of the Creator: 'If they incline unto peace, do thou also incline thereto' [Kor. 8:61]. I hope that we may both be saved thereby, and I promise to repay my debt and be grateful for the rest of my life."

"When I come to you you must welcome me warmly," said the mouse, "so that my attackers will see it and be aware of our friendship and give up. I will then break your bonds at leisure."

"I will do it," said the cat.

The mouse approached, and the cat greeted him warmly. The weasel and the owl gave up hope and left, and the mouse set about gnawing the bonds at his leisure.

The cat found him too slow and said, "You have tired quickly. I had greater expectations of your compliance. Having gotten what you wanted, have you changed your mind? Are you thinking of breaking your word? Know that a person's resolve and firmness are tested in affliction, for vicissitudes are the crucible of fidelity and the touchstone of men. This stalling does not conform to a noble character. You received the benefits of my friendship straightaway when the designs of your enemies were foiled. Now it would be more chivalrous to repay me and quickly break my bonds and free me from my fear, for this newly founded accord between us has ended our past contention. The benefits of fidelity and gratitude are known to you. The brand of treachery and deceit is a hateful mark, and a noble person will not sully his good reputation with such. If you want to play a crooked game, know that it will be known to all. Where nobility and gallantry are, nature abhors neglect of obligation. A good and gallant man steps into the field of sincerity on one show of affection, and if he sees in his mind any past fear or discord he quickly rids himself of it and considers it a good trade, especially when there has been a pledge affirmed by solemn oaths. It should be known that traitors are soon punished, and a false oath soon undermines the foundation of life, as the Prophet said, 'A false oath leaves homes empty.' Anyone who cannot be persuaded by humility and pleading to cease harm and does not engage in pardon and forgiveness is stripped of his good name and hangs his head before people."

"May anyone who breaks his oath of fidelity to you have his heart and back broken by the vicissitudes of fate," said the mouse. "Know that friends are of two sorts: the first is one who enters into friendship willingly and heartily, and the second is one who forms an association out of necessity. In neither of the two cases can one be unaware of the quest for benefits and the probability of detriment, but the one who enters a friendship with pure intention free of fear can be relied upon in all situations and one can live in safety from him at all times, while in the case of the one who takes shelter in an association out of necessity there are differing relations: sometimes the associates mingle happily and sometimes they avoid each other. A clever person should always be leery of some of the requests of such a person and grant them only gradually, and while doing so he should guard himself, for self-preservation is necessary in all cases to be known for virtue and good sense.

"All associations in the world are for immediate gain. I am doing what I said I would do while taking the utmost precaution for self-preservation, for my fear of you is even greater than my fear of those from whom I was saved by you, and the acceptance of a truce with you was to ward off their attacks. The favor you did me was for an exigent need and avoidance of imminent harm. How can one who neglects foresight be said to have a view toward consequences? I will break all your bonds, but I am watching for the right time. I will keep one bond as a guarantee of my life and will sever it when you have something more urgent to do than to attack me."

The mouse cut all the bonds but left one strong one. Thus they spent the night. The next morning, when the phoenix of dawn flew from the east and spread its bright wing over the earth, the hunter appeared from afar.

"Now it is time for me to discharge the remainder of my obligation," said the mouse. So saying, he gnawed away the last bond, and the cat was so in fear of his own death that he forgot about the mouse and bounded up a tree. The mouse scurried into his hole. The hunter, finding his trap cut, left in despair.

The next day the mouse came out of his hole and saw the cat from afar, but he did not want to get near him. The cat called out and said, "Why are you avoiding me? You have gained something precious and earned friendship for your offspring and descendants. Come closer and enjoy the reward for your compassion and manliness."

The mouse shrank back, but the cat said, "Do not deprive me of the sight of you, for anyone who rejects a hard-won friendship will be deprived of the fruits of amity and other friends will despair of him. I owe you my life, and you did what no one else could have done. I will never forget my obligation to you so long as I live, and I will not neglect to repay and reward you."

Of course it was to no avail. The mouse replied, "When a situation looks threatening, if based on past experience one can expect amity, if one is of good cheer and mingles no fault can be found, but when there is inner suspicion, even though the outward aspect is free of signs of vengeance, one should not neglect self-preservation, for the detriment can be great and the outcome disastrous. It is like sitting on an elephant's tusk and going to sleep: of course one will wind up under the elephant's feet and be destroyed with the least movement.

"People are inclined to friends for benefits, and they avoid enemies because of potential harm. If a wise person is in trouble and can only be saved by the efforts of an enemy, he will seem friendly and amicable, and if he sees opposition from a friend he will avoid him and exhibit enmity. The offspring of beasts run after their mothers for milk, and when they no longer need them they leave them without any past experiences of fear or doubt. No reasonable person would attribute that to enmity, but when the benefit ceases it is wiser to cease the association. So too does a wise man do things according to the season and put on a raincoat when it rains. He comes up with a plan for every situation according to the time and lives with his enemies and friends in dread or relaxation, anger or good humor, forwardness or deference as befits his interests, and in all cases he should be calm and even-tempered.

"At the base of our nature is enmity. It has grown over time and become entrenched in our beings. A friendship formed on the basis of need cannot be relied upon, for when the cause is removed each will revert to type, like water, which is warm as long as you keep fire under it. When you remove the fire the water reverts to its original cold state. There is no enemy more harmful to a mouse than a cat. Only exigent circumstances and need forced us into a truce. Now that the cause no longer exists the enmity will doubtlessly be renewed.

"There is no benefit for a weak rival in association with a strong one or for a weaker opponent to be near a stronger one. You have no yearning greater than to make a meal of me, but in no way am I going to be deceived by you. How could a mouse ever trust the friendship of a cat? It is much safer for the weak to avoid associating with the powerful, for otherwise something will happen and the weaker will be taken unawares and dealt grievous harm. Only rarely does one who is taken in and is negligent rise again.

"When a wise person takes matters into his own hands and there is no longer any exigence he should not delay in separating himself from an enemy. No matter how steadfast and dependable he may see himself, he should not imagine the enemy to be the same and ought to seek distance from him. Nothing is more appropriate to foresight and safety than that you should avoid the hunter and I should beware of you. When there is no longer kindness or understanding between friends can they still be loyal and have mutual understanding? It is impossible for us to meet, and it would be far from wise to do so."

The cat, upset and distressed, said, "My heart has often told me that one day you would be separated from me. I had suspected it would be so, but not that you would lay aside our friendship."

With these words they bade each other farewell and parted.

This has been the story of an enlightened wise person who did not pass up an opportunity to befriend an enemy in time of need, and after attaining his goal he did not fail in foresight and precaution. A weak little mouse, when surrounded by calamities and overwhelmed by enemies, did not lose heart and succeeded in snaring one of them with guile, by means of which the threat was done away with. He kept his promise to the enemy, and after achieving his end he was vigilant in self-preservation. If the wise, the perspicacious, and the clever take these experiences as models they too will enjoy success and attain happiness in this world and the next.

Chapter Eight

The King and the Bird Finza

The Raja said to the Brahman, "I have heard the story of a person who was surrounded by implacable enemies and overwhelming opponents and threatened on all sides. Like it or not he approached one of them and made a truce with him to escape the others. He kept his bargain with the foe, and after attaining his goal he wisely looked to self-preservation and with foresight remained safe from the enemy. Now tell me a story of implacable enemies who are best avoided. If one of them is placated should one rely on him?"

The Brahman replied, "Anyone who has a sound mind will recognize the necessity of maintaining the utmost precaution and weighing benefits against disadvantages, and he should have the discrimination to realize that it would be better to avoid a friend who asks for too much and poses a danger and to evade his deceit and treachery, especially when one can see his inner hostility and changeability, for he who is taken in by a smooth tongue and affected amiability and does not protect himself will make his own life the target of an arrow of calamity and attract the blade of catastrophe with the magnet of his own foolishness. Appropriate to this is the story of the bird."

"How was that?" asked the Raja.

The King and the Bird Finza

It has been related that there was a king named Ibn Madin, and he had a bird called Finza that had good sense and beautiful speech. The bird laid an egg in the king's palace and hatched a chick. The king had them taken to the harem and commanded that great care be taken of the bird and the chick. The king had a son on whose brow the light of good fortune shone. In short, the prince and the chick grew fond of one another and played together. Every day Finza would fly to a mountain and bring back two pieces of a fruit that had no name among men. She would give one to the prince and the other to her own child, and the children loved the sweetness of the fruit and ate it eagerly. The effects were immediately apparent in their growth and development, and in a short time they grew tall and strong. For this service Finza's intimacy with the king increased every day.

When some time had passed, one day when Finza was away, her child leapt upon the prince and hurt him. In a rage the prince, forgetting all his friendship with the chick, grabbed him by the legs, hurled him to the ground, and killed him. When Finza returned and found her child dead, she was filled with grief and dismay, and her lament rose to heaven. "Alas for anyone who is afflicted with the company of tyrants," she said, "for they soon forget their promises, and the cheek of their fidelity is easily scratched by the talon of cruelty. Sincerity and advice are of little importance to them, and service and honor have little weight. Affection and hostility depend upon the occurrence of need and the termination of benefit. Pardon is forbidden in their religion of vengeance, and in their code of pride and vainglory it is allowed to neglect rights. The fruits of loyal service are seldom remembered, and punishment for errors is never forgotten. Major infractions on their own part are considered minor and unimportant, and small slips on the part of others are deemed major and serious. I at least will not let an opportunity for redress go by without taking revenge for my child from this merciless traitor who has killed his friend and companion." With this she flew into the prince's face and pecked out his eyes, and then she flew off to the battlements.

When the king was informed he went into a rage over his son's eyes and wanted to get hold of the bird to subject it to torment. Then he went up on the ramparts and called out to Finza, saying, "You are safe. Come down."

Finza refused and said, "I am obliged to obey the king, and doubtless my separation from him will be long and endless. I have always had the good fortune to serve at his court, and if my life were any compensation I would give it willingly. I thought I would live safe in the king's shadow for the rest of my life, but now that my son has been slaughtered in his harem can I have any hope of that? The safest course of action for me is to refuse this command, and I hope that the king will be merciful enough to excuse me. It is certain that the king will not allow a criminal to live. If the sentence is stayed in the short run, in the long run it must be expected. The more time passes the greater the desire for revenge will grow, and even if destiny allows me to escape, in the end I will taste its bitterness and be dragged down. The king's son was treacherous to my child, and in grief over my offspring I replied in kind. I must not trust you or allow myself to be deceived by you."

"Actions have been taken on both sides," said the king. "Now I have no justifiable reason to hate you, and you will not be harmed by me. Believe me and do not needlessly sentence yourself to a painful separation. Know that I consider revenge to be reprehensible and would never engage in it."

"To come back to you will never be within the realm of possibility," said Finza, "for the wise have advised against associating with a friend with a grudge. They say that the more offended people seem compassionate and kind, the more their loathing and hatred increase and the more they should be avoided. The wise consider mothers and fathers as friends, brothers as companions, wives as helpmates, relatives as debtors, and daughters as opponents, but sons are wanted for the perpetuation of one's memory and as intimates with oneself on a level no one else can share. When anything untoward happens all others hide themselves and cannot be coaxed out for any reason."

The Old Woman and Her Daughter

An old woman in the village of Chekao had a daughter named Mahasti and two cows. The daughter, who was as beautiful as a stately cypress, was struck by the evil eye one day and fell ill. She withered away, and the world turned dark in the old woman's eyes. She grieved and lamented, for she had no other darling like her. By chance one of the old woman's cows, while looking for something to eat, put its snout in a pot and got stuck. The cow ran out of the kitchen toward the old woman like a demon out of hell. The old woman thought it was the angel of death and cried out, "O angel of death, I'm not Mahasti. I'm just a poor old woman. If you want Mahasti, go take her and leave me alone."

Before calamity struck she was her darling, but when the old woman was threatened she readily turned her over. You may therefore know that when push comes to shove no one is anything to anyone else.

✳ ✳ ✳ ✳

"Today I am free of all bonds. I have reaped so much grief in your service that my saddlebags are heavy-laden with it. What animal could bear them? I have lost not only my darling child but also my companionship with you. Moreover I have no security of my life, and it would be the height of foolishness to be taken in by smooth talk. I have no recourse save separation and forbearance."

"If you had initiated what happened avoidance would be advisable, but since you acted in retaliation and retribution, and it was justified, what prevents trust and causes aversion?" the king said.

"Anger causes pain in the mind, and aversion engenders agony in the heart," said Finza. "If words contrary to this are heard they should not be trusted, for the tongue will not be expressing the truth. Hearts, however, truly reflect one another's thoughts, and your heart is not in conformity with your tongue. I well know the force of your fury, and I can never be safe from your wrath."

"Rancor and spite often occur between friends," said the king, "for there is scant possibility that people can keep the doors of offense and antagonism closed. Anyone with intelligence and wisdom will try to keep them from flaring up and will avoid letting them be kindled."

"Old dogs cannot be taught new tricks," said Finza. "I have seen what the world has to offer and have watched fate play out its game. Many a precious thing have I lost to a roll of the world's dice, and I have amassed stores of experience and know truly that anyone on this earth who sees that he has a free hand will turn against anyone and trample virtue underfoot in retaliation for an injury. You needn't waste your time trying to fool me. What the king says is true, but it is forbidden in the code of wisdom to believe in the forgiveness of those who harbor hatred, for therein lies great danger, and the stakes are high. Unless you are a skilled player, the dice are not loaded, and your opponent is trustworthy, you should not play. It is impossible to imagine that an adversary will ignore the causes for his anger or fail to watch for an opportunity for retaliation, and many are the enemies over whom one cannot get the upper hand by mere force—only with cunning and deceit can one get them under one's power, like a wild elephant that is lured into a trap by a tame elephant. At no time and in no situation would I feel safe from the king's vengeance. A day in his service would be like a year, for my weakness and confusion would be obvious, and his might and power would overwhelm me."

"A generous person does not abandon a friend or sever friendship on a mere suspicion even in a case of mortal danger and fear for one's life," said the king. "This trait is found only in animals of the lowest order."

"Hatred and resentment are essentially dreadful, especially when they take root in the minds of kings," said Finza, "for kings are immovable in their code of vengeance. They do not allow excuses to get in the way of their wrath and animosity, and they will seize any opportunity for retribution. They take great pride in exacting retaliation for errors and mistakes by offenders. If anyone expects otherwise he will be embarrassed when he sees what fate has in store for him.

"So long as vengeance pent up in the breast has nothing to stir it up and remains like an ember without kindling, even if presently there is no trace of it, as soon as an excuse or cause is found it will rage forth like fire fallen on fuel. That fire can never be quenched by any amount of words, kindness, or pleading on the part of the offender or by any advice from the well-meaning, and so long as the accused is alive the wrath will not subside, just as fire will burn as long as there is kindling. Despite all this, if there is any possibility for an offender to curry favor and seek the pleasure of his friends and assist in acquiring the benefits and repelling the harms, it is possible both that the wrath may disappear and that the friendship of the offended party may be won and that the fearful heart of the offender may be soothed with safety and security.

"I am too weak and feeble to imagine anything like that or to think that my service could negate the cause for complaint or create amity. If I were to come back I would be constantly in fear and dread, and every day, nay every hour, I would envision a new death. There can be no benefit in my returning. I cannot pay blood money, and I will not sacrifice my head."

"No one is capable of benefiting or harming another without the will of the Creator," said the king, "and the amount of each is dependent upon destiny and the decree of fate. Just as the hands of created beings are incapable of creating and giving life, they are also unable to take it or end it. My son's initial action and your requital of him were decreed by fate and divine will, and you and he were merely secondary causes of the decree. Do not blame us for heavenly decrees. If our separation takes place it will cause distraction of my mind, and happiness and joy are only enjoyed when one's followers and retainers have a share in it."

"The inability of created beings to ward off the Creator's decrees is obvious," said Finza, "and it is certain that good and evil and benefit and harm are meted out according to the will of the Lord and cannot be hastened or delayed by any amount of effort. However, all are unanimously agreed that one should not neglect precaution and must protect oneself from harm. 'Hobble your horse and then trust in God.' There is a great distance between what you say and what you do. You have many opportunities to attack, and I am weak. I must avoid danger. You want to soothe the pain in your heart by killing me and to entrap me by guile, but my soul rejects death. No animal would willingly drink this potion, and as long as the reins of free will are in its hand it would see avoidance as the right way. It has been said that grief is an affliction, poverty is an affliction, nearness to enemies is an affliction, separation from friends is an affliction, incapacity is an affliction, fear is an affliction, and death is the chief of all afflictions. The Sufis call it the great disaster. One who has been repeatedly afflicted with its grief and tasted its bitterness can divine what is in the mind of an afflicted person. Today I can judge what is in the king's mind by what is in my own heart since I can see his pain and grief with my inner eye. I am certain that every time the king thinks of his son's eyes, and every time I think of my child, anger will rage internally, and it is impossible to know what will come of it. There can no longer be any comfort in our association. We had best be parted."

"What good can there be in a person who cannot disregard the mistakes of his friends, cannot rise above hatred and resentment so that no trace of an offense can ever be found on his heart, and does not cheerfully accept his friends' apologies?" said the king. "The

Prophet said, 'Behold, I will tell you of the worst of people: he who does not accept an apology and does not forgive an offense.' I at least see that my own heart is pure, and I find no trace of those things that have been mentioned in my mind. I have always been ready to forgive my followers and reward my servants."

"I know that I am guilty," said Finza, "and although I was not the initiator I was still an aggressor. If someone has a wound on the sole of his foot and insists on paying no attention to it and walking across rocks, the wound will reopen and his foot will be useless for walking on even soft ground. Anyone who has an inflammation in his eye and faces the north wind will be courting blindness. My association with you would be like that. My avoidance of you is prescribed by the law: 'Throw not yourselves with your own hands into perdition' [Kor. 2:195]. People can do no more than take care to protect themselves so that they can justify themselves, for anyone who does not rely on his own power and strength will fall into fear and dire straits as he rushes headlong into perdition, and anyone who does not know his own limits of food and drink and eats too much for his stomach to digest, or who takes a bite too big for his mouth and it gets stuck in his throat, must be reckoned as his own enemy. Anyone who is deceived by an opponent is considered wayward and foolish by the wise. No one can know to what he is fated and whether he can expect happiness from the world or live in expectation of misery, but it is necessary for all to base their actions on correct thoughts and to see the necessity of caution and wisdom, to hold tight onto the reins of passion, and to do good to friend and foe in order to enjoy good fortune. If anything good should come it will be due to that.

"Things in this world proceed according to heavenly decrees, and neither can they be increased or diminished nor can they be hastened or delayed. A person can be known to be absolutely intelligent who avoids doing injustice and harming living beings. So long as the path of caution is open to him he will not stand in a position of fear and trepidation. I have many routes of escape, and it would be a pity for me to remain and tarry in a place of confusion and hesitation, for the king's wrath wants my blood and considers licit that which is forbidden by religion and gallantry. I hope that wherever I may go I will live happily. He will enjoy life, will achieve his goals wherever he may go, will not be deprived of the companionship of friends, and will acclimate himself to the strangeness of exile who has five traits: avoidance of malefactors, avoidance of danger, adopting good character, making one's slogan harmlessness and beneficence, and having good manners at all times. When an intelligent man cannot be safe in his homeland and among his kith and kin, he must accept distance from his family, friends, children, and people, for they may all be compensated for.

"The most wasted money is that which is not profited from and not spent; the most useless of women is she who does not get along with her husband; the worst of children is one who refuses to obey his father and mother and is intent on being disowned; the vilest of friends is he who ignores friendship in times of need; the most negligent of kings is he of whom the innocent are afraid and who does not strive to maintain his realm and care for his subjects; the most decadent of towns is one in which there is little safety. However generous the king may be and however he may reassure me with solemn oaths, I have no security with him and cannot live safely in his service or near him since fate has separated us in a way that does not admit of our being joined again. In the future every time I have a yearning for him I will see his splendor in the faces of the sun and moon and ask the zephyr for good news of him. Of me in exile the king may assure himself that 'when the zephyr blows the breeze will carry my greetings and praise to you.'"

With these words their conversation ended, and the bird bade the king farewell.

This has been a tale of being wary of being deceived by an overwhelming enemy and avoidance of falling for the guile of an irresistible opponent. An intelligent person will understand that the purpose of relating these tales has been that the wise may follow them as examples when they experience vicissitudes.

Chapter Nine

The Lion and the Jackal

The Raja said, "I have heard the story of a wounded enemy who could not be placated despite all attempts. Now tell me a story of something that happened between kings and their intimates. After the infliction of cruelty and punishment and an accusation of crime and treason, can reconciliation be imagined and can the re-establishment of trust be relied upon?"

The Brahman replied, "If kings close the door to forgiveness and indulgence and cease to rely on anyone in whom they see the slightest mistake, affairs will not be tended to and they will be deprived of the pleasure of pardon. Ma'mun said, 'If criminals knew how much pleasure I derive from pardoning their crimes they would commit more.' Of all traits that may adorn a person none is more beautiful than forgiveness and none stands out more clearly than indulgence. The Prophet said, 'Behold, I shall inform you of the strongest of you: it is he who controls himself in anger.' The most praiseworthy characteristic of kings is self-control in the face of vicissitudes and never at any time to allow one's character to be devoid of kindness or to perpetrate violence without injustice. Things should be carried out with a mixture of fear and hope: neither should the loyal be made despondent nor should the disobedient be emboldened. An authority was asked to explain the meaning of the verse, 'Who bridle their anger, and forgive men; for God loveth the beneficent' [Kor. 3:134]. 'The outward meaning of the verse is self-evident in the law and needs no elaboration,' he replied, 'but the elders of the path have said that to swallow wrath means not to mete out excessive punishment, pardon means to erase all trace of abhorrence from the page of one's heart, and beneficence means to return to the basis of friendship and companionship, for in the code of generosity maintaining means is obligatory and in the law of gallantry the neglect of rights is forbidden.' It should be known that God has taught his servants good character and encouraged them to have praiseworthy customs. Anyone who is slated for happiness will obey the injunctions of the Koran. It is clear from the verse that things should be based on clemency and kindness, and in all cases leniency and benevolence are of importance. The Prophet said, 'If clemency were a person people would see no one more beautiful, and if harshness were a person people would see no one uglier.' When one reflects on the preceding and understands the virtues of forgiveness and benevolence, one should concentrate one's efforts on acquiring those characteristics and realize that one's best interests lie therein. It is no secret that human beings are rarely immune to error, negligence, and mistakes, and if severity is applied as retribution for them it will be to one's detriment.

"One must recognize the loyalty, counsel, virtue, and competence of a person against whom an accusation has been made. If one can assist him and ward off impugning his honesty, one will be making strides to renew one's reliance on him and realize that he should not be doubted. One should follow the dictum that says, 'Indulge the mistakes of those of good qualities,' for it is impossible to control a kingdom without ministers and assistants, and one benefits from one's servants when they possess wisdom, righteousness, virtue, and rectitude and their minds are adorned with good counsel and allegiance.

"There is no end to affairs of state, and kings need competent counselors who are worthy of being privy to secrets and can manage affairs. Those who possess righteousness, trustworthiness, piety, and honesty are few, and the correct way is to ascertain the good and bad qualities of one's followers and to be aware of what each can do and for what job he is suited. When a king informs himself with certainty and insight he must assign each to a post appropriate to that person's worthiness, bravery, intelligence, and competence. If in addition to a person's skills a flaw is found in him, it should not be overlooked, for no person can be free of faults. Great care must be taken in this regard, for if a person fails in a task to which he is assigned he should be removed to prevent affairs from falling into chaos since the reason for taking on competent people is to get things done, and if an otherwise competent person fails at his job, of course it is just as necessary to get rid of him as it is to get rid of the ignorant and incompetent. Competence should never be a cause for complication, and even though it is sometimes necessary to discharge persons of virtue and competence for the acquisition of a goal, in the end it is better not to regret the loss of persons of ignorance and error.

"After they have understood the preceding it becomes imperative for kings to examine their employees minutely and keep track of the affairs they have entrusted to their competence so that they will know if the loyal have performed satisfactorily and done good service and if the disloyal have slipped by and been negligent. They can then reward the loyal abundantly and chastise the disloyal according to their offenses. If either one is neglected the loyal will become lethargic and apathetic and the corrupt will become emboldened and presumptuous; complicated affairs will fall into disarray and be neglected, and it will be difficult to rectify them. Here the story of the lion and the jackal is apropos."

"How was that?" asked the Raja.

The Lion and the Jackal

It has been related that in the land of India there was a jackal who had turned away from the world. He lived among his peers, but he eschewed eating meat, shedding blood, and harming animals. His friends adopted an opposite stance, saying, "We are not pleased by these characteristics of yours, and we think you are mistaken in your opinions. Since we do not eschew each other's company we expect compliance in habits and customs, and no benefit can be seen in spending one's life in torment since one day life will end and you might as well take what pleasure you can from the world. 'Forget not your share of the world' [Kor. 28:77]. You must know that neither can you bring back yesterday nor can you count on tomorrow. What is the use of wasting today and neglecting enjoyment?"

"My friends and brothers," the jackal said, "enough of this nonsense. Since you know that yesterday is past and tomorrow may not come, provide yourselves today with something that can serve as provision for the road, for this deceptive world is flawed from one end to the other, and the only virtue it has is being a seedbed for the hereafter in which one can plant seeds that can be harvested in the next life. You should concentrate on performing good deeds and charitable acts. Do not rely on the agreeability of the treacherous world, but rather set your hearts on eternity and do not deprive yourselves of the fruits of health, life, and youth. The Prophet said, 'When you awake in the morning do not talk to yourself of last night, and when you go to bed do not talk to yourself of the morrow. Enjoy your health before you fall ill, your life before you die, and your youth before you grow old,' for the pleasures of the world are as impermanent and fleeting as a flash of lightning and the darkness of a cloud. To set one's heart on an abode of tribulation and annihilation is far from wise. An intelligent person seeks nothing of the world other than a good name and memory because happiness, comfort, success, and the good things of the world all pass away.

"If you want happiness in this world and the next listen to these words and do not destroy animals for the sake of a morsel for yourselves, the enjoyment of which ceases the moment it is down the throat, and be content with what you can get without inflicting harm, for enough to ensure the continuance of the body and soul is never lacking. The Prophet said, 'The holy spirit inspired into my heart that no soul dies until its allotted sustenance is fully used up. Therefore fear God and seek the good.' Hear this advice and do not ask me to conform to what is rejected by reason, for my companionship with you causes you no detriment, but conformity with your blameworthy actions would cause me torment. I am with you in companionship, but in my heart I flee from you."

His friends excused him, and as he sat all the firmer on the carpet of piety and rectitude his renown spread throughout the world and he attained a reputation for rectitude and honesty that no one could aspire to.

In the vicinity was a meadow of great beauty and fragrance, and in it were many beasts. The king of the beasts was a lion whom all obeyed and in the shelter of whose might and mastery they passed their days. When the lion heard of the jackal he summoned him and put him to the test. After several days the lion met privately with the jackal and said, "Our kingdom is extensive and involves many affairs. We are in need of advisors and helpers. We had been told that you had attained a high degree in asceticism and abstinence, but when we saw you it became clear that you were even greater than we had heard. Now we wish to assign you a position of trust that will elevate you to the elite of our intimates."

"Worthy kings are they who choose competent helpers to carry out their tasks," said the jackal. "It is also incumbent upon them not to impose a job on anyone, for when a task is imposed on a person by force he cannot discharge it satisfactorily. Long may the king live! I would detest working for a ruler and have no knowledge or experience in it. You are a magnificent monarch and have many beasts in your service who are both capable and competent and who also crave worldly tasks. If you would take one of them your mind would be free of care, and they would be happy with the rewards they would reap."

"What is the use of this rejection?" asked the king. "Of course you will not be exempted."

"Working for a ruler is for two persons: one is a headstrong deceiver who gets what he wants by deceit and craftiness; the other is a weak, negligible person who is used to suffering humiliation and in no way would be respected, obeyed, or honored but will only fall prey to envy and enmity, for, as you should know, intelligent people are always deprived and envied. I am neither of these: I am not dominated by greed and will not perpetrate treachery, and I do not have a lowly nature that would suffer humiliation. No one who serves a ruler with good advice, trustworthiness, continence, and honesty and guards himself against hypocrisy, ambition, suspicion, and treachery will last long. Friends will throw up shields of enmity and contention in his face, and enemies will make of his life a target for arrows of calamity. Friends will vie for his position out of envy, and enemies will contend with him to offer advice. When friends and enemies join forces and unite in their enmity, of course he will not be able to live in safety no matter how high he has risen. A traitor is at least safe from a king's enemies even if he is afraid of his friends."

"My intimates will have no opportunity to attack you when you are in favor with us," said the king. "Do not fret, for our good opinion will ward off completely the plots and calumnies of enemies. With one reprimand we will block the way for their intrigues, and we will grant you your heart's desire."

"If the king's intent is empowerment and beneficence," said the jackal, "it would be kinder, more merciful, and more equitable to let me wander safely in this countryside and be content with water and forage from the good things of the world and not have to worry about the enmity and envy of worldly people. It is certain that a short life in safety, comfort, and leisure is better than a long one in fear and dread."

"That is all true," said the lion, "but you must put all fear out of your mind, for you most certainly will be close to us."

"If this is how things are," said the jackal, "I must be given assurance that when friends conspire with underlings in hopes of gaining my position and overlords intrigue in fear of their own status, you will not be instigated by them against me and that you will be constant and take all precaution."

The lion made a solemn pact with him. Turning over his possessions and treasuries to him, he promoted him to the highest rank and station among his followers and consulted with only him in various affairs. Every day the lion's estimation of him grew greater.

The jackal's intimacy and station were hard for the lion's confidants to bear. They conspired with one another and spent their days plotting against him. They sent someone to steal a bit of meat the lion had set aside for a meal and hid it in the jackal's quarters. The next day when it was time for the lion's meal he asked for it.

"We can't find it," they said. The jackal was absent, but all his foes were there, and when they saw that the fires of the lion's hunger and wrath were both raging, they sprang their trap.

"We have no choice but to inform the king of what we know, although it will not be pleasing to some," one of them said. "I have been told that the jackal carried that meat off to his own quarters."

"Even though you may not believe it," another said, "it must be considered, for it is difficult to know people, and rightly has it been said, 'Do not praise a man until you have tested him; and do not vilify without experience.'"

"So it is," said another. "It is impossible to be aware of what is in people's minds, but if this meat is found in his quarters, of course the treachery that is being spoken of will be proven."

"One must not fall prey to delusion," said another. "A traitor never escapes, and treachery can in no way be kept hidden."

"One of his cohorts told me everything," said another, "but I hesitated to give it credence until I heard it from you. It is a good adage that says to be well informed before detaining your enemy."

"His cunning and deceit have never been hidden from me," said yet another. "There is no limit to his vileness and guile. I knew what he was up to all along. I knew this so-called ascetic would be unmasked as disreputable and would make a huge mistake and commit a major crime."

Another said, "If this pious ascetic, who considered taking on the king's affairs to be so burdensome, has committed such an act of treachery, it is truly amazing."

"If this accusation is true it is an act of ingratitude and lèse-majesté," said another. "No one would label it as mere disloyalty."

Another said, "You are all honest people and cannot be accused of lying. If the king orders us to search for the meat in his quarters, there will be proof and everyone's doubts will be confirmed."

"If caution is to be taken, no time should be wasted," said another, "for we are surrounded by his spies, and no place is free of them."

"What's the use of searching?" said another. "If his crime is revealed he will only use his guile and cunning to hoodwink the king."

In this manner they fanned the flames of the king's anger until hatred took root in his heart. Summoning the jackal, he asked him, "What did you do with the meat?"

"I turned it over to the kitchen to be served to the king at his mealtime," he said.

The chef was one of the conspirators, and he denied it and said he knew nothing about it. Then the lion sent a group of his trusted intimates to search for the meat in the jackal's quarters. Of course they found it and brought it to the king.

The wolf, who had not spoken until that time in order to appear unbiased and unwilling to rush to judgment without a thorough investigation, and seeming to be friendly to the jackal, stepped forward and said, "Now that this cad's crime is clear to the king, he should punish him, for if he ignores such a crime criminals will no longer fear being exposed."

The lion had the jackal arrested. Then one of those present said, "I am astonished that this traitor's actions could have been kept from the king's mind, which is so enlightened that the sun is no more than a dust mote by comparison. How could he have been unaware of the vileness and deceitfulness of his nature?"

"Even more amazing is the fact that he has let it go on so long," said another.

The lion sent a message to the jackal, saying, "If you have any excuse for this crime, say it." They brought back a strident reply that the jackal knew nothing about. This enraged the lion and so clouded his mind that he broke all his promises and gave the jackal's foes a free hand to kill him.

News of these events reached the lion's mother, and she knew her son had been hasty and lost self-control. To herself she thought, "Let me go as quickly as possible and save my son from the whisperings of the devil, for when the king is filled with wrath the devil has taken over, as the Prophet said, 'When a ruler is angry the devil is in control.'"

First she sent a message to those who had been ordered to kill the jackal and told them to stay his execution. Then she went to the lion and asked what the jackal's crime was. The lion told her.

"My son," she said, "Do not give yourself cause for confusion and regret, and do not deprive yourself of forgiveness and beneficence. 'Forgiveness only increases a man in stature, and humility only makes him more esteemed.' Kings, above all men, should reflect and be prudent. A woman's honor is tied to her husband, a son's dignity is tied to his father, a pupil's knowledge is due to his teacher, an army's strength depends upon a powerful leader, veneration for ascetics depends upon religion, the safety of subjects depends upon a king, and order in a kingdom is based upon righteousness, intelligence, steadfastness, and justice. Major components of judiciousness involve knowing one's followers, appointing each to his proper station and position, patronizing them according to their skill and competence, and realizing that they will accuse one another. If a king listens to their connivances against each other, whenever they want they will be able to accuse a loyal person and make a traitor seem honest, and they will misrepresent the king's good deeds to the people as evil. The envious will get persons of merit ousted, traitors will accuse honest men and drag the innocent into a maelstrom of destruction. Without doubt, as this continues, all will become involved, those present will refuse to accept tasks and those absent will resign their posts, and the king's orders will not be carried out.

"Without absolute certainty it is not proper for a king to allow himself to have a change of heart toward those he trusts. He should rather encompass everything within his clemency and knowledge and consider well his servants' past deeds and not allow disrespect for their positions. When a mistake has been unintentional he should not impugn their loyalty or punish them for it. He should not listen to the words of base, ignoble people when they bad-mouth competent persons of virtue. In all cases his own reason and opinion should be impartial referees with true discrimination.

"The jackal has advanced to a high position in your state. You have always spoken in praise of him and honored him by deliberating with him in private. Now you should stay your intention to kill him and protect yourself and him from the connivance and conspiracy of enemies by holding a judicious investigation, as befits your steadfastness and dignity, so that you will be justified to yourself and before all your military and civilian subjects, for what he is accused of is beneath anything such an honest and trustworthy servant would stoop to. You know that as long as he has been in your service, and before that too, he has never eaten meat. Do not be hasty before the truth is ascertained, for the eye and ear have often come to hasty conclusions based on surmises, just as in the darkness of night a person may see a firefly and think it is fire, but when he catches it he sees that he was mistaken and rushed to judgment before being certain. An ignorant person's envy of a learned one, a malefactor's of a benefactor, and a coward's of a brave man are all well known.

"Most probably his accusers put that meat in his quarters, and it would seem to be the least part of their plot. The jealousy the recalcitrant harbor is well known, especially when the stakes are high. Birds high in the air, fish at the bottom of the sea, and beasts in the field cannot be safe from attack. When a hawk hunts, it catches both birds that fly higher and those that are lower, and dogs fight with each other over a bone they find on the road. Your servants who occupy positions lower than the jackal's are envious: it would not be strange for them to contend for higher position. Reflect well and exact retribution as befits your greatness. If the accusation is determined to be true then it will be possible to have him killed."

The lion listened to his mother's words intently and weighed them in the balance of his mind. Then he called the jackal forth and said, "Based on past experience, we are more inclined to accept your defense than to believe the reports of your foes."

"I cannot be free of the accusation unless the king ascertains the truth by means of a ruse," said the jackal, "even though I am certain of my own innocence and honesty and am confident that the more you investigate the more my loyalty and counsel will outweigh that of your other retainers and servants."

Kalila & Dimna

"How should we proceed?" asked the lion.

"Summon those who have slandered me," he replied, "and question them meticulously how I happened to be singled out and others who are meat eaters were omitted from consideration, for the affair will not become clear without such a proceeding. I am hopeful that if the king orders this—and when they growl and grumble he will roar and tell them that if they tell the truth they will be pardoned—the veil of false suspicion will be lifted from the truth and my innocence will be proven."

"How can I bring myself to pardon someone who has admitted making an attack on me and my kingdom?" asked the lion.

"Long live the king," replied the jackal. "Any pardon given from a position of full power and dominion is virtue itself, and the king's objection cannot make the slightest difference in that, especially when the perpetrators repent and submit obediently. Of course then they will no longer have any cause for vengeance and will deserve to have their offenses overlooked. The wise have said that the search for a way out of evil action is a major entryway into doing good."

When the lion heard what he had to say and realized how true it was, he separated those who had conceived the plot from the others and made an investigation into the depths of the affair and promised them amnesty if they would not conceal the truth. Some of them confessed and admitted to the entire conspiracy. The others necessarily followed them, and the jackal's innocence was proven.

When the lion's mother realized that all doubt had been removed from the jackal's truthfulness she said to the lion, "This group has been given amnesty, and it is impossible to go back on that. You have gained valuable experience in this affair, and you can learn a lesson from it. Be suspicious of those who gain intimacy by bad-mouthing and defaming your counselors, and do not listen to intrigue unless you have proof that precludes all doubt. The drivel of the self-interested who find fault with your intimates and confidants should be given no weight no matter how insignificant it is, for eventually it will grow and reach a point at which it is impossible to counter. When fresh grass is collected, rope can be made from it that an elephant cannot break. One should seek the reason behind everything, major or minor, that is reported and decide whether to listen or not.

138

"You should beware of having eight sorts of people around. The first is he who is unappreciative of his benefactors. The second is he who gets angry for no reason. The third is he who is overly proud of a long life and thinks he is exempt from obligations. The fourth is he who indulges in deceit and chicanery and disregards their seriousness. The fifth is he who bases his labor on enmity and not on truth and honesty. The sixth is he who indulges his lusts and follows passion. The seventh is he who is suspicious of people for no reason and accuses the trustworthy without a clear reason. The eighth is he who is known for immodesty, jocularity, and shamelessness. There are also eight types who should be encouraged. The first is he who recognizes the necessity of gratitude. The second is he whose promise is not broken with altered circumstances. The third is he who venerates patrons and the generous. The fourth is he who abstains from treachery and abomination. The fifth is he who can control himself in anger. The sixth is he who can be generous when called upon. The seventh is he who maintains modesty and rectitude. The eighth is he who avoids associating with profligate and foulmouthed people."

When the lion realized how compassionate his mother had been in this affair he thanked her and apologized, saying, "Thanks to your good guidance a way that was dark has been illuminated and a difficult labor has been made easy. Proof has been had of the innocence of a knowledgeable and competent counselor, and an innocent person has been cleared of accusation."

The lion's trust of the jackal increased, and he was honored and patronized even more than before. He summoned the jackal and said, "This accusation should be considered as having increased my trust in and reliance on you, and affairs that were entrusted to you are back where they belong."

"It cannot be," said the jackal. "The king broke his promise and allowed the impossible allegations of enemies into his mind."

"You should not think of such things," said the lion, "for there was no shortcoming in your obedience or counsel or in our favor or patronage. Be strong of heart and perform your service."

"I escaped this time," the jackal said, "but the world cannot be cleared of the envious and detractors. As long as I enjoy the king's favor the envy of associates will be in place, and the mere fact that the king listened to the words of instigators makes the king look gullible. Every day they will come up with a new intrigue, and every hour they will try to create doubt in you. When a king lets the honeyed words of a conspiratorial schemer into his ear and pays attention to the chicanery of an informant, serving him will mean risking one's life and would best be avoided. There is a well-known adage that says, 'Leave one whose sack is slack.'

"I have one more thing to say if the king will allow it," said the jackal. "The most appropriate persons to listen to testimony and give redress are kings and rulers. If, in this case, the king had mercy on me and renewed his trust, it is due to his excellence, which can be called a blessing. However, because of the haste with which he rushed to judgment, I have become suspicious of his generosity and lost hope in regal favors, for he needlessly forgot his patronage of me and my service to him on the basis of an accusation that, even had it been proven, would have been of little importance. A master's heart should be as wide as the sea and his clemency should be as immovable as a mountain: neither should intrigue cause a ripple in the one nor should anger move the other."

"What you say is good," the lion said, "but it is harsh and severe."

"The king's heart is harsher and more severe in allowing falsehood than mine is in telling the truth. Since he so easily listened to calumny and slander he should not have any difficulty in listening to the truth. Do not attribute my words to boldness or disrespect, for they contain two obvious pieces of good advice. One is that the tyrannized can be placated by vindication and their minds wiped clean of vindictiveness, and what could be better than for me to express what is in my heart so that my presence and absence are alike for the king and nothing remains that would be a cause for enmity or grief? The other is that I wanted the referee of this case to be the king's enlightened mind and justice, and a verdict is better given after listening to the words of a plaintiff."

"Thus it is," said the lion. "We have been steadfast in your case and ordered you released from this whirlpool."

"If my release was due to the king's kindness, the haste in condemning me was also by his order," came the reply.

"Do you not think that saving you from the brink of disaster was a greater act of benevolence?"

"It is so," the jackal said. "I will never, no matter how long I live, be able to repay the king's kindness to me, and this pardon and mercy, after his having disowned and sentenced me, outweighs all favors. Prior to this I was loyal and obedient to the king and his counselor and would have sacrificed my life for his pleasure. I am not saying what I say to prove to the king that he made a mistake in my case or to find fault with him, but the envy the ignorant have for the virtuous and competent endures and cannot be ended. What's the use of all this? The poor things take friends, subject them to debasement, plot against them, scheme against their king, and endeavor to destroy the realm, relying on the blandishments of a world that is surrounded by false promises, and all they get is regret and remorse, for truth is always victorious and falsehood is always vanquished. God grants a praiseworthy end to people of rectitude and honesty: 'God willeth no other than to perfect his light, although the infidels be averse thereto' [Kor. 9:32]. Nonetheless, I fear that, God forbid, foes will find a way to intervene between me and the king; otherwise I was and still am your servant."

"Who could do such a thing?" asked the king.

"They say, 'In the heart of your servant fear has been created because of what you did to him, and now he bears a grudge for that injury.' It is right to be suspicious, and it is especially right that persons who have been cruelly punished, who have fallen from their positions, who have been discharged, or who have seen inferiors promoted over their heads should be suspicious of kings. Even if none of those things could ever be thought possible, a wise man should keep in mind that after such things trust on both sides may be more firmly established since if there is any animosity in the master's mind because of a shortcoming or act of neglect on the part of the servant, once his anger subsides and an appropriate reprimand is given, all trace of it passes away and nothing remains. He will recognize the schemes of detractors and no longer listen to intriguers' drivel, and the servant's loyalty and counsel, as well as his virtue and competence, will be more firmly established, for unless a servant is competent and loyal neither will he be the object of envy and enmity nor will his associates scheme against him. Rightly have they said, 'Have nothing and escape calamities.' If there is any fear or dread in the heart of a servant, once he has been chastised he is safe and has no further expectation of calamity. There are only three reasons for a servant to have a grudge: the status he enjoyed is diminished by his master's neglect, foes come out against him, and the goods he amassed are lost. When the master's pleasure has been obtained reliance on him is renewed, foes are crushed, and wealth is gained, for apart from life itself it is possible to compensate for everything, especially in the service of kings and nobles. When these things have been made up for how can a grudge remain? The value of these things first and last, once they come together, can be appreciated by persons who will be mentioned for the rectitude of their forebears and known for personal integrity.

"Despite all of this, I hope that the king will excuse me and not drag me back into a snare of calamity and that he will allow me to wander safely and comfortably in this wilderness."

"What you have said is eloquent and reasonable. Be strong of heart and take up your service again, for you are not one of those servants of whom any accusation could be made. If anything is reported of you it will not be listened to. We have come to know you and realize that you are patient in affliction and grateful for favor and consider both qualities to be dictates of wisdom and loyalty. To deviate from them you would think absolutely forbidden in the code of service, dignity, and gallantry, and you would eschew and regard as vain and futile anything contrary to gallantry, honesty, and trustworthiness. Do not let yourself fear or worry needlessly and have confidence in our favor, for our presumptions of your honesty and truthfulness have been confirmed and the expectations we had of your wisdom and perspicacity have been verified. Never again under any circumstances will the words of a foe be listened to, and any skulduggery they engage in will be attributed to manifest vilification."

In short, the lion persuaded the jackal to take up his duties again, and every day he honored him more and grew more confident of his rectitude and righteousness.

This has been a story of what happens between kings and their followers after an outburst of wrath. Anyone who is slated for heavenly assistance and felicity will focus his attention on understanding these pieces of advice and unraveling the riddles of the wise.

Chapter Ten

The Lioness and the Archer

The Raja said, "I have heard the story of the disagreement, treachery, cruelty, and punishment that transpire between kings and their servants and how they re-establish trust, for it is incumbent upon kings for the regulation of their realm and maintenance of their best interests to follow the dictum that says, 'Reversion to the truth is better than adherence to falsehood.' Now tell me a story of a person who, to preserve his life and in his own best interests, had to harm others and cause injury to animals."

The Brahman said, "Injury to living beings is only allowed by ignorant persons who cannot distinguish between good and evil and between benefit and disadvantage and who in their foolishness are blind to consequences and cannot see the end of things, for the knowledge of the wayward falls short of comprehending their own best interests and the veil of ignorance prevents them from enjoying happiness. How could an intelligent person allow for another like himself what he does not like for himself? The Prophet said, 'How is it that you see a splinter in your brother's eye and do not see a tree trunk in your own?'

"It should be known that every action has consequences that will redound upon the perpetrator, and one should not be fooled by any delay in them that may happen, for what will happen will happen though it may take some time. If anyone thinks he can gild his evil deeds or disguise himself fraudulently and dishonestly as a benefactor so that people will praise him and his fame will spread far and wide, he will never rid himself of the consequences of his reprehensible deeds and eventually he will taste the fruits of his own vileness. Then he may heed advice and adopt praiseworthy characteristics. It is like the story of the lioness and the archer."

"How was that?" asked the Raja.

The Lioness and the Archer

It is related that a lioness and her two cubs lived in a forest. One day while she was out of the forest in search of prey an archer came, killed her two cubs, and skinned them. When the lioness returned

143

and saw her children lying on the ground in that condition her cries rose up to heaven. When a jackal who was a neighbor of hers heard her outcry he went to her and asked, "What is the cause for your distress?"

The lioness told him what had happened and showed him her children.

"Know that every beginning has an end," he said, "and when the period of life is over and the time for death comes not a moment's respite can be imagined. 'When their term is expired, they shall not have respite for an hour, neither shall they be anticipated' [Kor. 7:34]. The foundation of this ephemeral world is laid upon the assumption that on the heels of every happiness one must expect grief, and on the heels of every grief one should anticipate some happiness. In all cases one should be content with one's fate, for in the face of vicissitudes one can but forbear. Cease your rage and be just. 'Whatever evil befalleth thee, it is from thyself' [Kor. 4:79]. There is a proverb that says, 'Your hands tied the neck of the water-skin and you blew it up.'[1] Much worse has been done to others than what the archer did to you, and they went into the same useless rage and fury before finally giving in to forbearance. 'Have the forbearance for the pain of others that they had for yours.' Have you not heard the saying 'As you requite so will you be requited'? He who sows a seed will doubtlessly reap it. Adopt clemency and nonviolence and do not frighten beings so that you may live safe."

"Continue," said the lioness, "and bring forth proofs of what you say."

"What is your age?" he asked.

"One hundred years," she said.

"During this period what has constituted your sustenance?"

"The flesh of animals," she said. "Beasts and humans I have hunted."

"Then did those animals on whose flesh you subsisted all those years not have mothers and fathers, and did their loved ones not grieve over being separated from them? If back then you had known

---

1. The Arabic proverb is applied to someone who is responsible for his own fate because he failed to secure the waterskin adequately and is drowning in a river crossing.

the results of your actions you would have abstained from shedding blood and never done it."

When the lioness heard these words she realized how true they were and was certain that her loss had resulted from her own hubris. She forswore inappropriate actions and eating meat and vowed to content herself with fruit. Rightly have they said that an ignorant person does what an intelligent one does in the face of calamity but only when it is too late.

When the jackal saw that the lioness was eating the fruit on which he lived he was pained and said to her, "You neglect your own sustenance and have taken to eating the food of others, which has nothing to do with you. Plants are not enough for you. The trees, the fruit, and the persons whose sustenance they are will soon die now that their food has been usurped by a fierce foe and unassailable opponent. Signs of your tyranny used to be seen in the deaths of living things; today the results of your abstinence are apparent in nonliving things. In no case can the people of the world escape your cruelty regardless of whether you are fierce and vicious or pious and righteous."

When the lioness heard this she stopped eating fruit and vowed to spend her days in acts of worship and thought to herself, "How long will I worry about air, earth, fire, and water? How long will I fret over winter, autumn, summer, and spring? The colors of camphor and musk of day and night have enfeebled you and dried your brains. Forget about this fool-seducing caravanserai and leave behind this man-eating station."

This has been the story of an intrepid evildoer who subjected the people of the world to torment without thinking of the consequences until she was afflicted with the same fate and only then saw the right way, for the lioness did not cease to shed blood until she saw her two cubs skinned on the ground. When she had this experience she turned away from this deceptive world and said, "Anyone who puts his hopes in you makes a mockery of himself, for only someone as disagreeable as you would take you as his darling. I will sever my heart from you, for one of your eyes weeps while the other laughs."

Wise are they who understand what this means and make these experiences models for their minds and natures and base their works in religion and the world on them: do not do unto others what you would not like for yourself and your children so that the beginnings and ends of your actions may be remembered for good and you may be free of the censure of evildoing in this world and the next.

Chapter Eleven

The Ascetic and His Guest

The Raja said to the Brahman, "I have heard the story of an intrepid evil-doer who was very harmful, but when she was struck by a disaster similar to what she inflicted she took refuge in repentance. Now tell me a story of a person who abandons his own calling and takes up another but, when he is unable to do it well, cannot go back to his own calling and is left perplexed and regretful."

The Brahman replied, "'For every job there are those to do it.' Anyone who turns away from his hereditary calling or acquired skill and tries to do a job for which he is not fit will doubtlessly fail and be unable to profit from it, but then it will not be possible for him to return to his first job. As they have said, 'A skill is not forgotten, but its fine points can be forgotten.' A person should remain in his own calling and not stretch his hand out in longing for every new limb or be tempted by the beauty of its blossoms and leaves since one cannot be certain of the sweetness of its fruit. The Prophet said, 'He who is granted a thing should stick to it.' Appropriate to this is the story of the ascetic."

"How was that?" asked the Raja.

The Ascetic and His Guest

It has been related that in the land of Kannauj there was a righteous man. He was observant of his faith and careful of his religious duties, focused his attention on the customs of the wise, spent his days doing charitable works, abstained from love of the world and illicit acquisition, and was free of any taint of sanctimoniousness, spite, and hypocrisy.

One day a traveler was welcomed warmly as a guest in the ascetic's dwelling. When he had settled in the ascetic asked, "Where are you coming from, and where are you going?"[1]

---

1. What follows relies mostly on Kashifi's version (pp. 478–84). Nasrullah's text at this point becomes so difficult to follow that massive corruption of the text has to be

The guest replied, "My story is a long one. If you would like to hear it, I will recount some of it in brief."

"Anyone with good sense can learn something from listening to any tale," said the ascetic, "and can make his way over a bridge of metaphor to the path of truth. Tell your tale without fear, and recount to me all the benefits and disadvantages you have found in your travels."

"Know, O ascetic of the age, that I am originally from the land of the Franks. I was a baker there, and the oven of my breast was constantly inflamed with the fire of greed, and with all my endeavor scarcely did I receive so much as a loaf of bread from the table of destiny. I was friends with a farmer, and we constantly trod the path of friendship and sincerity. In friendship and in order to assist me the farmer would send to my shop wheat I could use. I paid him for it over time, and it was easy for him to give me a lot of time to pay. One day he took me to one of his orchards and hosted me as gentlemen are wont to do. After we had partaken of food we began to converse and he asked me how much profit I made. I told him and said, 'My capital in the shop is twenty loads of wheat, and the profit I make on it is enough to feed my family, which is about ten or twelve.'

"'Goodness,' said the farmer, 'the profit from your labor is not enough to base anything on. I had imagined that you made great profit and had a large income, but I see I was mistaken.'

"'Sir,' said I, 'what is your work like, and what is your profit and capital?'

"'I have little capital but great profit,' he said. 'For the handful of seed I plant I get large crops, and we would never be satisfied with a return of ten times what we put into it.'

"I was astonished and said, 'How can this be?'

"'Do not be surprised,' said the farmer, 'for there is great profit in it. When a poppy seed, which is the smallest of all seeds, falls into good ground and grows it sends up around twenty stalks or more. On every stalk there is a poppy pod with more seeds than can be counted. From this you can see that the profit from our labor is beyond reckoning.'

---

suspected. Kashifi seems to have concurred, replacing it with what is translated here and adding a couple of short anecdotes.

"When I heard this a craving for the profit of farming took root in my head. I closed my shop and started getting together implements of agriculture. In my quarter there was a dervish known for his good character. When he realized that I was abandoning my trade and taking up a new calling he summoned me and chided me, saying, 'Master, be content with what you are given and do not seek more, for the label of greed is shameful and the greedy come to an ignominious end. Anyone who enjoys contentment is a king, and any who suffers the stigma of greed sinks to the level of demons and beasts.'

"'I do not derive so much profit from the labor in which I was engaged,' I said, 'and I have realized that the benefits of farming are many. I imagine I will profit from it and make an easy living.'"

The old ascetic said, "You have been making your living from a trade that enabled you to make a decent living. The work you now propose to engage in is laborious. You may not be able to do it. Not everything that emerges from the hidden recesses of wishing accords with desire. Do not be a fool and do not abandon your job, for he who abandons his trade and takes up work for which he is not suited suffers what happened to the crane."

"How was that?" the guest asked.

The Washerman and the Crane

It is related that a washerman worked on the bank of a river. Every day he would see a crane standing on the river's edge catching worms in the mud, and when it was content it would return to its nest. One day a sharp-taloned hawk appeared and caught a fat partridge. The hawk ate some of it, left the rest, and departed. The crane thought to itself, "This bird with such a small body hunts large animals while I, with such a huge body, content myself with miserable ones. This can only come from lack of ambition. It would be better for me henceforth not to bother with small things but rather to cast the lasso of my ambition to the crenellations of the celestial sphere." Therefore it stopped hunting worms and waited to hunt doves and partridges. When the washerman saw the crane's consternation and how it abandoned its labor he was amazed and watched. By chance a pigeon appeared in the sky. The crane flew up to catch it, but the pigeon headed down to the edge of the water and got away. The crane followed it down and landed on the riverbank, but its feet got stuck in the mud, and the harder it tried to fly off the more it sank into the mud and its feathers got covered in it. The washerman came, grabbed it, and started home. Along the way he met a friend who asked, "What is this?"

"This is a crane that wanted to do the job of a hawk and did itself in," he replied.

* * * *

"I have told this story that you may know that everyone should stick to his own job and not take up a trade for which he is not suited."

"When the old ascetic told this story, my ambitions became even greater, and not only did I not listen to his words, which had been spoken in sympathy, but I also remained fixed in my resolve. I gave up baking and used the little capital I had to outfit myself for agriculture. I planted some seed and waited for my crops. At this point I got into financial straits because what I had derived from the bakery shop had covered daily expenses, but now I would have to wait a year before I saw any profit. I told myself I had made a mistake by not listening to the words of elders. Now I was faced with daily expenditures and had no income from any source. I would have to borrow a sum, reopen my bakery, and go back to my old job. I therefore went to one of the merchants in town, borrowed some money, and reopened my shop, putting one of my employees in charge of it. I went back and forth, sometimes going out into the fields to see to the farming and sometimes coming to the market to see to the shop. After two or three months had passed that employee had embezzled everything, and there was nothing left of either my capital or my profit. All sorts of disasters struck my crops, and I got back not even a tenth of what I had spent.

"I went back to that neighbor and told him of my situation in detail and explained how I had taken up two jobs and lost on both of them. The old ascetic laughed and said, "How like is your condition to that of the man who sacrificed his beard to the wiles of women!"

"How was that?" I asked.

The Man Who Lost His Beard

It has been related that a man had two wives. One was old, and the other was young. The man's beard was salt-and-pepper. He loved both his wives very much, and he would spend a day and night in the house of each. It was his custom, when he came into either house, to lay his head in the wife's lap and sleep. One day he went to the old wife's house and, as usual, laid his head in her lap and went to sleep. The old woman looked at his salt-and-pepper beard and said to herself, "What could be better than for me to pluck out the few black hairs in this man's beard so that it will be totally white and not appeal to that young wife? When he sees no desire on her part he will understand that she has grown tired of him and the fire of his love for her will be quenched. He will stop loving her and be totally devoted to me." Therefore she plucked from his beard all the black hairs she could.

The next day he went to the young wife's house and as usual put his head in her lap and went to sleep. The young wife saw white hairs in his beard and thought to herself, "These white hairs should be plucked out so his beard will be completely black. When he sees himself with a black beard he will detest the old wife and want only me." Therefore she plucked out what she could of the white hairs. When this had gone on for a time one day he put his hand up to stroke his beard and realized that there was no hair left. He cried out, but it was to no avail.

❊ ❊ ❊ ❊

"Your situation is just like this. You spent some of your capital on the bakery shop and lost some on farming. Now you see neither bread baked in your oven nor crops harvested on your farm."

"When I heard this I realized that what the old ascetic was saying was true: I had gotten nothing from my labor but regret. All I had would not suffice to repay the loan, so I figured I should put into practice the saying 'Flight from what cannot be borne is a custom of the apostles.' That night I fled from the city and proceeded stage by stage in terror until I had traversed a vast distance. After a time I received news that my family had died and my creditors had taken all my possessions to satisfy the loan. Despairing of returning to my homeland, I kept going and have been consoling myself by meeting with sympathetic people until this moment, when the mirror of my heart has been polished by meeting you. Such is my tale."

The ascetic said, "Your words have the aroma of truth, and my heart testifies to the veracity of your story. If you have endured the torment of exile and the travail of travel for a few days, you have acquired good experiences and learned something of the manners and customs of others. Henceforth you will pass your time with ease of mind and freedom from worry. 'The evening of grief is ended, and the dawn of enjoyment has broken.'"

The guest was glad at the sight of the host, and the host, delighted to have an opportunity to talk with his guest, began to expound. Now the ascetic was one of the children of Israel,[2] and he spoke Hebrew well and conversed charmingly in it. The guest liked his manner of speech and wanted to learn that language. First he praised him and said, "I have never seen such eloquence or heard anything more expressive." Then he said, "I have every expectation that you will teach it to me, and it would befit your gallantry to grant my request since without any prior acquaintanceship you have honored me as your guest. Now that our affection and companionship are confirmed, if you would have compassion and grant my request I would be most grateful."

"I will obey and do as you request," said the ascetic. "If your desire is true and you are determined to do it, I will consider it a duty to teach it to you."

The guest tried hard for a long time, but in the end the ascetic said one day, "You have taken on a difficult labor and gone to a lot of trouble. No one who abandons his own language and opposes his forebears in their tongue, craft, or anything else is likely to succeed."

"To follow one's fathers and forefathers in ignorance and error is a result of mindlessness and foolishness," said the guest. "To acquire new skills and attainments is a sign of wisdom and perspicacity and proof of intelligence and discernment."

"I have instructed you," said the ascetic, "but I fear that the results of your efforts will be regret—just like the crow that wanted to learn to strut like the partridge."

"How was that?" asked the guest.

---

2. At this point we return to Nasrullah's text.

The Crow That Wanted to Walk Like a Partridge

It is related that a crow saw a partridge walking. The partridge's manner of strutting appealed to him, and he yearned for the harmoniousness of its movements and agility of its limbs since natures are attracted to beauty and seek it out. In short, the crow wanted to learn how to do it. It tried for a time and ran after the partridge, but it never learned how to do it, and in the meantime it forgot its own manner of walking and could never get it back.

"I have told this story that you may know that you are making vain efforts and wasting your time. You have abandoned the language of your ancestors but cannot learn the Hebrew tongue. It has been said that the most ignorant of men is he who takes on a labor for which his skill and lineage are unsuited."

❀ ❀ ❀ ❀ ❀ ❀

This chapter has to do with the prudence and caution of kings. Any ruler who is inclined to control his realm, see to the welfare of his subjects, patronize his friends, and eradicate his foes will see the necessity of protecting himself and not letting vile, unworthy persons think they are as good as the highborn or that they are equal to persons with whom they are unfit to be compared. The adoption of servants and maintenance of stations are of great importance in regal affairs and the code of policy, and only by maintaining honor can the distinction be made between a ruler and a farmer. If the distinctions among classes are done away with and the lowest people are equal to the middle classes, and the middle classes equivalent to the nobles, the grandeur of the king and the awe of rulership will be lost. The harm and disruption will be great, and the consequences grave. The histories of kings and nobles of the ages show the importance of keeping this door closed.

This has been a story of somebody who abandoned his trade and took up a job for which he was unsuited by heredity and disposition. It takes a wise man to read these chapters for understanding, not for amusement, so that he may benefit from them and in order that his character may be free of flaw and blemish.

Chapter Twelve

The Superiority of Clemency

The Raja said, "I have heard the story of a person who turned away from the calling of his fathers and forefathers and vainly conceived a notion at which he would not succeed and was then unable to return to his former calling. Now tell me which quality is most praiseworthy in rulers and the most suited for the interests of the kingdom, the stability of the state, and the winning of hearts. Is it clemency, generosity, or bravery?"

The Brahman replied, "The best quality for kings, in order that they themselves may be held in awe and respect, that both the military and civilian populations be content and grateful, and that both the kingdom and state remain stable and long-lasting, is clemency. God has said: 'If thou hadst been severe, and hard-hearted, they had surely separated themselves from about thee' [Kor. 3:159], and the Prophet has said, 'Good character is a sign of a person's good fortune.' The benefits of generosity are necessarily limited to a few, and bravery is needed only occasionally in a lifetime. Clemency, however, is needed by young and old alike, and its benefits extend to elite and commoner and to military and civilian. One of Mu'awiya's sayings is the following: 'If there were a hair between the people and me, no amount of tension would break it. If they let go I would pull on it, and if they pulled on it, I would let go.' That is, his clemency was of such a degree that he was able to live and get along with everybody in the world, and even in a time when many of the Prophet's companions were still alive, he was able to gain control of the community and reign over the face of the earth.

"Anyone who aspires to this must pay attention to these words, for the most beautiful ornaments for kings are judiciousness and clemency. Since the commands of kings affect the lives, marriages, land, and property of the people and their orders are carried out absolutely, if a ruler does not possess the qualities of clemency and judiciousness, with one harsh word a world can be destroyed, people can be harmed and alienated, and many lives and much property can be lost.

"At the base of clemency lie consultation with the wise, sound judgment, and experience, consorting with wise and loyal persons and intelligent and compassionate ones, and avoiding reckless traitors and harmful ignoramuses, for nothing influences people like their companions. The Prophet said, 'A pious companion is like a perfume maker: even if he doesn't give you any of his perfume, some of the aroma sticks to you. An evil companion is like a stoker: even if he doesn't burn you with his fire, some of his stench sticks to you.'

"With generosity a king can enrich the world, and with bravery he can win ten battles, but if he is devoid of clemency, with one outburst everything can be destroyed and everyone can be alienated. Even if he is deficient in the first two, with clemency he can keep the whole world grateful and crush his enemies by having sound judgment. Clemency without judiciousness is not free of defect either, for though many expenses may be borne and much care may be taken, if the end result is imprudence all will be lost and pointless. The Prophet said, 'A clement man is not given to cursing.'

"When a king who is surrounded by all the paraphernalia of rule does not follow his passion when forgiveness and clemency are called for and does not obey the devil when punishment and wrath are needed, and when his commands and prohibitions are based on reflection and deliberation, his kingdom is safe from attack by enemies and foes, but if there is any negligence in following this conduct, all enjoyment that might have been obtained by the favorability of fate and that would have assisted in keeping things under control and maintaining order in the kingdom can be lost with the slightest curse or harsh word, and its consequences can be disastrous and lead to regret.

"The foremost of all felicities is leadership, but its continuance is tied to the king's wisdom and perspicacity and his minister's loyalty and good counsel, for when a king is clement and knowledgeable and has a wise and intelligent advisor known for his righteousness and competence and who is also experienced and compassionate, he will be victorious and triumphant in all affairs, and no matter in which direction he turns success and good fortune will follow him and he will subdue his enemies. Even if he gives an order on a whim or fails to maintain prudence, with his ministers' and advisors' counsel and their clemency and kindness it can be rectified, as was the case in the hostility between the king of India and his people."

"How was that?" asked the Raja.

156

The King and the Brahmans

It is related that in the land of India there was a king named Habla. One night he had the same terrifying dream seven times and woke up at the end of each. When he awakened the last time he was terrified and spent the rest of the night moaning and writhing as though he had been stung by a scorpion. When the veil of darkness was lifted by the dawn and the king of the stars appeared in the east he arose, summoned the Brahmans, and told them all he had seen. Listening carefully and seeing traces of fear and dread on his face, they said, "It is a terrible dream, and no more frightening dream has ever been heard of. If the king permits, we will withdraw for a while, consult our books, and reflect with the utmost of scrutiny, and then we will report our interpretation with all certainty and insight and come up with a plan for warding it off."

"So be it," said the king.

They left him and sat together in private, saying to one another, "Recently he has killed twelve thousand of us. Now we are in possession of his secret, and that gives us the means to exact our revenge. He has made us his confidants, and if there were another dream interpreter in all the realm he would never have relied on us, for traces of his enmity and aversion to us are still obvious in him. Haste must be made before the opportunity slips away. Here's what we should do. We will speak to him as forthrightly and severely as possible and so frighten him that he will do whatever we suggest. We will tell him that the only way he can be absolved of the blood on his hands is to put to the sword a group of his intimates in our presence. If he asks for a list of names we will say his two sons,[1] their mother Irandukht, his secretary Kak, the white elephant he rides, the other two elephants he is so attached to, and the Bactrian camel

---

1. The text is corrupt here. It becomes clear later on that there are two boys, and that is what Kashifi (p. 496ff.) has as well. In the Old Syriac version the boys are the king's son and a brother's son (Bickell, Syriac text p. 96, German trans. p. 94), and Ibn al-Muqaffaʻ (p. 179) has "your wife Īrākht, her son Joyar [read Jōbar], and your sister's son." In Nasrullah's version this becomes "the boy Jōbar [variously "two boys"], the boy's mother Īrāndukht," et al. In the later Syriac version (Keith-Falconer, p. 221), they are "Īlār, the queen and mother of Gobar your son, who is dearer to you than all your [other] wives, and Gobar your son, whom you love more than all your [other] sons," et al.

that can traverse a clime in a night. All these he must put to the sword, and the sword must be broken and buried beneath the earth with them. Their blood must be put in a large jar, and the king must sit in it for a while. When he comes out four of us will come to him from all four sides and recite incantations and blow on him. We will rub blood on his left shoulder and then cleanse his body, wash him, anoint him, and take him safely into the throne room. If he complies with all this and leaves us alone, the evil portent of this dream will be warded off. If he does not do it, he must expect great disaster along with the end of his kingdom and life. If he does as we say we will have our revenge, and when he is alone, weak, and unprotected, we will put an end to him."

They agreed on this plot and returned to the king, who sent everyone away and listened to what they had to say. He was much taken aback and said, "Death would be better than this plan you suggest. If I kill those beings, who are as precious to me as my own life, what benefit or comfort would I derive from living? Under no circumstances will I remain in the world forever, of course the end of every human being is death, and endless kingship is unimaginable. You will have to come up with a better plan, for between my own death and that of my loved ones there is no difference, especially when so many benefit from their existence."

"Long live the king," the Brahmans said. " 'Your brother is he who tells you the truth.' The truth is bitter, and advice untainted by hypocrisy and treachery is harsh. How could the king equate others with himself and sacrifice his life and kingdom for them? It is necessary to listen to the advice of the compassionate and give it weight. The dictum is well known: 'Obey the commands of those things that make you weep, not the commands of those things that make you laugh.' The king should consider himself and the kingdom recompense for all things that may be lost, and he should undertake without hesitation that in which there is great hope of salvation. People attain independence only after much pain, and kingdom is won with endless effort. To abandon both of these is far from sound judgment and lofty ambition, and it will result in regret when it is too late. As long as the person of the king remains, women and children can be had, and as long as the kingdom remains stable, servants and the paraphernalia of luxury are possible."

When the king heard these words and saw how forthright they were in their speech, he was pained. Leaving them, he went to his quarters, put his head on the ground, wept bitterly, and flailed about like a fish out of water. To himself he said, "If I sacrifice my loved ones I will be deprived of the benefits of kingship and the comfort of life. It is clear that I will live only a certain time, for the end of every human is death and kingdom will not last forever. Of what use is kingship to me without my son who is the apple of my eye? Since he will fall into the hands of foes, what difference can it make whether it happens sooner or later? And then there is the son in whom all signs of good fortune can be seen and who would be certain to follow his noble forebears in acquiring honor and ruling.

"Irandukht possesses a beautiful countenance, shining cheeks, and tresses like the night, she is unfailing in her kindness and charming to be with, and she is harmonious in her movements, refined in her character, and soft in her body. How can I enjoy life without her? My minister Bilar is the most competent and cleverest of men, his mind can fathom the secrets of treacherous time, and his second sight can delve into the mysteries of the turning celestial sphere. Without him how can the realm be managed, how can affairs be carried out, and how can income and expenses be balanced and the treasury maintained? The designer of the heavens learned his craft from my secretary Kak, from him the scribe of the sky, Mercury, learned to write, every one of his words is a priceless pearl, with one of his rescripts a hundred thousand soldiers are mustered, and with a stroke of his pen a hundred thousand spears are lifted. Without him how can the needs of the far-flung ends of the kingdom be known, and how can one learn of the situation of enemies and the intentions of foes? If these two competent and knowledgeable counselors, who are like my hands and eyes, are done away with and I am deprived of the benefit of their advice and counsel, how can affairs be carried out, and how can things be managed? The white elephant's body shines like a full moon and is as adorned and grave as the celestial sphere, and his howdah is like a charming palace and an impregnable fortress. Without him how can I go out to face enemies? The other two elephants are like thunderclouds and as swift as the wind, their trunks are like dragons suspended from the top of a mountain and crocodiles suspended in the sea, in attack they carry off men like whirlpools, in battle they crush opponents like roaring torrents. Without them how can I defeat my foes in battle? Without my Bactrian camel, which leaves the wind in the dust, how can I be informed, how can I send messages? Without my glittering sword, how can I perform in battle?

"If I am deprived of all these things and kill my loved ones and helpers, what pleasure can I have in living? Separation from dear ones is a bitter potion, and managing affairs without a friend and servant is a vain effort and impossible task."

In short, the king's distress became known. His minister Bilar thought to himself, "Were I to initiate an inquiry into the reason it would be inappropriate for a servant, and were I to ignore it I would be disloyal." Therefore he went to Irandukht and said, "He has fallen into such a state, and from the day I entered his service he has kept nothing from me and never deliberated on major or minor affairs without consulting me. He has summoned the Brahmans once or twice and conversed with them. Now he has shut himself up and is lost in thought and wretched. You are the queen of the age, the refuge of the army and the subjects, and second only to the king's mercy and kindness are your concern and compassion. I fear those charlatans may be encouraging him to do something that will result in regret. You should go find out what has happened and inform me so that I can think up a remedy."

Irandukht said, "There have been harsh words between the king and me."

"It is known that when the king is lost in thought his servants cannot interrupt him," he said. "It isn't just you. Many times I have heard the king say, 'When Irandukht is with me, even though I may be sad, I am glad.' Go, do this as a great favor for all his servants and retinue and for the people."

Irandukht went to the king, bowed, and said, "What is the cause for your concern? Tell your servants what the accursed Brahmans have said to you so they can console you. One of the requisites of service is partnership in all things, good and bad, welcome and unwelcome."

"You shouldn't ask about something that would pain you if you knew," said the king.

"May the king not be distressed," said Irandukht. "If, God forbid, there is any cause for concern, it must be confronted with patience and forbearance, for you know that anxiety only increases pain, as is said, 'Where a patient person has one affliction an anxious one has two.' There is nothing in the realm of possibility over which one should grieve. Any affliction or worry that befalls can be dealt with. A successful monarch is he who, when something happens, knows how to deal with it wisely. Escape from such events is possible only with intelligence, forbearance, wisdom, and dignity."

"If what the Brahmans have told me were to be told to a mountain," the king said, "it would crumble and turn black. Do not persist in asking, for you would be pained if you heard it. Those accursed ones have said that you and your son, all my faithful servants, the white elephant, the other elephants, and the Bactrian camel must all be killed to avert the evil of a dream I have had."

Irandukht was very clever, and when she heard this she said without a flinch, "'Make it easy for yourself and have no compunction.' The king should not be worried over this. The lives of his servants are willingly sacrificed to his interests. As long as the king's person remains women and children can be had, and so long as the kingdom lasts there will be no lack of servants and luxury. However, once the evil of this dream has been averted and the king's mind is at ease, he must never again rely on that group, especially when it involves killing any living being, for the shedding of blood is a weighty thing and to engage in it without reflection has disastrous consequences. Regret and remorse are to no avail since the past cannot be recalled and the dead cannot be brought back to life.

"The king must remember that the Brahmans do not love him. Just because they are erudite it does not mean that they can be trusted or should be consulted for advice. He who is vile by nature cannot be made beautiful by any ornament, and knowledge and wealth do not give him fidelity or nobility. If you endeavor to train him it is like putting a jeweled collar on a dog or plating a date pit in gold. The Prophet said, 'Giving knowledge to the unworthy is like hanging jewels and pearls on swine.' The aim of these scoundrels is not to let their opportunity slip away to assuage the rancor lurking in their hearts from the king's punishment. First they want to destroy the son who is like the king himself—and may it never be that one has to be content with a substitute! Then they want to eliminate a son with so much nobility, promise, wisdom, and perspicacity and then compassionate servants to whose competence the permanence of the kingdom is tied. Next they want to snatch away the paraphernalia of rule like elephants, the camel, and the sword. I have no importance, and there are many like me in your service, but when the king remains alone and they have gained domination over the kingdom and its people they will do whatever they want. Up to now they have kept themselves in the background because they were weak. Seeing the king's might and his servants' allegiance, they did not dare to come forward. Had they seen the slightest defect in either or detected any dissatisfaction in the minds of the king's servants, they would have split the kingdom up long ago, for nothing stimulates a foe's boldness like aversion in confidential servants and dissension in the ranks of the military and civilian population. The histories of those who came before us are eloquent on this subject and filled with examples.

"In short, if there is any relief in what they say, by all means do not delay. Carry it out at once. If, however, there is any room for delay, one precaution remains that can be taken."

The king said, "Speak. What you have to say will be listened to and heard, and no doubt or uncertainty will be allowed to cloud it."

"The wise Kar-Idun is here," she said. "Although his origin is near that of the Brahmans, he is more honest and truthful than they are and is more worldly-wise. His view of consequences is more penetrating, and he possesses both erudition and clemency. And what could be better than these two? The Prophet said, 'Nothing was ever combined with anything better than clemency with knowledge.' If the king grants him intimacy and discloses the Brahmans' interpretation of the dream to him he will inform him of the truth. If his interpretation accords with theirs, then all doubt will be eliminated and their recommendation should be carried out. If he indicates something to the contrary the king will know how to discriminate between the truth and falsehood and between good advice and treachery. Nothing stays or impedes the king's command, and when he gives an order not even the celestial sphere can countermand it."

These words were agreeable to the king, and he ordered a horse saddled and went in secret to the wise Kar-Idun. When he met him he showed him great veneration, and the wise man bowed respectfully to the king and said, "What has compelled the king to come? If an order had been given I would have come to court. What could be more appropriate than for servants to appear before the king? Are these signs of distress that are perceived in the royal countenance?"

"One day I went to rest, and while I was asleep I heard seven terrifying sounds, after each of which I awoke in terror. After that, when I went to sleep, I had the same terrifying dream seven times, awaking after each. Every time I went back to sleep I had another dream. I summoned the Brahmans and told them. They gave a dreadful interpretation, and that is the cause of the distress you see."

The wise man asked about the details of the dream. When he had heard all he said, "The king made a mistake. He should not have told them that secret. The king knows well that those accursed ones were not worthy to hear it, for they have neither guiding intellect nor religion to cling to. On account of this dream the king should rejoice and give alms, for it is filled with signs of felicity and portents of good fortune. I will tell him the interpretation now and hold up a brazen shield against their plots. Surely there are loyal supporters and servants in allegiance to repel the treachery of foes before they can attack.

"The interpretation of the dreams is this: The two red fish you saw standing on their tails mean that an emissary will come to the king from King Humayun. He will bring two elephants laden with four hundred rotls of rubies, and they will stand before the king. The two ducks that arose from behind the king and landed in front of him are two horses that will be brought as gifts from the king of Balanjar. The snake that slithered across the king's foot indicates that the king of Hamjin is sending a sword. The blood the king smeared over himself means a suit of gem-studded purple cloth is being sent to the royal wardrobe from the land of Kasrun. The white camel on which the king was seated means a white elephant that the king of Kaydiun's emissary is bringing. The thing that glowed on the king's head like fire is a crown the king of Jad is sending. The bird that pecked at the king's head is an ill omen even though its effect will not cause much harm except that a person dear to the king will turn away from him. This is the interpretation of the king's dreams. That he saw them seven times means that emissaries will bring gifts seven times and the king will be glad and happy of their presence, the receipt of the gifts, the permanence of his state, and the length of his life. Do not let the Brahmans deprive the world of his justice and clemency or remove the ornament of his kingdom and state from this age. In the future the king should not make unworthy persons privy to his secrets, and he should not consult on any affair with a wise person until he has tested him. He should realize the necessity of absolutely avoiding associating with base and vile people."

When the king heard this he was glad, thanked the wise man, rewarded him amply, and departed happy. He waited for the arrival of the emissaries for seven days, and on the seventh day they brought gifts just as the wise man had said they would. The king rejoiced and said, "It was a mistake to tell them my dream. If it were not for heavenly mercy and Irandukht's compassion the directions of those accursed ones would have resulted in my death and the deaths of all my loved ones and followers. Anyone upon whom fortune smiles should hold dear the advice of loyal people and take care of those who are compassionate, and he should never initiate action before reflecting or neglect judiciousness and caution."

Then he turned to the minister, the secretary, his sons, and Irandukht and said, "It is not good that these gifts should be taken to our treasury. It would be more appropriate for them to be distributed among you, for you were all in great danger. Irandukht should be especially singled out, for she made great efforts in dealing with this affair."

"Servants exist to make shields of themselves during troubles," said Bilar, "and they consider it a benefit of their lives and fruit of their good fortune. If fortune smiles on a person and he follows these rules of conduct, he cannot expect praise or reward. The queen, however, has played a large role in this affair. The crown and the robe should go to her. They are in no way suitable for the others."

"Both should be taken to the harem," the king said as he arose.

At once Irandukht and the other women of her rank presented themselves. The king said, "Both of these things should be placed before Irandukht for her to choose one of them." The crown seemed better to her, but she cast a glance at Bilar to confirm that what she had chosen was approved of by him. He motioned to the robe, but just then the king turned his attention to them. When Irandukht realized that the king had noticed their communication she picked up the crown so the king would not be aware that there had been any collaboration between her and Bilar, and he too quickly averted his gaze so the king would not realize that he had motioned with his eyes. He lived for another forty years, and every time he went before the king he similarly averted his gaze so the king's suspicion would not be aroused. Were it not for the minister's intelligence and the wife's cleverness neither one would have escaped alive.

It was the king's custom to spend one night with Irandukht and the next night with another wife. One night when it was Irandukht's turn he went there as usual. She came before him with the crown on her head and stood holding a golden platter filled with rice. The king was partaking of it, conversing with her, and admiring her beauty when one of her fellow wives passed by wearing the purple robe. The king saw her and took his hand from the food in astonishment. Inflamed by lust and desire, he praised her greatly. Then he said to Irandukht, "You did not do right to choose the crown." When she saw how taken the king was with her fellow wife she flew into a fit of jealousy and dumped the platter of rice over the king's head, and thus the interpretation the wise man had given came true.

The king had Bilar summoned and said to him, "Look at the mockery this ignorant woman has made of the king. Take her away and have her beheaded so that she and others may not think that when they are so bold we will pardon them."

As Bilar led her away he thought to himself, "There is no necessity for haste in this action, for this is a peerless woman and the king will miss her, and thanks to her so many escaped the brink of death. I am not certain the king will soon forget. Some time will be necessary for him to calm down. If he repents she will still be alive and I will receive praise. If he persists in his tyranny it will be possible to kill her then. By delaying I will receive three benefits. First, the credit for saving a living being. Second, the king will be glad she is still alive. Third, the subjects of the realm will be grateful to me for saving a queen from whose benevolence all benefit."

Therefore he took her to a house with a group of intimates who served in the king's palace and ordered them to take care of her. Then he smeared a sword with blood and went back before the king looking sorrowful and sad. "I have carried out the king's command," he said. As soon as the king heard these words—his wrath having subsided—he thought of Bilar's wisdom, intelligence, and rectitude and was pained, ashamed that he had been hasty and acted with such importunity. He had also been confident that Bilar would delay the execution and would not do anything that could not be undone.

When the minister saw traces of remorse on the king's countenance, he said, "The king should not be sad. The past cannot be brought back, and what is done is done. Sorrow and regret are debilitating to the body and diminish right thought. Sorrow results in nothing but pain for one's friends and joy for one's enemies, and anyone who hears about this will doubt the king's resolve and steadfastness and will say that he gives such an order impulsively and when it is carried out he shows signs of regret. This is especially true of something that cannot be rectified. If you allow it I will tell you a story appropriate to this situation."

"Tell me," said the king.

The Pair of Doves That Stored Up Grain

It is related that a pair of doves gathered grain to fill their nest. The male said, "It is summer, and there is much grain in the field. Let us keep this grain for the winter, and when we find nothing more in the fields we can live on it." The female agreed, and they parted ways.

When they put the grain away it had been damp and filled the nest. When summer came and the heat affected it the grain dried out and the nest looked less full. The male was away. When he returned and saw less grain he said, "This was supposed to be for the winter. Why have you eaten it?" No matter how much the female insisted she had not eaten it, it was to no avail. He beat her until she died.

During the winter, when the rains were constant, the grain got damp and returned to what it had been. Then the male realized what the cause for the decrease had been. He wailed and moaned and said, "The worst part is that remorse has no benefit!"

* * * *

"A wise and intelligent person should not be hasty to end a life lest, like the dove, he suffer remorse. The benefit of having perspicacity is that one sees consequences and is not heedless of what is right at the time and for the future. If one has all the means of greatness at his disposal and does not use them at the proper time he will be deprived of their benefits. A successful monarch is one who reflects on the end results and consequences of his actions and who inflicts little harm, does good, and listens to the words of his counselors.

"It is certain that the king has good judgment and a penetrating mind and does not need to hear these ravings, and any command he gives can only be informed by fortune and felicity. It is also certain that the king considers the advice he receives from his counselors as excessively long-winded. All this has been stressed so that the king will not allow worry over one woman to cloud his mind to the extent that he deprives himself of the enjoyment of the twelve thousand women who serve in the palace."

When the king heard this he really worried about the death of his wife and said, "You acted on a word we spoke in anger and put an end to an incomparable being. You did not reflect and deliberate as would have been proper for a counselor, and words have been spoken that have made me exceedingly regretful of Irandukht's death."

"Two persons should always worry," said the minister. "One is he who is impetuous in doing evil, and the other is he who fails to do good when he can. They both derive little enjoyment of the good things of this world and have much regret in the next."

"I would be better away from you," said the king.

"One should distance oneself from two persons," said the minister. "One is he who thinks good and evil are much alike and who denies torment in the next life, and the other is he who does not restrain his eyes from looking at forbidden things, who does not close his ears to profanity and gossip, who does not keep his loins from impropriety or his heart from greedy, envious, and harmful thoughts."

"You are a man with ready answers, Bilar," said the king.

"Three persons are like that," the minister replied. "A king who shares his treasures with his army and his subjects, a woman who is ready for her husband, and a learned man whose deeds are crowned with success."

"Your condolences pain me, Bilar," said the king.

"Such pain is befitting for two persons," replied the minister, "a rider of a beautiful horse who bears bad news and the husband of a beautiful young wife who does not honor or respect him and from whom he constantly hears rebuke."

"You killed the queen unjustly with wasted effort," the king said.

"The effort of three persons is wasted," said the minister, "somebody who puts on white clothing and makes glass, a washerman who aspires to fine clothing and spends all day standing in water, and a merchant who chooses a beautiful young wife and spends his life traveling."

"You deserve to be severely tortured," said the king.

"Two persons should be subjected to that," said the minister. "One is he who punishes an innocent person, and the other is someone who persists in questioning people and refuses to listen when they apologize."

"You deserve the label of foolishness, and the garment of shamelessness fits you well," said the king.

"Three persons deserve those labels: a carpenter who stores wood chips up in his house until there is no room in the house, a barber who is not skilled in his job and nicks people and is thus deprived of his wages, and a rich man who resides abroad and whose property falls into the hands of enemies and does not go to his wife and children."

"I wish I could see Irandukht," the king said.

"Three persons wish for something and do not get it," said the minister, "a worker of corruption who expects to be rewarded by the virtuous, a miser who has expectations of praise by the generous, and an ignorant person who cannot rise above his lust, anger, greed, and envy and wishes he were equal to the good."

"I have given myself this grief," the king said.

"Three persons give themselves trouble," the minister said, "he who does not protect himself during battle and suffers a serious wound, a greedy merchant without an heir who amasses wealth by usury and illicit means and who is attacked by an envious person and winds up in calamity, and an old man who marries a strumpet by whom he is berated every day until he prefers death, and in the end he dies in that state."

"We must seem much demeaned in your eyes that you speak thus," said the king.

"A master is demeaned in the eyes of three people," said the minister. "First is an outspoken servant who does not know the etiquette of conversation with masters and is with them at all times, and the master is fond of levity and profanity and the master has no inkling of demeanor befitting his station and the appropriateness of rebuke. Second is a treacherous servant who takes over his master's possessions so that in a short time he has more than, and imagines himself superior to, his master. Third is a servant who undeservedly gains a position of trust in his master's household and learns secrets."

"I find you to be a wastrel spendthrift and an empty-headed profligate, Bilar," the king said.

"Three persons can be accused of this," said the minister. "One is he who invites a foolish ignoramus onto the right way and encourages him to seek knowledge. When the ignoramus is thus emboldened much nonsense will be heard from him, and regret will be to no avail. Next is he who lets a fool gain a position of dominance over himself through improper intimacy and betrays his confidences to him. Every moment lies will be heard from him, evil deeds will be ascribed to him, and regret will not help. Finally there is he who tells his secrets to a person not known for self-control."

"I take this to be a sign of your shamelessness," said the king.

"Ignorance and levity are apparent in three persons," said the minister. "One is he who entrusts his property to a stranger and lets an unknown person judge between him and an adversary. Second is he who claims bravery, patience, wealth, the intimacy of friends, and the ability to control his actions and then can offer no proof of any of them on a day of battle, in a time of adversity, among the wealthy, when facing the wrath of enemies, or when he has an opportunity to dominate. Third is he who says, 'I am free of carnal desires and enjoy only spiritual pleasures,' and then falls prey to every whim and indulges in wrath and lust."

"Do you want to teach us how to be a king and display your false competence to people?" asked the king.

"There are three persons who think they have mastery but are still sunk in ignorance," said the minister. "One is a novice musician who, try as he may, cannot get his instrument in tune with his fellows and can neither distinguish treble from bass nor tell the difference between a crescendo and a diminuendo. Another is an inexperienced painter who claims to be able to depict but doesn't know how to mix paints. The third is a lightweight jokester who boasts of something but when put to the test has to ask his underlings for help."

"You, Bilar, had no right to kill Irandukht," said the king.

"Three persons have no right to what they do," said the minister. "One is someone who boasts unjustly and cannot have his words and deeds put to the test. Another is an indolent person incapable of anger. The third is a king who informs any- and everybody of what he intends to do—especially when great affairs are involved."

"We are afraid of you, Bilar," the king said.

"There are four things whose fear is baseless," said the minister. "One is a little bird that sits on a slender branch and, fearing that the sky may fall, flies up into the air to escape. Another is a crane that fears to put its two legs on the ground because of the heaviness of its body. The third is an earthworm that eats dirt and fears there may not be any more. Last is the bat that does not come out during the day in fear that people will be attracted to its beauty and imprison it in a cage like birds."

"I must bid farewell to all pleasure in life with the death of Irandukht," said the king.

"Two people are perpetually deprived of happiness," said the minister. "One is an intelligent man afflicted with the company of the ignorant. The other is a grouch who can find no escape from his own ill humor."

"You do not distinguish between reward and punishment or between good and evil," said the king.

"There are four persons who do not do these things," said the minister. "One is someone who is afflicted with a terrible chronic disease and thinks of nothing else. Next is a dishonest, faithless servant who succeeds in confronting his master. Third is a person who does battle with a brave enemy without having his mind set on ending the affair. Fourth is a tyrant who falls into the hands of a tyrant mightier than himself, for he can only expect great catastrophe."

"You have spoiled all good things," the king said.

"This is a characteristic of four persons," said the minister. "One is he who considers cruelty and temerity as virtues. Another is he who is pleased with his own opinion. Next is he who consorts with thieves. Fourth is he who is quick to anger and slow to pleasure."

"One should not have confidence in you, Bilar," the king said.

"The wise have no confidence in four persons," said the minister. "A riled snake, a hungry beast, a merciless king, and a dishonest referee."

"Consorting with you is forbidden to us," said the king.

"Four things do not consort with each other," said the minister, "piety and corruption, good and evil, light and darkness, and day and night."

"Our trust in you is ended," the king said.

"Four persons should not be trusted," said the minister. "A rash thief, a disobedient servant, a wounded slanderer, and a feeble-minded ignorant."

"My pain is endless because the sight of Irandukht used to be the remedy for my other cares, and I see no remedy for the pain of separation from her," said the king.

"Five types of women should be grieved over," said the minister. "One is she who has a noble character and great beauty and is renowned for her chastity. Another is she who is knowledgeable, forbearing, sincere, and devoted. The third is she who offers good advice and respects her husband in his presence and in his absence. The fourth is she who is agreeable and submissive in good times and bad. The fifth is she from whose companionship much benefit is derived."

"If anyone were to bring Irandukht back to us, we would give him more wealth than he could desire," said the king.

"Material gain is dearer than life to four persons," said the minister, "he who is hired to fight, he who tunnels under massive walls for the sake of little gain, he who engages in commerce on the sea, and he who works in a mine."

"You have made a wound in our heart that cannot be remedied," said the king.

"Enmity between four types is like this," said the minister, "wolf and ox, cat and mouse, hawk and partridge, and owl and crow."

"With this one act you have negated a lifetime of service," said the king.

"Seven persons have this defect," said the minister. "One is he who negates his beneficence and virtue by placing obligations on and annoying others. Another is a king who patronizes the indolent and liars. Third is an ill-tempered person whose irascibility outweighs his charity. Fourth is a doting mother who indulges a disobedient child. Fifth is a generous man who thinks a promise-breaking schemer can be trusted with his property. Sixth is he who takes pride in bad-mouthing his friends. Seventh is one who does not consider veneration for holy men necessary and cannot distinguish between their external appearances and their inner selves."

"You have deprived me of Irandukht's beauty by killing her," said the king.

"Five things negate all good qualities," said the minister. "Ire disgraces a man's clemency and makes his knowledge look like ignorance. Grief clouds the mind and emaciates the body. Perpetual battle on the field exposes one to annihilation. Hunger and thirst reduce living beings to naught."

"After this we will have nothing to do with you, Bilar," said the king.

"The wise should not be acquainted with six persons," said the minister. "One is he who consults with someone who is devoid of knowledge. Another is an impatient person who is frustrated by worthwhile acts. Next is a liar who is pleased by his own opinion. Fourth is a greedy person who prefers property to his life. Fifth is a weak person who goes on a long journey. Sixth is a conceited person whose conduct is not liked by his teacher and master."

"You, Bilar, were better untested," said the king.

"There are ten persons who can be tested," said the minister, "a brave man in battle, a farmer at harvest time, a master in distress, a merchant in settling accounts, a friend in need, a relative during calamity, an ascetic in the acquisition of reward, a poverty-stricken person in penury determined to be pious, and a person who claims to have the self-control to forswear property and women."

When he reached this point and saw signs of anger in the king's countenance, Bilar fell silent and said to himself, "Now it is time to make the king glad by the sight of Irandukht, for his yearning for her is at its maximum, and he has turned a blind eye to all the nonsense I have been telling him." Then he said, "Long live the king! I know of no one like him on the face of the earth, there is no sign of his likes in the histories that have come down to us, and there will not be anyone like him until the end of the life of the world. With my feeble power and lowly status I have dared to speak and gone beyond my bounds. Of course the king was not moved to ire. His person is so adorned with clemency and calm and ornamented with patience and solemnity, and his clemency and knowledge are limitless. His forgiveness encompasses all his servants, and his benevolence includes all people. He does little harm and his clemency encompasses all. If any catastrophe comes from the turning of the celestial sphere or any vicissitude strikes to sully the good things given by heaven no one sees the king sorrowful, and his person is devoid of the marks of rage and disquietude. In all difficulties he maintains control of himself nobly and knows that it is imperative to be content with one's lot. Although he possesses total dominance and all the paraphernalia of power and magnificence, he regally turns a blind eye to the faults of his loyal servants, and if those in a position of privilege are somewhat conceited and insubordinate and either implicitly or openly do something that looks confrontational, they are reprimanded as required by majesty, and thereby the elite and common folk alike, as well as military and civilian, are cowed into obedience. When they witness his might and bow their heads in submission, so much generosity and favor is shown them that it will be recorded in histories of the world.

"Despite such power and might, the king has listened to my immoderate words. How can a servant express his gratitude for this? A sharp sword is present and I am at your mercy. What prevents punishment other than the king's clemency and generosity? I confess my fault, and if punishment is ordered I deserve it, for I have committed an offense and delayed the execution of the king's order out of fear of being reprimanded. Now I tell you that the queen is alive."

When the king heard this he rejoiced and beamed. Then he said, "What prevented me from punishing you in anger was my knowledge of your loyalty and counsel, and I knew that you would delay carrying out the order and that upon consideration you would conclude that Irandukht's offense, great as it was, did not deserve such punishment. There will be no retribution for your deliberations, Bilar, since you wanted to be certain of our resolve before you carried it out. With such prudence your wisdom and sound judgment have been tested even more, and our reliance on your good service and obedience has increased. Your service has found a position as pleasing as possible, and we will award you the fruit of it as much as possible. Rightly has it been said, 'Burden an old camel or leave it.'[2] Now go and deliver our sincerest apology to Irandukht and say, 'Without your countenance the sky is without a moon; without your stature the meadow is without a cypress.' Be quick that you may return all the sooner so that our joy, which has been renewed by news of her life, may be complete and that we may give an order for a happy meeting to take place."

Bilar said, "That would be right, and there should be no delay in carrying out the order." Then he went out to Irandukht and gave her the good news of her salvation and the order for her to present herself. Immediately she prepared herself to go to the king, and the two of them went to him together.

Irandukht kissed the ground and said, "How can I express my gratitude to the king for this pardon? If Bilar had not had all confidence in the complete clemency, generosity, and mercy of the king he would never have hesitated."

"You have done us a great favor," the king said to Bilar. "I always had complete confidence in your advice, but today it has increased. Be strong of heart, for you have a free hand over our realm. Your command will be obeyed by all who obey us, and there will be no objection made to whatever you think correct in managing affairs."

"May the king's fortune always increase," said Bilar. "It is incumbent upon servants to obey, and if they succeed in that they have no

2. The Arab proverb means to ask a person of age and experience or else leave the affair alone.

174

right to expect praise. In addition to the fact the king's past favors to his servants are obvious, if one spent a thousand years in seeking his pleasure and contentment, it would not suffice for a thousandth of the gratitude demanded. It is only asked that the king not be hasty henceforth lest the results bring regret and remorse."

"We accept this counsel," said the king, "and in the future we will give no order without reflection, consultation, planning, and augury." And he gave Irandukht and Bilar great rewards. They both bowed and gave their opinion that the Brahmans who had interpreted the dream as they had should be killed. The king ordered them tortured, and some were hanged. The wise Kar-Idun was summoned and given great gifts. An order was given that he should be shown the Brahmans as they were.

"This is how traitors and betrayers should be requited," he said.

When he left, the king said to Bilar, "You should leave and give us rest so that we may go into our private quarters, for it is not right that there should be 'a beauty in the world and we be deprived; a draft in the goblet and we be sober.'"

This has been a story of the excellence of clemency and its superiority over all other regal characteristics. It is well known to the wise that these examples should serve as lessons to readers. Anyone singled out for eternal favor will be guided by the experiences of the ancients and the wise and will lay the foundation of present and future deeds on wisdom and sound judgment.

Chapter Thirteen

The Goldsmith and the Traveler

The Raja said, "I have heard a story of clemency and how it is superior to other characteristics of kings. Now tell me a story of how kings choose their servants and what should be sought in them that it may be known who is best for patronage and who is the most grateful."

The Brahman replied, "The most important criterion is knowing where and how to employ servants, for a king must put his intimates to various tests to determine the level of wisdom, loyalty, and ability to counsel that each one has. Modesty, chastity, piety, and rectitude are most reliable, for the basis of service to kings is righteousness, and the mainstay of righteousness is fear of the Lord and piety, and no one has any more powerful characteristic, as the Prophet has said, 'You are all human beings and equal. The only superiority any of you has over another is in piety.'

"The quality of piety gains beauty when one's forebears are known for honesty and chastity and renowned for self-control and abstinence. When one's father has such noble characteristics, when the relationship to the father is ensured by the mother's virtue, and when personal worth and good traits adorn these qualities, worthiness for good fortune and preference is clear. If there be doubt of any of these things, of course that person should not be admitted to intimacy or share in state secrets, for much harm will ensue and become obvious in the long run. He will be detrimental, and no benefit can be imagined.

"Only when much caution is taken can a servant's truthfulness and his avoidance of falsification and misrepresentation be proven and his honesty and truthfulness in word and deed be verified—the brand of liar being serious and best avoided by a king's intimates. If somebody combines all these good points but his gratitude and fidelity are not well known and his loyalty is not proven with regard to others, the trust of prudent kings is not warranted, for a lowly villain does not appreciate reward or favor and sways however the wind blows. A wise, virtuous, and competent person would rather lose his life than to be branded with this hideous label. It is better for kings' attention to be focused on their servants' good qualities rather than on their external adornment and wealth, for what would adorn a king's servant is intelligence, perspicacity, knowledge, and competence. 'Those to whom knowledge is given, superior degrees' [Kor. 58:11]. Superficialities have no weight in the view of persons of insight.

"In some natures there is an inclination to single out those close to the throne for honor and promotion, to seek out members of ancient families, and to prefer nobles and grandees. This having been said, intelligent people know that a man's 'family' is his wisdom and knowledge and his 'nobility' is his honesty and self-denial. Noble and elect is he whom the monarch of the age selects and ennobles. One of the kings of Persia said, 'We are time: he whom we elevate is exalted, and he whom we demote is debased.' It is the enduring custom of time to crush the noble and nurture the base, and no one with any intelligence would gainsay it. Any time a base person rises to prominence one must expect catastrophe for a noble person. Kings are prone to employ their own protégés and to rely on those who have profited from the kings' good fortune, and that is not devoid of benefit, for when a servant thinks about his own unworthiness he will be grateful for his preferment because he cannot imagine that he himself was a cause for his being patronized. However, this happens only when hereditary traits and acquired virtues are combined and learning and honesty result. Without these things a person cannot be called a good servant, and he will not be grateful.

"When someone has all these good qualities, passes the test described above, and has been proven in all respects, he may be patronized and gradually admitted to the various degrees of intimacy until he becomes known and respected, and not promoted to the top at once, for that would only give detractors a reason to scheme against him.

"It is well known that if a physician prescribes medication after one glance, the patient will expire after the first dose and there will be no need for a second. An expert physician is one who asks about his patient's state, the length of the illness, and its symptoms, takes the patient's pulse, and seeks the cause. Only after informing himself of all aspects of the illness does he begin to treat it, and he keeps track of daily improvement or lack thereof until finally recovery and health are attained.

"In sum, it is incumbent upon a king to know his servants and to assess the level of competence of each lest he rely on someone injudiciously and live to regret it. Apropos is the story of the goldsmith."

"How was that?" asked the Raja.

The Goldsmith and the Traveler

It is related that a group of hunters dug a pit in the wilderness to catch beasts. A tiger, a monkey, and a snake fell into it. After them a goldsmith also got trapped in it, but the beasts were too injured to harm him. Days passed, and finally one day a traveler passed by, saw them, and thought to himself, "I should save this man from adversity and be rewarded for it in the afterlife." He let down a rope, and the monkey clung to it. The next time the snake got to it first. The third time the tiger got out.

When those three were out they said to him, "You did each of us a kindness, but this is not the time for reward."

"My homeland is in the mountains near the city of Burakhur," said the monkey.

"There is a forest in that vicinity," the tiger said, "and I live there."

"I have a home in the city walls," said the snake. "If you should ever go there we will repay your kindness. Now we have a piece of advice: Do not take that man out for men cannot be trusted and will repay good with evil. Do not be fooled by their external beauty, for their interior hideousness is much greater—and especially that of this man, who has been with us for days. We know his character. He is not to be trusted, and if you do, one day you will be sorry."

The traveler did not believe them and refused to take their advice. He let down his rope and got the goldsmith out of the pit. The goldsmith thanked him and charged him to come see him sometime so that he might repay him.

With these words they bade each other farewell, and each went on his way. Sometime later the traveler happened to be in that city. The monkey saw him on the road and, greeting him humbly, said, "We monkeys have no quarter, so I cannot offer you hospitality, but do stop for a while so I may bring you some fruit." He came back straightaway and brought him a lot of fruit. The traveler ate as much as he could and set off on his way.

From afar he spied the tiger. He feared it and wanted to avoid it, but the tiger said, "You are safe. Even if you have forgotten what you did for us, we remember our obligation to you." The tiger came forward and thanked him profusely. Then it said, "Can you wait for me for a moment?" The traveler stood while the tiger went into an orchard, killed the daughter of the prince, and brought her jewelry to the traveler. The traveler took it, thanked the tiger for its kindness, and set out for the city.

Along the way he remembered the goldsmith and said, "There was such goodwill among the beasts, and their gratitude earned me much reward. If the goldsmith learns of my arrival he too will be as kind and welcome me. With his help I may get a good price for this jewelry."

When he arrived in the city he sought out the goldsmith, who welcomed him warmly. They conversed for a while and listened to each other's news. During the discussion the traveler mentioned the jewelry and showed it to the goldsmith. He brightened up and said, "This is my work."

Now this vile man, who had been in the employ of the daughter of the prince, recognized the jewelry and said to himself, "This is a great opportunity. If I ignore it and let it go to waste I will be deprived of the benefits of prudence and skill and the advantages of intellect and perspicacity." He therefore decided to commit an act of treachery and went to the court to inform the prince that he had caught his daughter's murderer with her jewelry.

When the poor fellow realized how things were he said to the goldsmith, "You have killed me with your friendship, and never has anyone killed another more vilely with enmity."

The prince, thinking that the traveler was guilty and that the jewels were proof of his guilt, ordered him to be paraded around the city and then hanged. As he was being paraded the snake that was mentioned at the beginning of this story saw him, recognized him, and went to him where he was being detained.

When the snake heard the tale he was pained and said, "I told you that he was a vile, untrustworthy man and that he would repay good with evil and kindness with meanness. The Prophet has said, 'Guard yourself against the evil of him unto whom you have done a kindness.' Anyone who expects virtue from a base villain and seeks his assistance in warding off vicissitudes is, as the Arab says, like an overburdened camel that seeks assistance from its chin.[1] I have thought up a solution for this affliction of yours. I have bitten the prince's son, and no one in the entire city is able to come up with a

---

1. The Arab proverb refers to an overburdened camel that tries to use its chin to get up. The proverb is applied to someone who seeks assistance from the wrong source.

treatment for it. Take this plant. If you are consulted, after explaining how this happened to you, give it to the boy to eat, and he will be healed. Only by this means will you be delivered, for I cannot think of any other way."

The traveler thanked the snake and said, "I erred in making an ignoble person privy to my secret."

"There is no need to apologize," the snake said. "Your generosity has already been proven."

Then the snake went up on a hill and called out in a loud voice to all the people in the palace—but no one could see it—and said, "The imprisoned traveler has the remedy for snakebite." At once they took him out and brought him before the prince. First he explained his situation, and then he healed the boy, and when signs of recovery were evident the traveler's innocence was obvious to the prince. He gave him a large reward and ordered that the goldsmith be hanged in his stead because the punishment for lying in those days was that if an informant put someone in jeopardy, and if false testimony was revealed, the accuser would suffer the fate that would have befallen the one falsely accused.

Beneficence is never wasted, and requital for maleficence cannot be put off for any reason. An intelligent person must refrain from doing harm and injustice and make provisions for the next life by rectitude and doing as little harm as possible.

This has been a story of kings in their choice of intimates and recognition of followers as well as avoidance of making snap decisions, from which great harm may arise.

Chapter Fourteen

The Prince and His Friends

The Raja said, "I have heard the story of kings' choice of friends and how precaution is necessary lest an ignorant maleficent who will neither appreciate patronage nor be grateful for employment gain the upper hand. Now tell me a story of how an intelligent noble person can fall into the snare of affliction and how a vile, ignorant fool can pass his days in the shadow of comfort, with neither the one's being assisted by intelligence or perspicacity nor the other's being brought down by his foolishness and ignorance."

The Brahman replied, "Intelligence is the mainstay of felicity and the key to success. Anyone who possesses that quality and is clement and steadfast will be worthy of fortune, glory, and high status. Its fruits, however, are tied to destiny. A prince wrote over a city gate, 'The base of felicity is destiny, and all intervention is useless,' and thereupon hangs a tale."

"How was that?" asked the Raja.

The Prince and His Friends

It has been related that four persons met on a road. One was a prince in whose every movement the purity of his lineage and the nobility of his rank were obvious and in whose deeds and character signs of fortune were clear. The second was the adolescent son of a rich man to whose beauty the angels would have prostrated themselves, and he combined youthfulness with grace and great elegance. The third was a merchant's son, and he was intelligent, competent, prudent, wise, and judicious. The fourth was the son of a farmer, and he was powerful, strong, skilled in all forms of agriculture, proficient in improving land, and as steadfast as a mountain in his labor.

They were all far from home and had fallen into poverty and destitution. One day the prince said, "Things in this world are tied to destiny in the other world. No amount of striving or effort on the part of a man can make the slightest difference. It would be better for an intelligent man not to strive to acquire this world or to waste his precious life on such carrion, for it cannot be imagined that what is allotted could be increased or decreased."

The rich man's son said, "Beauty is of great consequence in attaining happiness, glory, and comfort, and wishes can be attained only by it."

The merchant's son said, "The benefits of good strategy and planning outweigh all others. If anyone's foot hits an obstacle he has no recourse other than his own intelligence."

The farmer's son said, "'Whoever do their utmost endeavor to promote our true religion, we will direct them into our ways' [Kor. 29:69]. The blessings of work and the felicities of endeavor give people success and bring happiness. Anyone who is determined to find something will of course succeed."

When they were near a city they stopped a while to rest. To the farmer's son they said, "We are all exhausted and would profit from your endeavor. Think up a way to get us sustenance, and in the coming days, when we are rested, each of us will take a turn to get something."

He went to the city and asked what the best job in the city was. He was told that firewood was very dear. Immediately he went to a mountain, gathered a load, took it into town, sold it, and bought food. Over the city gate he wrote, "The fruit of one day's labor fed four persons."

The next day they said to the rich man's son, "Today you think up some way to get provisions with your beauty so we won't have to worry."

He thought, "If I come back without provisions my friends will suffer." With that thought he went into town and sat down with his back against a tree, looking sad and sorrowful. Suddenly the wife of a rich man passed by and saw him. Smitten with him, she said, "'This is not a mortal; he is no other than an angel, deserving the highest respect' [Kor. 12:31]." Then to her servant girl she said, "Think up a ruse."

The servant girl went to him and said, "My lady says that if she could host you with your beauty for an hour she would attain eternal life and you would suffer no loss."

"I will obey," he said as he got up and went to her house. He spent a day in comfort and luxury, and when it was time to return he received a purse with five hundred dirhems with which he got provisions for his friends. Over the gate of the city he wrote, "The price for one day of beauty is five hundred dirhems."

The next day they said to the merchant's son, "Today we depend upon your intelligence and cleverness." He set off for the town. Recently a ship laden with precious commodities had come to the shore, but the people of the town were not buying and the goods were not moving. He bought them all at a discounted price and sold them all that day for cash, making a thousand dirhems in profit. With that he bought provisions for his friends and wrote over the city gate, "The result of one day's astuteness is a thousand dirhems."

The next day they said to the prince, "If your trust in God bears fruit it will have to keep us." With this thought in mind he set out for the town. By chance the prince of the city had just died, and the people were mourning him. He went to the prince's palace to watch and sat in a corner. When he did not participate in the others' wailing the gatekeeper spoke to him gruffly. When the bier was taken out and the palace was empty, he remained there. Once again the gatekeeper's gaze fell upon the prince, and he excoriated him and took him to prison.

The next day the grandees of the city gathered to decide who should rule, for they had no hereditary king. After they had discussed it at length the gatekeeper said, "Discuss this more in secret, for I have caught a spy, and he shouldn't learn of your deliberations." When the gatekeeper told them about the prince and his cruel treatment of him they thought he should be brought forth and questioned. Someone went and brought the prince out of prison.

"Why have you come here?" they asked. "In what city were you born and raised?" He answered politely and told them about his lineage, saying, "When my father departed this life and my brother took over the kingdom, I bade farewell to my homeland for self-preservation and thought it better to avoid useless contention."

A group of merchants recognized him and attested to the greatness of his house and the extent of his forebears' kingdom. His presence seemed fortuitous to the grandees of the city, and they said, "He is worthy to rule this region since he possesses distinguished looks and a noble lineage. Doubtless he will follow in his forefathers' just and bounteous footsteps and keep their good customs alive." Immediately they bowed to him, and thus kingship fell into his hands with such ease. Such was the great fruit his trust in God had borne. Anyone who is steadfast in trusting in God and also has good intentions will receive the best fruits in religion and this world.

It was a custom in that city for kings to ride through the city on a white elephant on their first day, and he too observed the custom. When he reached the gate and saw what his friends had written he ordered written next to them these words: "Hard work, beauty, and intelligence yield fruit when destiny is in agreement, as all the world can learn from my experience of one day."

Then he returned to the palace and sat on the throne, and the kingship was conferred on him. He summoned his friends and made the clever friend a partner to his ministers. To the possessor of beauty he gave a large reward and ordered him to leave the region lest the women be smitten with him and depravity ensue.

Then he summoned the learned men and grandees and said, "There are many among you who are smarter, braver, more skilled, and more competent than I am, but kingship can only be acquired by destiny. My companions strove to make money, and each got something. I neither relied on my ability to make money or on my knowledge nor sought anyone's assistance, and from the time my brother drove me from my hereditary kingdom I never expected such distinction. Well have they said that in the end things turn out contrary to expectations, so rejoice when sadness is at its utmost."

A traveler rose from among those present and said, "What the king says proves his wisdom, experience, and intelligence. No quality adorns a king like knowledge and wisdom, and the king's worthiness is as clear as the shining sun. The place for bestowing patronage is not hidden from the World-Creator: 'God best knoweth whom he will appoint for his messenger' [Kor. 6:124]. The good fortune of the people of this region has elevated you to this position and spread the light of your justice and the shadow of your clemency over them."

When he finished speaking another stood up and said, "Without any further ado, if so ordered I will relate an amazing story."

"Let us hear what you have to say," said the king.

"I was in the service of a nobleman. When I recognized the faithlessness of the world I realized that this old bride had gobbled up many young kings and brought down many self-sacrificing aspirants. I said to myself, 'You fool, you set your heart on someone who has rejected a thousand mighty kings and puissant princes. Know yourself, for time is little, life is short, and you have a long road ahead of you.' With this admonition I woke up and turned willingly and eagerly toward working for the next life.

"One day I was walking through the marketplace. A bird catcher was showing a pair of parrots. For my own salvation in the next world I wanted to free them. The catcher asked for two dirhems, and that was all I had. I hesitated because I found it difficult to spend my last two coins. Still, my mind was occupied with the birds. Finally I put my trust in God and bought them. Then I took them out of the city and let them go in a forest. When they perched atop a tree they called out to me and said, 'At present we cannot reward you, but there is a treasure under this tree. Dig in the earth and take it.' I said, 'Strange, you can see treasure under the earth but were unaware of the hunter's snare.' They replied, 'When fate strikes it cannot be warded off by any cunning. It blinds the intelligent and robs the negligent of sight, and destiny's decree will be done.' I dug in the earth and took the treasure. I tell this so that an order may be given for it to be taken to the treasury. If the king pleases he may give me a share."

The king said, "You sowed the seed of goodness. The harvest is yours for the taking."

When the Brahman reached this point and finished this story the Raja fell silent and asked no further questions.

"All that was possible I have presented to the king and done my duty," the Brahman said. "I hope for one favor, that the king will focus his mind on good thoughts and wisdom and the benefits of experiences."